BEFORE I LEFT

A gripping psychological thriller full of killer twists

DAISY WHITE

Published 2017 by Joffe Books, London.

www.joffebooks.com

This book is a work of fiction. Names, characters, businesses, organizations, places and events are either the product of the author's imagination or are used fictitiously. Any resemblance to actual persons, living or dead, events or locales is entirely coincidental. The spelling is British English.

ISBN- 978-1-912106-87-5

For all my wonderful family and friends, whose unending support and bad jokes mean so much. x

Chapter One

The clouds jostle for room in the dark sky, patterning the road with monstrous shadows. My head is wedged against the window and my body jolts to the movement of the lorry. I watch as the moon slashes a welt of light, giving a tantalising glimpse of a smooth oily blackness that must be the sea. I lift my head properly, blinking stupidly, my eyes gritty and one side of my body sticky with sweat.

Mary snores peacefully, lolling back against the rickety seat. She's pressed up against me, with her long pale fingers curled loosely over her stomach. Although we had to walk the first two hours, she was asleep from the moment we curled up together in the cab. I stayed awake from habit, one eye on the skinny, cheerful little man grinding the gears and humming to himself, the other on the counter on the dashboard clocking up the miles.

I don't feel safe yet. I may never feel safe again, but at least I know we've taken the first steps. Made a choice. Which is more than Mum will ever do.

The smell of salt and rotten vegetables mingles unpleasantly with the diesel fumes from the lorry, and the driver calls out, bus conductor style, "Brighton seafront, ladies. Everyone off!"

"Thanks, Mick," I tell him, shaking Mary awake and pushing her gently across the seat to the door. "We wouldn't have made it tonight if you hadn't come along." I mean it too.

"Glad of the company, love. Now hop out. I've got to be in Rye by dawn with this lot."

We wrench open the door, stagger out — half falling onto the pavement — and slam it shut quickly. Mick waves, little crumpled red face beaming, grey hair standing up in a tuft on his forehead as the lorry moves off with a roar.

"I feel sick," Mary says suddenly as we hover uncertainly on the seafront, stretching our cramped limbs and trying to chase away that floating, exhausted feeling that comes from a long night.

She clings to a line of green metal railings that divides us from the beach, while I rub her shoulder anxiously. I know she's okay really, because Mum was really sick with her last four pregnancies too. It's natural. Both of us take great breaths of night air, and the spring breezes whipping off the English Channel slice through our thin dresses, despite the warmth of the night.

Finally Mary lifts her head, and gives me a shaky grin. The moonlight turns her pale, lank hair into a mop of silver, and her blue eyes are dark pits.

"We've bloody done it, Ruby! We're in Brighton. I thought we were never going to make it. I really thought Derek would come back early, or your stepdad would see us on the main road." She sniffs, clearly overcome by our success, and wipes the back of her hand across her nose and eyes.

Excitement fizzes deep in my stomach, and just for a moment as we cling together, I allow myself a glow of triumph. The bruises on my body won't be joined by others tomorrow, and wherever we end up now, there will be no bellow of fury at lumpy gravy, or at fractious siblings who refuse to be quietened. No beer bottles will shatter the wall above my head, and no screaming babies will wake me from my sleep.

Except Mary's, of course. But that's different.

"Have you got the map, Rubes?" she asks. We turn from the sea to the city on the hill.

"Yeah. It should only take an hour or so to walk from here. Look, it's getting light so it must be about four o'clock. Even if she's doing a night shift, she'll be back home for six. We can wait outside if we need to." I haul the map out from my bag and spread out the crumpled sheet so we can both peer at it. The twist of unfamiliar street names leads all the way up to Elm Grove, which I have circled in red pencil.

We take a last look at the sea, which is now glittering pink and gold as dawn pushes gentle fingers through the dark clouds. Then we shoulder our bags, and head off up the hill.

* * *

"Oh my God, what have you done? And who is this?" Pearl says.

Mary instantly shrinks back into the shadow of the doorway, head down, and I'm reminded vividly of the day I first saw her. I'm also reminded — as if I needed to be — why we're doing this. For both of us.

"Hi, Pearl, great to see you! Can we come in please? This is Mary. You know, I told you about her. She lives down the road from us." I beam at my cousin, although I'm cringing inside at her reaction to our arrival.

Clearly deciding she has no choice, Pearl frowns, opens the door wide and waves us in. She is still wearing her starched student nurse uniform and shiny black shoes. It took a bit longer than we thought to walk up through the town, and at one point we went about two miles in the wrong direction, until a friendly milkman set us right. When we saw the sign for the hospital I knew we were going to be okay.

Pearl's mum is my mother's sister, and they named all their daughters after precious stones. She's small and curvaceous, with a sweet smile, and a pretty freckled face. I haven't seen her since Christmas, although of course we write every month. She has every right to be furious with me for pitching up unannounced — I definitely didn't mention that Mary and I were coming to Brighton. Just as I didn't tell her what happens at home when we aren't all assembled for a cosy family gathering.

She doesn't look that happy to see us. Her shocking red hair is neatly curled under her crisp white hat, and her pale face is scrubbed of makeup. She looks just as exhausted, after a long night shift, as we probably do after our eventful journey from Croydon.

"What have you done? Are you in trouble?" Pearl repeats, narrowing her eyes. She takes in our sweat-stained, bedraggled appearance, and the bulging paper bags at our feet.

"Peaaarrrl! Why do you always think the worst? We just wondered if we could — um — stay for a bit?" I flop down on her couch, pulling my cardigan sleeves down to hide the bruises on my arms. I really hope my brilliant plan isn't going to go horribly wrong at the very last turn.

Mary hovers in the kitchen, biting her nails. One hand gently caresses her stomach, even though she isn't showing at all yet. Pearl's bedsit is pretty small, and the bed is crammed next to the sofa, which is right opposite the sink. She told the family all about it at Christmas. There are around twenty students in this block, and they only get one shared bathroom. But she gets to be independent, to have her own (tiny) space. Even now I can remember the pang of longing I felt when she described moving into her own place.

Somewhere to be completely alone when you need it, and to just be yourself with nobody yelling or screaming, and no sick guilty feeling in your stomach because you know you should pick up the crying baby, but you don't really want to.

Pearl folds her arms across her chest now, and surveys us both with a stern expression, and one that suddenly makes me think she'll be a brilliant matron one day. "I'm not stupid, Ruby. You send me letters every month, and not once did you mention an early morning visit. How did you get here anyway? The milk train?"

"We hitched a lift for most of the way. We missed the last bus because I couldn't get away until after . . . um, after my husband went out." Mary joins the conversation, nervousness jumbling her words. She tugs at the chest of her dress with shaky fingers and straightens the faded green fabric. Her blonde hair falls forward to hide her face.

"Mmmm." Pearl studies her shrewdly, "Ruby talks about you all the time in her letters. In other circumstances I'd say pleased to meet you. How's your mum, Ruby? Does she know what you're up to?"

I avoid the question. "Oh, you know. She seems happy, and she's due next month. Hoping for another girl, I think! How's the training going?"

Ignoring my obvious subject change, Pearl pulls a face, "Seven kids! Rather her than me." Finally pausing in her interrogation, she turns to her tiny cooker and takes a pan from under a yellow spotted curtain that hangs round the sink.

My shoulders sag with relief and I try to catch Mary's eye, but her head is still down. I jump up from the couch, swallowing a hard ball of emotion and look through the yellowing nets at the small grimy window. All the while, I'm fighting to get rid of that choking fear that keeps swimming to the surface. This has to work. But if it doesn't, I'd rather sleep on the streets than go back. I rub my bruised arms again and turn to face the other girls, waiting for the next question.

"And Mary's husband? He's clearly not come with you."

Mary nods, sneaking a quick glance at my cousin from under her lank fringe. I swing back around to the window, unseeing, waiting.

Eventually, Pearl stops clattering drinks, and touches my shoulder gently. "Ruby? If you're in trouble I'll help, you know that, but you need to tell me the full story." Her voice is suddenly gentle, her blue eyes are softer, and I want to cry. I want so much to cry. But I need to stay strong.

"Thanks Pearl. We just wondered if we could stay for a couple of days while we find some work. Then we'll find a place of our own. Find jobs. Because . . . well . . ." I'm so ashamed I can't speak. A tear falls off my lashes, wetting my chin. I turn away from the window and carefully roll up my sleeves to show her my arms.

"Oh God, Rubes! Have you been in a fight? Was it a boyfriend?" Pearl takes my wrists and turns them carefully, wincing more than me at the bruising. Her cool fingers press gently and expertly at an older injury. "That burn needs dressing. Ruby?"

"It was George," I tell her, tears coming faster now. "He gets so angry all the time, and everything's wrong. He doesn't hit the little kids. He just ignores them unless we have someone round. It's just me. Me and Mum. But she never tries to stop him, to stand up to him." In fact she cowers in a corner, apologising over and over again, as George's fists rain down on her head, her face, her already battered body.

I know it isn't my fault, any more than Mary's husband pushing her downstairs after he gets back from the pub is her fault. But nobody speaks about things like that. If I said anything to most people who live round us, they'd just shrug it off, and tell me to deal with it, it's what men do. Must be your fault, they'd say. Clean the house better, keep the little kids quieter, work harder at teacher-training college, and make sure the men are happy.

"And your mum lets him hit *you*?" Pearl's eyes are wide and shocked, "He always seems so gentle, and he adores you all. No, of course he doesn't if he does this to you, but still . . . *George*. I would never have guessed. Does he get drunk?" She studies me, tilting my head gently with a professional hand. Clocking the marks on my neck, she casts a doubtful look at Mary, who seems to be trying to shrink into the soft furnishings. "And Mary?"

"Mary's husband hits her, after he's been down the pub. He gets really jealous if she talks to anyone, and last week he said the baby wasn't his, and he . . . he pushed her down the stairs. I tried to tell Mum about Mary, but she didn't want to know. She thinks you should just keep quiet and take it."

I wonder suddenly what Mum will do when she finds I'm gone. I was so focused on escaping I never thought about my empty space in bed this morning. Garnet will be pleased to have the narrow covers all to herself, but will she miss cuddling up to her big sister? I reckon Mum will only care when all the kids keep howling, and nobody else goes to sort them out.

The milk boils over with a hiss, and the smell of burning. Pearl curses. She wipes up the mess with a dishcloth and pours us drinks in chipped blue enamel mugs, biting her lip with concentration, "I can't believe this. I mean I do, of course I do, but God, what is wrong with people? And Mary is pregnant — that complicates things. How far gone are you?"

"Only about nine weeks . . . I don't really know because my . . . my you-know-whats have been a bit funny for ages."

"Mmmm. I suppose you haven't been for any check-ups?"

Mary flushes, narrow shoulders hunched forward, and hands resting lightly across her flat belly in a protective gesture, "I couldn't, I mean I did want to see the doctor but Derek, that's my husband, he said no, because he's a man. The doctor, I mean."

Pearl narrows her eyes, "Unbelievable — no, not you, sweetheart, your bloody husband. No pains or bleeding since he shoved you downstairs?"

"No! I mean, I'm really tired, and I feel sick a lot of the time, but nothing else."

Mary and I sit in silence. She chews her already ragged thumbnail, and I try to calm my frantic heartbeat. *Please say yes, please say yes* .

Finally Pearl yawns, and sits carefully on her neatly-made bed, sipping her drink. "Okay. Yes, of course. You can stay until we decide what to do with you. First I need some sleep. I've had a hell of a night. Then we'll think of a way forward. You two can sleep in the bed, and I'll have the couch. If you want to wash you can boil the kettle and there's a basin over in the corner. The taps at the sink only run cold water, and there isn't a plug. The toilet is on the left out of the door."

"We don't want to give you any trouble, Pearl. We'll get whatever jobs we can, and find a place of our own," I tell her. Guilt rises somewhere in my stomach. But as well as guilt there is a tidal wave of relief so violent and bone-shaking I nearly start crying again.

Pearl smiles at us both and wanders over to the radio. She switches it on and The Ronettes' 'Be My Baby' blares out. She taps her teeth with one scrubbed white finger, concentrating. "I have a friend who owns a hairdressing salon. He has a hard time trying to get apprentices, because the pay is rubbish. Bit like nursing, really. Anyway, I bet I can get you set up there, and find you a room. Then it's up to you. Right, now get some sleep!"

"Deal," I say, my shoulders sagging with relief, while Mary just smiles. Her eyes, like mine, are wet with tears.

Within half an hour I'm curled up next to Mary again, but this time on rough, clean sheets, and with Pearl snoring softly across the room. The tiny bedsit smells pleasantly of disinfectant, and everything is immaculately tidy. I let my eyes rove around, taking in the little crate of enamel mugs, the two wooden chairs, and the tin bath leaning up against a tall cupboard. On the makeshift worktop, two clean dishes lie next to a chequered tea towel. A few cooking utensils hang neatly on the wall, just above a half-full bottle of ginger beer.

Even though the sink might be missing a plug, it is spotless, with a bar of pink soap sitting neatly in a metal dish. The battered lino floor is clearly mopped every day. But the walls are spotted with damp and the ceiling has a large stain running right across the entire width of the room. Two tall cupboards make a sort of wall between the 'bedroom' bit and the 'kitchen' bit, and rows of shoes are stacked in cardboard boxes alongside them.

On a rickety little table, Pearl has a glass fruit dish filled with makeup, and a pretty jewellery box decorated with sequins. I remember both from her room at Aunt Jackie's.

People stamp past outside the window and their voices carry into the tiny space. On either side, in other bedsits, music accompanies the clang of dishes and the sound of water rushing into sinks. Cooking smells mingle with the salty scent of spring, which slides in at the window. At last, after a long winter.

The walls are thin, but the noise is comforting. The net curtain allows streams of sunshine to dance into the room. I close my eyes.

Chapter Two

It's after four in the afternoon when I finally wake up. Groggy and slightly disorientated, I prop myself onto an elbow, pushing the sheets away. Pearl is dressed in a cotton wrap over her short blue nightdress and already pouring drinks. She flicks on the radio again as she takes out a small pie from under the sink, carefully slicing it into three pieces.

"Come on then, you two. Time to get ready to meet your new boss!" She grins and pushes her mass of red curls away. Unpinned, her hair reaches almost to her waist.

"Now? You want us to come out with you?" Mary asks, biting her nails again. She is still blinking sleepily.

"Yes. That was my last night shift for the week, and tomorrow I have a day off. Time to head out and party, girls!" Pearl does a few dance steps round the kitchen. She stops suddenly, "I haven't forgotten why you're here, or what you've been through, but as far as I can see you need a fresh start. You're only nineteen, Rubes, and Mary, you're not much older, are you? You can be whatever you want. But first, jobs, and that's what we'll get tonight.

Johnnie is a character, but he has a big heart. Up to you what you tell him, and how much, but try to be honest up to a point."

"We haven't brought any clothes for going out," I say. I don't want to kill her enthusiasm, but I remember how she wrote to us about glamorous party people, and the pubs and clubs she frequents. "We don't want to show you up."

"No problem. I may not have enough food in the house for a proper feast, but I have plenty of the more important things." My cousin's smile shows her dimples. She hands us mugs and plates, and I feel another rush of gratitude.

Pearl bustles through cupboards in her tiny home, flinging around clothes, makeup, and shoes in a mad high-energy rush. I remember she was always like this at home, and used to drive Aunt Jackie crazy — neat and prim one minute, then chucking herself into one thing after another. Mary and I are obviously her new project.

We're ready by seven. Pearl looks amazing in emerald green, with a fitted bodice halter-type top which shows off her figure. Her skirt spills in luscious gauzy nets down to her knees, and her long red hair curls in perfect waves. Green heels, a little silver charm necklace, and a quirky black-and-white elephant bangle finish the outfit perfectly.

"You look fab," I tell her and turn to Mary. She's still looking uncomfortable, but has allowed herself to be made over and looks pretty in a navy blouse and gathered flower-patterned skirt. Her big blue eyes are highlighted with masses of mascara, and her lank blonde hair coaxed into a million curls. Her slightly pinched face and long nose are disguised by big slashes of blusher, and her full lips are bright pink.

"I look . . . Derek would never let me go like this!" Mary says, staring half terrified, half in awe at her reflection. She darts a worried look at the door, "I keep thinking that he'll have got my note by now. Do you think he'll come after us?"

"Well, assuming you aren't both total clods, and didn't leave an address for anyone to follow up on your little goodbye notes, I can't see how anyone could guess where the hell you are," Pearl tells us. Her voice softens, "Harder for you than for Rubes at the moment, because you're actually married to your monster, but we'll sort that out, don't worry! Not all men are flakes. Even though you've both been through an awful experience, we'll get through it."

They both look at me, and I nod in agreement, shoving the memories into a locked drawer at the back of my mind. I glance quickly in the mirror and for the first time in a while I smile properly. My eyes are blue like Mary's, but so dark they're almost black, and my skin is olive. I've already picked up a slight tan from the unusually warm spring sunshine. Dark brown hair falls long and straight from a high ponytail, drawing attention to my sharp cheekbones. Mum said once that I'm the image of my dad, who was half-Spanish. He didn't stick around long enough to meet me.

I spin around. The dress really is gorgeous. It's a red, high-necked shift, with long sleeves to cover my arms, and a short skirt to show off my legs. Black flats complete the look, so at least I'll be able to dance without falling over.

Pearl tilts my head to brush away a stray hair, and then sighs with pleasure, "You both look so cute. And Rubes, I would die for your lips. That perfect little bow and dimples!" She laughs. "Time to have some fun, girls!"

A knock makes us all jump, but Pearl swings the door wide, and a tall blonde woman strides into the room. She's wearing a stunning blue halter-neck dress, with so many nets underneath that the skirt sticks out like a ballerina's tutu.

"Hi, sweetheart! Are you ready? What's that horrid smell, have you been cooking again? Oh!" She clocks us peering round the door. "Sorry, I didn't realise you had company."

Pearl grabs both our hands and drags us forward, "This is Victoria. We work on the same ward up at the hospital, but she's a year ahead of me." She grins. "On the partying and the nursing."

"Leave it!" Victoria lights a cigarette and laughs.

"This is my cousin Ruby, and her friend Mary. They're coming to live down here, so I thought I might see if Johnnie would take them on." Pearl accepts a cigarette and offers the packet to me.

"Thanks." I lean over as Victoria strikes another match. Her bright green eyes study us through the haze of smoke.

"Hairdressing? Are you sure that's what you want to do?" She raises an eyebrow, pursing her scarlet lips.

"We'll take what's on offer. We were both doing teacher-training before, but it was . . ." I glance at Mary. "It was pretty boring."

"Suit yourselves," Victoria says. "Probably pays better than nursing!"

"Are you saying we made the wrong career move?" Pearl smiles and hands her a beer bottle from a little stash under the sink. She passes one to me, takes another, and offers one to Mary.

"Not drinking, love?" Victoria asks. Mary shakes her head firmly. Not that we're big drinkers, but since she got pregnant the smell of certain things makes Mary vomit — alcohol and coffee being two of the worst offenders. Pearl quickly changes the subject.

I plonk myself down on the couch with Mary, while the other two girls chat on the bed. With four people, the tiny bedsit is full to bursting, but I like it. I feel safe in a crowd, and Victoria is one of those stunning girls whom you could easily just sit and watch. Her blonde hair is smooth and glossy, her eyes are that perfect vivid green and her long slim legs are casually crossed. Delicate silver sandals reveal shiny red-painted toenails, and as she talks, she idly swings one foot in time to a Beatles tune on the radio. She looks like a Vogue model, all big eyes and slim lines.

"Are you okay?" I ask Mary softly. "Because if you don't want to go out, I can meet this Johnnie person and I'll explain that we both need jobs."

She leans over and squeezes my hand. "I need to do this too, Rubes. Pearl's right, it's like a new beginning. You know, I never went out until we walked to that coffee bar after class. My parents didn't let me go out after school, and then Derek always said it was better for us to eat together at home."

It's nice to see the new sparkle in her eyes. "We can do this. It's all going to be all right." Am I talking to my best friend or myself?

* * *

Two hours later and I truly believe it is going to be okay. Better than okay. In fact I'm having a riot. We've been to a coffee bar, 'looked in' on a private party, and now we're with a group of about ten of Pearl's friends, dancing and drinking the night away at another place called Whisky-a-Go-Go. As we arrived, Victoria whispered to me that the owner's wife was shot dead in a flat above the club, and the place is being run by a doorman while the murder investigation continues. It's a real scandal. Initially I shiver, despite the heat of the crowd, but soon forget this titbit of gossip. Nothing is going to ruin my first night out.

It's crammed. When we got here, there was still just enough room for Mary to sit on the long, low bench seats running round the walls, and there were tables to park our drinks, but now the crowds have arrived, the furniture has been moved and there are so many people that partygoers are pushed against the walls. The music is amazing, with all the latest stuff from the US. I lean against the wall and let the hits flow over me — 'Walk Like A Man' and 'He's So Fine' followed by the fab 'Telstar.' Perfect.

The sophisticated chatter bubbles all around. I've already been bought three drinks, and despite feeling I have to keep a watchful eye on Mary, I accept another. My stepdad George could be on another planet. I work hard to keep this feeling of floating happiness, beaming at everyone and accepting random offers of dates — which gets me another drink.

Pearl appears through the heaving mass of sweaty bodies, shoving her way ruthlessly through the hot crowd and dragging a tall young man by the hand. She pushes us together. "Ruby, this is Johnnie. He runs the hairdressing salon I was telling you about, and if you talk to him really nicely he might even let you start tomorrow!" She's flushed and fizzing with enthusiasm — the life and soul of every party.

Before I say a word, another friend grabs her hand and they spin off onto the dance floor in the frenzy of an Elvis hit. My cousin is a great dancer, light on her feet and just clever enough to avoid any steamy embraces. The room is spinning slightly after my last drink. I try to haul my thoughts together and to slice through the haze of laughter, smoke and coloured lights to make a good impression on my potential new boss.

"Hi, Johnnie. Nice to meet you!" I have to raise my voice to be heard, and lean close enough to smell the alcohol on his breath.

"Pearl says that you and another girl want to work for me. Got any references?" His lazy smile suits his slightly long, elegant face. He is wearing a well-cut suit and has an upper-class accent. He stands out against the men in leather and shirtsleeves, or black suit jackets over T-shirts. He should look old-fashioned, but actually he looks a lot like Paul Newman. More Mod than Rocker, but not really fitting neatly into either gang.

My heart jumps at the mention of references, but I take a breath. I move closer to make sure he can hear me. "Actually no. We've just dropped out of teacher-training college and we want to have some fun in Brighton. But we'll work bloody hard, and turn up on time every day." I smile. Too much alcohol makes the blood feel hot in my veins, and the music pumps up my heartbeat. I cross my fingers behind my back.

Johnnie nods slowly, taking his time to finish his bottle of beer. His slightly feline blue eyes flicker over my face. "Where's the other girl?"

I point over to the last remaining benches, where Mary is with some of Pearl's friends. She's still sipping water, and her eyes are shadowed with exhaustion, but that whole strained, pale, housewife persona has almost vanished. She looks five years younger, and about a foot taller. And she is smiling for once.

"Anything else I should know?"

"She's pregnant. And married. But not for much longer." Best give it to him straight out, I think. Sooner rather than later, Mary's condition is going to become obvious. Even though I know our futures could depend on this lazy-looking man, I feel slightly better as he finally grins back at me.

He flashes a cheeky glance at my stomach. "And you?"

"Not married, and not pregnant — and not likely to be. But I do have my reasons for wanting a job quickly, and for keeping a job."

Johnnie sighs with apparent pleasure. "I sense a bit of scandal. Excellent. I only like to work with really interesting people. Gossip is fine, scandal is good, and if you can work hard and turn up on time . . . I take it you know nothing about hairdressing?"

"I know Marcel waves went out with the ark," I tell him, because a large black-haired girl in green is barging past in an effort to get nearer her boyfriend. Her hair might be old-fashioned, but her boyfriend has his nose level with her impressive cleavage, and doesn't seem to have any complaints.

Johnnie's catlike face registers real amusement. His lips turn upwards and his eyes narrow to show a fan of fine lines in his tanned skin. He flicks his cigarette away with long, elegant fingers, grinding it carefully underfoot. I wonder for a split second if I've blown it. I'm actually just copying something Victoria said when she saw the girl earlier, and surely Victoria wouldn't be wrong about a hairstyle.

Then he bursts out laughing, "Darling!" Again the exaggerated, lazy upper-class accent. "I love you already. Especially with those luscious popping lips! Be at mine at eight tomorrow with your scandalous little friend, and I'll sort out the paperwork. We start the proper work at nine. Four months' trial to see if you actually like it, and then you can start your apprenticeships for real." Another man calls him away, and he flutters a hand in farewell, before disappearing into the painted crowds.

Stunned and exhilarated, I make my way over to Mary, dodging dancers, smiling at everyone, and bend down to shout in her ear. "Guess what? We start our new jobs tomorrow morning!"

Her mouth opens in a classic 'O' of surprise, and I laugh. She immediately starts asking questions but I can't hear any of them because someone has turned the volume up, and the room is going crazy. Pearl swoops down on us, dragging both of us out to dance, and we join the sweaty, smoky crowds, swaying to the beat. I want to remember this moment for ever. I'm nineteen, in Brighton, just got my first real job and I'm out with the party girls.

* * *

By the time we leave the club we're down to just seven of us. Pearl leads the way, holding hands with a pretty wild-haired brunette called Linda. Mary, Victoria and I straggle along with a couple of good-looking boys, who tease us about joining Pearl's 'gang,' and tell us stories about wild nights out, where apparently everyone ends up making out on the beach.

Pearl takes it pretty well, occasionally turning to tell them to shut up when their tales get too risqué. The night is warm, and we're all sweaty from the dance floor, with glistening foreheads and cheekbones. I can feel damp patches under my arms and I really hope it doesn't show. I jam my elbows into my ribs just in case.

The other girls peel off their cardigans, and we kick off our shoes to walk barefoot on the stony road. We pass a huge clock tower and jumbled rows of houses, shops, and coffee bars, all cloaked in darkness. The balmy black shadows mingle with the heat of the town, and I can't stop smiling. I shake my hair free from its elegant ponytail, dancing a few steps down the road.

Kenny laughs, taking my hand to spin me around and around. He is the shorter of the two boys, with a clean-shaven innocence and flopping, slightly-too-long black hair that contrasts with his stocky muscular figure and boxer's nose. His hand is sweaty and sticks to my palm, but his grey eyes are kind and bright with fun.

It feels special to be out at this time, to be out free and barefoot when everyone else is asleep, finding our way by the buttery glow of tall streetlamps and the pale wash of the moon. Last night, as we walked up from the seafront to Pearl's bedsit, I felt out of place, terrified, and worn down by everything we had been through. Tonight, I belong. This is my home, and this is my new life. I say that to Mary, as we wander along, arm in arm.

"How many drinks did you say you've had?" she laughs, squeezing me close as I ramble on about our new home.

I take in the maze of roads, and the tall embellished buildings. A new town and a new life. Scanning the empty streets, which spin slightly after all that beer, I spy just a few shadowy figures walking home after a night out, and a stray cat slinking along a high wall. No bulky male figure waiting to yell at me for being late, no jobs waiting, and no bruised parent to be patched up. This is what happiness feels like.

"Where are you going now? This is the wrong way!" Victoria calls to Pearl suddenly, as we make our way through a muddle of back streets, stumbling slightly on uneven flagstones.

"Mary and Rube's first night out. We need to head down to the beach and finish off with a swim!"

"Down Ship Street?" Victoria frowns, pausing to look at a street sign.

"How much have you had? If we cut down Dukes Lane it's the quickest route from here!" Pearl dances on ahead for a moment.

"*Swimming?* No way!" Kenny waves his hands in protest, and pretends to run away. Victoria and Pearl promptly put their arms round his waist and start to drag him along. He's laughing so much, he can hardly walk.

"I'm going to head home if that's what you're planning — you know I can't swim. You go and enjoy your freezing dip," Linda says, smoothing her silky dress. The other man in our group, Ted, offers to walk with her, ignoring Kenny's and Victoria's screams and whistles.

"She doesn't fancy you, Ted, you're never going to get in there!" Kenny yells, but Ted makes a rude gesture, and offers Linda his hand.

She winks, and takes it. "Of course he isn't, but I like a good-looking man to walk me home. See you tomorrow night, crazy people!"

The pair turn quickly into a back street. Linda's pink dress is a flash of vivid colour under the streetlight, and her nut-brown curly hair bounces on her shoulders. Ted's slightly high voice floats back on the breeze as he chatters away, his hair golden in the moonlight.

Pearl shakes her head. "I would love it if those two finally got together, but much as I adore little Ted, he's not the catch of the century, is he?"

"Great dancer, though." Victoria hums a tune under her breath, swinging Kenny's arm in time to the beat.

Pearl begins to plan tomorrow night out loud as we wander down the hill, suggesting various parties and bars, which of course I've never heard of. Victoria and Kenny gossip about various relationships they have both had, argue whether sex is better if you're a man or a woman, and debate whether you should go all the way before you get married.

"Are we really going for a swim?" Mary asks nervously, stepping round a pile of broken wooden crates. She winces as her bare foot hits a sharp stone.

"Only if you can! If you can't swim, then just paddle on the edge. It's really warm tonight, and I promise the sea at night is the most beautiful way to end your first evening," Pearl says, swinging her purse as she walks and jumping cracks in the road like a little girl.

I move nearer the buildings to avoid a parked car and my bare feet slip in a wet patch. Yuck, it must be vomit or spilt alcohol. I recover my balance and look down. The oily liquid oozing across the stone is dark and slick, and my feet are stained red in the moonlight.

"Ruby?"

For a moment I can't breathe, although my heart is slamming against my chest so hard I think I might pass out. I put a hand down to check, and my fingertips come away spotted with scarlet. The others are clustered around now, exclaiming over the pool of blood and wrapping gentle arms around my shoulders, but I'm out on my own, drowning in memories. Is it possible for the dead to come back? All traces of my alcohol-blurred high are gone, and I'm icy cold and sober — with blood on my hands.

"Rubes, it's okay, sweetheart," Victoria has walked right into the narrow alley between two dark buildings, and is poking around. "I know it must be awful to have your feet covered in blood, but it must be from a delivery to the butcher, or something. Look, there's some packaging. Or maybe it's just a fight. Those bloody London boys coming down here for the weekends always . . ." Her voice trails away. "Bloody hell!"

"What is it?" Kenny follows her into the alley, and makes a disgusted noise.

"Tell us then!" Pearl's voice shakes. She peers quickly up and down the street, which not surprisingly, stays clothed tightly in its shadowed secrets.

I take a step into the darkness and blink hard. As my eyes adjust and focus I feel bile rising in my throat. At the edge of the pool of blood, up against the wall, is a dead cat. It lies spread-eagled on its back. Its throat has been cut and its glistening innards are on display.

"Sick bastards!" Victoria's sharp voice slices through the shadows. She tip-taps back. "Someone has gone and killed a cat. Slit its throat and started their own little autopsy too, by the look of it. There are some weirdos around here."

Kenny takes my arm, guiding me back to the road, "Might just have been that a car hit it and the driver thought he was putting it out of its misery," he says sensibly, if unconvincingly.

"No bloody way. That was not a cat that has been hit by a vehicle — it was a cat that has been sliced by a knife," Victoria says firmly. "Tomorrow morning I'm going to report it to the police."

"Do you think they'll take any notice?" Pearl asks, still sneaking horrified looks behind to the poor animal, but not going any closer.

"I don't care. It's a crime to murder humans, and it should be a crime to murder animals as well. I bet it *is* one of those stupid gangs. There've been too many fights and stuff since that all kicked off."

Mary has her arm firmly around my shoulders and her body shakes against mine, but her voice is surprisingly firm. "Come away, Ruby. We'll keep going down to the sea and you can wash your feet."

I nod, doll-like and mechanical, as Pearl agrees with Victoria, "It's okay, Ruby. You'll feel better when you're cleaned up. It — it only looks like a lot of blood because it's running downhill, I'm sure."

My breathing eases a little, and that tight feeling in my chest relaxes. Just a dead cat. I've seen them before, drowned in the gutter, and even though it upsets me, it isn't the end of the world (which is another of Mum's favourite sayings). I know some people are sick.

Just my mind playing tricks, and creating bloodstained monsters from the past. There is something that I haven't told anyone, something that I know will haunt me for the rest of my life. If I'm lucky that's all it will do, and the memory will fade from all-too-vivid colour to blank darkness. But now isn't the time to mention it.

A dark-shadowed alley should just be a passageway between buildings, not a place of death. These empty streets are as safe as any I've been through before. I'm a city girl, I know these things. *Just a cat* . . . But tears trickle hot and fierce down my cheeks. My feet are sticky and I can feel the dust and grime collecting on my heels and toes as I walk. "Let's get down to the beach. I need to wash this off."

Pearl recovers quickly, but then she probably sees blood every day in her job. Before long she is encouraging us all to run headlong down the main street, dodging a disdainful black cat, who may or may not be the ghost of the victim at the top of Ship Street. Victoria is still ranting about cruelty to animals.

"Just a quick dip. But it really is amazing swimming at night, like being awake in a dream," Pearl explains, waving her arms to demonstrate swimming on her back.

Despite our scare, Mary and I manage a giggle.

"I'll swim if you promise me a date for next week," Kenny offers, walking between the two older girls. "Mind you, it doesn't even have to be a date because I am *so* broke — we can just go back to my place and make out!"

Victoria snorts with laughter, and Pearl shakes her head, cracking up at his increasingly lurid suggestions. Unperturbed, he carries on walking with us anyway, as we cross the road to the seafront, and those same green railings. The pier lies skeletal and deserted, stretching long weed-clad limbs into the oily blackness of the sea.

Concrete steps take us down to the pebbly beach, and we crunch down to the foamy water's edge, laughing as the waves slide over our feet. Pearl tells us it's just past midnight, and because there is a full moon we should all make a wish.

Kenny loudly wishes to go on a date with her. Or Victoria. Or me. Or anyone who is female and under the age of forty.

"Idiot!" Pearl pushes him so he stumbles and falls into the next breaking wave. "Why do we put up with you?" But she's laughing again, kicking up spray with both feet, soaking us all.

Kenny comes up from the shallows spitting water, and he sends another wave of foam over the little group. His trousers are wet and the front of his shirt is spattered with seawater, but he still seems happy enough. "You love me really, Pearl, it's just taking you a while to recognise it.

Victoria lights a cigarette, cupping her hand to shield the flame from the salt breeze. "She does, Kenny. You keep right on believing that, sweetheart!"

Pearl unzips, and steps casually out of her dress, standing for a moment in her pink lacy underwear. Clearly this happens quite often, because nobody says anything as she wades in and dives into the darkness. A moment later her sleek, wet head, haloed by the moon, appears nearer the pier. "Come on, Ruby — I know you can swim!"

She's right. Mary shakes her head and accepts a cigarette from Victoria. They both collapse on the pebbles, and Victoria continues her banter with Kenny. Ignoring the chatter of thoughts racing through my brain, I slip my own dress over my head and follow Pearl into the water. It's freezing cold, and the icy ripples make me gasp, but I shake out my own hair like a mermaid, revelling in the freedom.

The sea murmurs into the night, and the hypnotic rise and fall of the dark waves brings me closer to Pearl. She's drifting on her back, hair spread out, studying the moon.

"Have you wished yet? Do it now!"

Obediently, I too flip over onto my back, staring at the star-dotted sky. I can see shadows across the moon, but its silvery glow still lays unearthly train-tracks of light across the waves. It must be the alcohol, because I don't believe in all that superstitious rubbish, but tonight I wish, moving my lips, but not making a sound. The words run softly inside my head, banishing the other chatter: *"I wish for Mary and me to be happy and safe here in Brighton . . . for her baby to be healthy . . . oh and I want to have some fun too."*

I think that might be three wishes, but never mind. I'm sure nobody's counting.

"Can you two come in now? We're getting cold!" Victoria shouts from the beach.

I realise then how far out we have drifted in the current. We're towards the end of the pier. I'm close enough to make out the huge supports, hung with curtains of weed, and the black gloom beneath, where the water sloshes and slaps. The seaweed smells sour, and the salt on my lips makes me spit into the water.

As I start to swim back towards the others, I catch sight of a figure, higher up on the beach underneath the pier. My heart pounds harder, and I shiver, pausing in my swim, although there is no reason for someone not to take a night-time stroll along the beach. If that person happened to come across some crazy half-naked swimmers, he might even stop and watch.

But his stillness bothers me, and the shiver creeps along my wet skin, as the figure moves slightly and I catch a quick flash of yellow as he lights a cigarette. He's too far away for conversation, but near enough for me to smell the smoke, and pick out his angular face. Nothing more. No features, no obvious identity. I tread water uncertainly for another minute, still shivering.

When the figure turns slowly to face me full on, I can see his raincoat fanning out in the breeze. My stepdad George always wore a long coat when he went out. My salty wet hands are clenched and my legs cycle frantically underwater to keep afloat. The watcher under the pier takes another puff, without taking his eyes off me. Everything except my head and shoulders is hidden under the water, but his gaze seems to burn across my naked skin.

"*Ruuuuby!* You swimming to France or what?" Kenny yells.

The invisible thread that links me to the dark watcher snaps, and I splash loudly and quickly back to the safety of the beach. I haul myself through the shallows with numb limbs and wince as I tread on sharp wet stones.

"Probably some drunk," Victoria decides, when I eventually reach them, and explain. "Or a tramp. They do shelter under the top end of the pier, where the tide doesn't reach. Are you even sure it was a man?"

I think about this as I flip back my wet hair and grab my cardigan, suddenly very aware of my nakedness. My knickers and bra are white, and the water has soaked them transparent. *Could* it have been a woman watching me? No. "It was a man. He was pretty tall, and had a long jacket on, like a raincoat maybe. I could see the outline of his shadow against the beach."

Since we don't have any towels, Pearl and I scrub down with a mixture of cardigans and Kenny's jacket.

Strangely, I don't mind that Kenny stares lustfully at us as we pull our dresses back on, but I do mind that a faceless stranger was watching me in the sea.

My feet are rinsed clean by the grey salt water, which is now ebbing and flowing up the beach, like a giant heartbeat. It soothes my frazzled nerves. First the blood, the poor cat, and then some freak watching me . . . I order myself to calm down, and not ruin what has been a very promising beginning.

"Do you want me to go and have a look for the bloke who was watching you?" Kenny suggests, as the other girls gather purses and shoes. "Although Victoria's right. I hate to admit that, but lots of other people hang out on the beach late at night. You're always safe in a group, though."

I smile at him, tugging the sleeves of my dress down to my wrists. Kenny looks like he could probably see anyone off in a fight, despite his boyish expression. Yet he seems to have the sweetest nature, which is probably why I feel safe with him already.

"Come on, you two!" Pearl is finally dressed, and heads up the beach, marching briskly with her red hair now in two long, wet stringy plaits.

We trail after her. Kenny stays comfortingly close to me as we crunch back up the shingle banks to the green railings. The combination of damp, salty skin, and the fabric of my dress makes my bruises itch, and I rub my arms. When I take a quick look back from the road, we're too high to see under the pier anymore, and darkness has swallowed the solitary watcher.

Chapter Three

"Come on Ruby, get a wiggle on. I've got a wedding party coming in at ten!" Johnnie's in a bad mood.

He flounces off to yell at the senior stylists, and I fumble my way through some pin waves. Luckily these are quite easy. It's quite satisfying to transform a hank of hair into something pretty and neat.

"Sorry!" My client looks up from her magazine and frowns when I accidentally stick a pin into her neck. Okay, so I'm still making mistakes. She is a society lady, with her tweedy suit and short curled hair. She even wears a single strand of pearls around her neck. She's a relic of another time — I'm sure she wouldn't be seen dead in Pucci.

I get rid of her as quickly as possible. She does give me a nice tip, though. Mary sweeps up the floor and wipes down the chair and mirror. This place, with its opulent gilt and cherub-encrusted mirrors, is buzzing. Clearly Johnnie's is the place to have your hair done, because I've already seen everyone from office girls to old ladies, to models and musicians, coming through the pink-and-gold doors. Mary and I aren't allowed to do much cutting or try any of the harder styles, of course. We do a lot of cleaning and fetching towels instead. My hands are wrinkly from shampooing.

In between the hairdressing we give manicures, and I have a major weakness for the little cupboard of jewel-coloured polishes. Most clients have pink or red, but the younger girls are starting to ask for purple and blue. Johnnie has promised to nip into the wholesale warehouse next time he's up in London. He'll do anything to compete with Vidal Sassoon.

We've been here a whole two weeks now, and I'm surprised by how well I've settled in. After that strange evening, I was almost prepared to run again, but I've managed to dismiss the idea that I'm being watched. I'm determined to live in the present.

I'm also so proud of Mary. She's a star hairdressing apprentice even though she feels so sick. Most of the time I pretend I've always been here, slogging in the salon during the day and partying all night, with nothing else to think about and no memories to avoid. There's no time to think at work anyway and by bedtime I'm exhausted. Pearl was right about a fresh start. Nobody back home seems to be bothered we've moved out.

The big news in Aunt Jackie's most recent telephone call to Pearl is rather horrible. She phones every week on a Wednesday night according to my cousin, and won't end the call until she has caught up on all the gossip and imparted a lot of her own. She says my stepdad was attacked and killed on his way home from the pub. They found his body in an alley two doors down from Mum's house. Auntie Jackie didn't even mention that cousin Ruby had run away. She did say my mother wanted to grieve in peace and not have to put up with a whole load of family turning up. Odd. I wonder if Aunt Jackie knows I've run away. I would say Mum hasn't noticed, but I think she knew, deep down, that I would have to go. Does she guess where I am? If she does, she knows better than to speak up.

I grab my combs and brushes and shove them into a hot water and disinfectant solution. We told Victoria what happened to my stepdad, and she said it was fate. She's slightly daunting, but she has a lot of common sense, and as we see such a lot of each other, we've quickly become close. She didn't flicker a false eyelash when I gave her an edited version of our great escape either.

Pearl and Mary may have guessed there's more, but I know they'll keep quiet. It isn't as if they can do anything else. Sometimes I even forget, myself — just for an hour or so. Blood on my feet, blood on my hands . . .

"Do you want to go to the pictures tonight? I really want to see *Lolita* again!" Mary wipes the mirror with a soft cloth.

"Really? I didn't think it was your kind of film. I'd rather see something new — Johnnie said *Cleopatra* was stunning — but I don't think we've got time. Pearl said to meet the others at half seven at the Regent." The Regent Ballroom is a grand, pillared, dance venue on the corner of Queens and North Street, and it has a bouncy dance floor. It's an elegant relic of days gone by, a bit like my client from earlier, but it's a great place to start the night. "I wish we had a television. We could watch something while we get ready."

"Dream on! Maybe we can save up for one in our new place." Mary chucks an empty shampoo bottle in the bin, and lines the new ones up neatly, next to several gallons of lacquer. The glass bottles glitter in stray sunbeams. "We'll be lucky if we can afford food for tonight."

Johnnie glares at me again so I start sweeping the grey lino floor even though it doesn't need it. He doesn't pay us much but we can afford clothes and food. He's offered us the rooms above the salon rent-free, too. We'll move in next week once they've been cleaned up.

Catherine and Eve, the two senior stylists, regard us with a sort of world-weary disdain and give us all the rubbish jobs when Johnnie isn't around. But they dote on

Johnnie. They treat him rather like a naughty family member.

Catherine has a scrapbook of pictures of Johnnie's clients, which she cuts out from society magazines, and she constantly reminds us of the "standards" we are expected to uphold. To be fair, Johnnie did say the staff haven't always been reliable, so I make an extra effort to work hard, and do everything I'm asked. I know how lucky we are. Mum always said you made your own luck, but she clearly wasn't any good at it. When I once asked her if she was happy with George, *knowing* she couldn't possibly be, she just gave me this wistful little look, and said she was lucky to have a man.

I sweep harder, paying attention to the fiddly corners under the shelves and around the pink-and-white reception desk. If it wasn't for Johnnie, we might be stuck sponging off my poor cousin, who has already done quite enough for us, so I mean to pay him back in hard work. I'm never going to end up like Mum. It's my dearest wish, and I repeat it every day. Have done since I was about ten.

"Can you make up some more neutraliser, Ruby?" Eve calls across, cutting into my thoughts. She's about forty, a beady-eyed professional the size of a bus. Not fat, but muscular. No clients ever dare argue with her, and I bet her husband doesn't either.

I wave to let her know I've heard, stow the brush neatly into the cupboard next to the mop and bucket, and start measuring out the conditioning cream. *"Twenty-volume peroxide,"* I mutter, peering at bottles and tubes on the shelf unit near the back door. You mix it with water, and the chemicals work their magic on a client's hair. It's fiddly, and takes the skin off your fingertips if you aren't careful. Johnnie buys these huge plastic containers of hundred-volume peroxide, and gets us to dilute it down with distilled water. It stinks, making the back of my throat burn and my eyes water.

I beam at Eve, who is scowling at me, and trot over to her with the plastic dish. She glances briefly at my red thumb. "Did you get burnt?" I nod and she smiles grimly. "Only way to learn. Isn't it, Joyce?"

Eve's ageing client agrees in a gravelly drawl. "Green soap, we used in my day!" she adds, fiddling with her handbag. She insists on clutching that bag against her huge bosom even though Eve has to lean over her to get to her sparse fringe.

"Mrs Carpenter used to be a hairdresser too," Eve informs me. "Go and wash the towels now, Ruby. Make yourself useful!"

We have to hand-wash the towels every day, and hang them out to dry on the line in the tiny courtyard at the back of the shop. I gather the wet washing into a basket and go outside, banging the door behind me. It's a peaceful job and I take my time over it, half thinking about tonight and half watching a couple of noisy seagulls perched on the rooftops next door. You get a great view across the lower half of town from here, and you can get out into the street through the door in the rear wall. It's our quick route down to Brenda's Café for chicken and chips with lashings of salt and vinegar.

The sun misses the little courtyard totally, concentrating its rays on a little halo of dust on the doorstep, so I have no idea how the towels dry. I can only imagine how cold I'll be hanging out wet towels next winter. But, enclosed in the cobbled square, with the bustle and dust of the town behind me and the seemingly endless blue sky above, I almost feel happy again.

When I turn to step back inside, something makes me pause — a small sound that doesn't belong to the street bustle outside, or to the peaceful skies above. The back of my neck prickles uncomfortably, and I stop dead. I swing round, half expecting to see someone standing behind me.

The courtyard is still empty, but the noise comes again. Someone is rattling the handle on the outside door.

I freeze like a hunted animal. The courtyard goes from cosy to stifling. I look up at the neighbouring balconies, the high brick and stone buildings opposite, and the distant rows of new housing between the church and the grocer's. It's not like I'm alone in a side street with an assailant. There are loads of people around. I only have to scream.

The bolt on the inside of the door shakes a little, and the metal chinks against the brick wall, as though the person outside is giving it an impatient push.

"Hello? Is someone there?" My heart hammers frantically against my ribs, and I rub my sweaty palms on my pinny and tug my pink-and-grey uniform shirt down to my wrists. I take a deep breath. For a second I consider unlocking the door and confronting whoever is on the other side.

As I stand there dithering, a woman shouts from next door and I swing round, squinting up into the sun. One of my neighbours is hanging out her own washing on her second floor balcony.

"Oi, you! Get away from 'ere! I can see you spyin' on me. Get away, you peeping Tom!" The seagulls rise skyward, squawking. "*Harooooold!* I need you out here, love, some sicko spying on me from behind the wall."

I hear footsteps running in the road outside. Something comes over the wall, and lands with a chink at my feet. It rolls on the cobblestones, before coming to rest next to my shoe. What on earth?

It looks like a ring or a badge. I'm bewildered. Is it meant for me? How could anyone know I was hanging out the washing? One glance to my left shows me how. Just as I can look towards the sea, and see the streets spread out before me, anyone further along the road and higher up the hill can watch our courtyard. Most of the shabby balconies stretching into the distance have a line of clothes flapping in the breeze, a few plants or a bird cage, but the one directly to my left is dirty and deserted. Could he have been there, watching the salon? Or has he been across the road? Perhaps he was further up the hill, sitting casually on the bench by the telephone box.

The woman who shouted from next door is now chuntering away someone inside. I strain and just catch the words "peeping Tom." She thinks he was spying on her. "Dark hair and a suit. Tall bloke. Looked really smart but you get all sorts round 'ere now, don't you?"

Footsteps thump and a door bangs. Perhaps Harold has gone to have a look around.

Running my tongue over dry lips, I reach down and pick up the little bit of metal. It is indeed a ring. I roll it around my palm. The dull brass with a criss-crossed pattern and the emblem of a lion's head is a man's signet ring, chunky and dirty. Embedded in the engraving, among the other grime, I can see unmistakable dried bloodstains. I want to hurl it back out onto the street. Instead, I stagger towards the wall and vomit into a patch of weeds, retching painfully, clutching my stomach. My throat burns and my eyes stream. It can't be. It is.

George was wearing this ring that night, staggering home through the alley. And he was still wearing it when he lay drowning in his own blood as his assailant ran off into the night.

Chapter Four

I was sure he was dead, but men like that are survivors. There was always that chance nagging at my mind. The telephone call from Aunt Jackie was a welcome relief.

It can't be him. The dead do not return, or if they do, they don't get spotted by an elderly washerwoman with operatic lungs. My face is burning hot, and I realise I'm holding my breath, arms wrapped around my chest. If I don't move it didn't happen. I can smell rotten fruit, the heat of the day is suddenly blinding, and the springtime wash of blue that was so welcome before is too vivid, too strong.

"*Ruby*? What are you doing out there?" Eve shouts from the salon.

For a moment I consider running away. Again. Then common sense kicks in. So someone is watching me. So what? If it was the police, they would have arrested me by now. This thought calms me a little. I've been expecting them to turn up ever since we ran away. Every time I see a policeman on a bike round here, I get an icy, fearful feeling deep in my stomach.

The man watching on the beach must have followed me, and from further away than the seafront in Brighton. But if this watcher-man means to harm me, I'll get him first. This last thought shocks me a little, but I'm pleased that I'm not that cowering little girl shrinking away from someone's fist anymore. You make your own luck, don't you?

I pause for a moment in that bright patch of sunlight, taking a long slow breath. Sanity returns in a welcome rush of energy, so I shove the ring deep into my pinny pocket, and get back to my work.

A mirror in the back room is covered in dust but I can still see my reflection in it. I shake out my hair and yank it into a low pleat. Then I turn on the tap at the rickety sink, and splash some water onto my face, finishing with a good scrub round with a towel. I look a bit pale, but sane enough.

Mary looks hard at me as we pass each other in the corridor. I thought I looked pretty normal, but she knows me too well.

"What's wrong, Rubes?"

For a second I consider keeping it from her, but her concern makes me feel a bit teary. "I'll tell you later, after work, but you know that man I thought was watching me swim on our first night? I think he was here just now, outside the courtyard. Maybe trying to get in, maybe just trying to scare me. He threw this in for me to find." The dull brass ring teeters on my shaky palm.

Mary nearly drops her pile of fresh towels, "Is he . . . is he here?" She casts a furtive glance over her shoulder. "Oh my God, Rubes, you don't think it's Derek, do you? Did you get a closer look this time?" Her face loses colour and she bites her lips so hard I see a drop of blood against the whiteness of her skin. The hand not clenched over the towels fumbles protectively over her stomach.

"Oh Mary, I'm sorry I mentioned it. Look, if I'm sure about one thing, it wasn't Derek. I didn't see him today, because he was the other side of the wall, out in the road, and the woman next door just shouted and scared him off. The man watching me on the beach was taller and thinner, and why on earth would Derek have my stepdad's signet ring? My stepdad was wearing it the night he . . . the night we left. There is no way I could miss that. Please, sit down on the stairs a minute and I'll take your towels in." I'm horrified that I could have been so selfishly wrapped up in my own thoughts. I should have said *first* that there was no way it could have been Mary's husband.

"The ring belongs to *George?* How did it get here?" My best friend sits heavily onto the wooden stair, hunching over her towel pile, her skinny legs drawn up. Her eyes are big and bright, and her pale hair is pinned neatly back from her bony face. She looks younger than ever. She sniffs a bit, and takes a bit of tissue from her pinny pocket to dab her long nose. I wait.

"Ruby, is someone after you? You know, someone from home, who maybe knows what happened to . . ."

She doesn't finish, and I keep my own eyes fixed on her face. My heart flutters and I hardly dare breathe until she continues.

"Rubes, you can tell me anything. You know that. But I respect what you don't tell me too. I can guess what happened the night we left, and you got out of an impossible situation." Her blue eyes meet mine. "Me too. But if there is chance that anyone is following you, someone from Croydon, then you *must* tell me. It affects me too, and we can deal with it. We've got friends here now."

I open my mouth to answer, but Johnnie sweeps into the corridor and comes to an abrupt halt as he sees Mary crouched on the stairs.

"Mary? Are you not well? Is it the baby?" His usual flamboyant drawl is replaced with concern, and I think again how lucky we are to have found this job.

"I just felt a bit faint for a minute. Sorry, Johnnie, I really am."

"I'll do Mary's work for a bit. Maybe she can sit out the front in the sun for a bit?" I put in quickly.

Johnnie looks doubtful, but nods. "Now stop chattering, you two. I have that bridal party due in five minutes. Mary, take as long as you need, and Ruby, you can start helping with the bridesmaids. But get Eve to tell you what to do." He flashes me a look. "Then Mary can get on the reception desk for the rest of the afternoon."

Our boss retrieves a box of fresh flowers before vanishing back into the salon. The outside door bangs and we hear a stream of excited chatter. Clearly the bridal party has arrived early.

Alone, I hug Mary quickly, almost guiltily, grab her towels and run after our employer. He is now gushing over the bride, a dark-haired glamorous model I vaguely recognise from magazine covers.

"Can I take your coats?" I beam at the rest of the entourage, who smile politely and hand over light summer coats and a couple of pastel cardigans. When I hang them up I catch a glimpse of the designer labels — Biba of course, but also Pierre Cardin, Courrèges and a pink and purple silk Pucci creation. I'm fascinated by them, and by the whole party.

The bride is beautiful, of course, and after two hours of work her long dark hair is dressed with white roses, and a few clusters of tiny pearls, creating an elegant arty look. The other girls all have dark nail polish and pale skin with crowns of tiny purple buds around their glossy hair.

Eve is bustling around, snapping at me to fetch coffee and water for the customers. I try to pass her more flowers for the last bridesmaid but she pushes my hands away.

"Thank you, Ruby, I think we're all done here!" Catherine ruffles the dark mane to give a few more tousled curls before spraying a careful halo around her client.

One of the bridesmaids asks me kindly, "Are you new?"

"Is it that obvious?" I smile back, making my two elder colleagues glare.

The girl giggles. "Only to me, I expect. I'm a stylist so I'm always doing the hair and makeup on photoshoots for Anna." She gestures towards the bride, who is now sipping a glass of champagne. Johnnie clearly doesn't hold back for his best customers. "Even though really I should be just doing the clothes now she's all famous!"

Anna turns round to face me. Her doe eyes look enormous in her sharp-boned face. "You know, you have a great look for modelling too. Johnnie darling, you should get your new girl's hair cut. She has fabulous cheekbones."

Johnnie looks smug. Eve and Catherine clear up and stalk away in silence. They look rather cross with me, and when the reception phone rings I hurry to answer it. By the time I've booked in another client for next week, and then two more for tomorrow, the bride and her girlfriends have clattered out onto the street.

"Isn't she going to wear a wedding dress? What about makeup?" I wonder out loud to Johnnie.

"They're getting changed and having all that done at the town hall. I would have offered them space here, but of course there simply isn't room. Maybe I need bigger premises."

The wedding party soon disappears towards the town hall for the ceremony. Johnnie gushes about the reception.

"So glamorous, darlings. They're having a picnic at Glebe Hall — champagne, live music, party in the woods — so different from your usual stale sandwich and half-glass of flat fizz, and so much more *fun*!"

"I take it from the over-excitement that you've been invited?" Catherine sets cold cream on another client's grey head. She can talk out of the corner of her mouth, with her teeth clenched on a long-handled pink comb that pokes out the other side. I've tried to do this, but even putting pins in my mouth nearly choked me.

Johnnie beams. "Not properly, but I've been asked to 'look in.' There are some very influential people going, not to mention a rather hunky photographer I've had my eye on for a while. I'll just pop up there for an hour, because I have a few other things to do this afternoon. You don't mind closing up do you, Eve?" Eve nods and smiles. "Mary, do you want to nip out for another five minutes? Get a bit more sunshine, before the last few clients? I'm going to head off now. See you all later."

While Mary and Johnnie are out I tidy up the back room, wash up the tea mugs and stack the empty boxes from an earlier delivery neatly in one corner. Then it's time to take another turn on the reception desk. I can see Mary sipping a cup of tea at one of the little wrought-iron tables and chairs Johnnie has artistically arranged between the shop and the pavement. Sometimes he suggests clients sit outside in the sun to help their hair 'set.' I'm never sure if this works or if he is simply trying to manage the busy parts of the day.

It's lovely to see Mary happy. I jam my fingers down hard on the signet ring in my pinny pocket, and get on with my work. But every time the door opens to admit a new client, or when Catherine drops a tin dish with a clatter, my heart jumps. I really can't terrify my best friend any more, though, so I take deep breaths and down a glass of water.

"Ruby, can you give the window a quick polish inside while we're not too busy? I'm sure I can see finger-marks."

Eve hands me the cloths and a little basin of water, and I set to work, stretching to reach the top, and leaning right down to get the bit near the gold coving.

Everything's fine, Mary's fine, the dusty street outside is bustling with life, and I'm safe in the salon — then I see him again.

He catches my eye the second time I look across the road. He's leaning casually against the wall at the entrance to an alley with his hands in his pockets. Just far enough away so I can't see his face clearly. Just like any other office worker taking a late lunch break, with a paper tucked under one arm. But he's near enough to watch me. I clutch the cloth in one shaky hand and pause for a moment. Then I force myself to stare back this time. I squint into the sun, trying frantically to see if I can recognise anything familiar. I get nothing. A dark suit and dark hair. Tall. Not very old, but not a gangly teenager either. Taller than George, if I remember rightly, but the mop of dark hair is the same. Do ghosts come back younger than when they died? If I went outside and shouted, would he hear me?

Am I going mad?

A couple of men staggering down the alley with boxes bump against him and he drops the paper. He picks it up, waves away their apologies and leans back against the wall. He's not a ghost, at least.

For a couple of minutes the dark-haired watcher doesn't move, or shift his gaze. I move a little to the right so the sun is no longer directly in my eyes. Now I can look back properly at him, while I go on pretending to rub my cloth at a bit of stubborn dirt.

Some children run down the road, ignoring their mother yelling at them. They turn down the alley, and they too bump and scatter around the watcher. Once again he doesn't move. He keeps staring at me. Is it a contest? I'm going to prove I'm not scared of him, whoever or whatever he is.

A whole line of traffic — delivery vans with painted logos, and a few cars, and a motorbike — wends its way between us, but we stay as we are. I'm almost shaking now, though. Why doesn't he do something? It is like being watched by a corpse propped against the wall. If the delivery men and the children hadn't clearly seen him and run into him, I'd definitely think he was a ghost. Would George come all the way to Brighton to haunt me? Lots of men have dark hair. I shove away my crazy thoughts and make a decision. I'm going to find out what the hell he thinks he's doing.

I move away, quickly finish my job and turn to ask for five minutes' break, but all the time I know it's going to be too late. If he wanted us to meet we would have done so by now. I look back and the man has vanished, almost as though he could read my mind.

I narrow my eyes. My palms are wet with sweat and my mouth is dry. I stare uselessly up and down the road. From her chair in the sun, Mary catches me looking, waves and stands up. The big pink clock on the wall of the salon shows three o'clock. At least three more hours of clients and cleaning to concentrate on.

I try to bury myself in the work and take over from Eve with the shampooing. But my stepdad keeps intruding.

* * *

I can see him as he was on that last evening, shouting as usual and pushing Mum around the room. A big burly man with curly dark hair and a broad chest. He smashed some of the dresser plates for good measure, watched Mum creep away weeping and turned to me where I stood frozen in the doorway in my coat.

Mary and I had already made up our minds to go that night. We'd told Derek and Mum that the teacher-training college had laid on some extra night classes. All I needed was for George to finish his usual bullying routine, and go down the pub, so I could make my escape. He always went down the Kings Head, drank with his mates until closing time, came home and collapsed in a drunken stupor.

But tonight he was late. Late home from the market because he had been doing some deal, and late to eat the dinner Mum had cooked, which was dry and tasteless by the time she put it in front of him.

George's insults never really bothered me, although nobody likes being called a prostitute or a slag, or be accused of stealing the housekeeping money, day after day. I was even used to being hit. But that evening his fist smashed into my stomach like a sledgehammer, making me double up in agony. He leant close over me. His breath was already sour with drink and anger. "Just checking you haven't got any brats brewing, like your slag friend."

His second blow caught the side of my head, and knocked me right out. Only for a couple of minutes, though, because when I opened my eyes he was still stamping clumsily around the kitchen. He dipped into the old bean tin where we kept the housekeeping money, and pulled his boots on.

I lay where I had fallen, playing dead, as my head pounded and lights flashed behind my closed eyes. My outstretched hand was sticky and wet with blood.

* * *

Finally the last client is dispatched into the warm evening with her neat curls and bright pink nails. Time to grab some food and get ready to go out. Not much food, though, because we spend every penny on our nightlife. There are so many places to explore, so many new friends to join up with. Sometimes we go out with Pearl's crowd, but lately we've joined up with a big gang of Johnnie's friends too. We hit the dance halls, the coffee bars, the ice rink, and my personal favourite, The Blue Gardenia, which is above our first-ever coffee bar, the Whisky-a-Go-Go.

"Make sure you both come in a bit early tomorrow. I want to get started at eight. We've had so many bookings, I'm squeezing a few in at the top end of the day," Catherine tells me, patting her peroxide curls. Eve nods. On top of the fact we're new, we are out partying every night, which means we aren't "nice girls" waiting for some dumb clod of a boyfriend to come along and marry us. I also made the mistake of telling Eve we tried teacher-training and didn't like it.

Both Catherine and Eve have numerous kids, and I can see how hard they work, and how their eyes are shadowed if "the baby" has had a bad night. I suppose for lots of girls you marry your childhood sweetheart, have babies and work your arse off to keep them warm and fed. Life isn't about having fun, it's about surviving and keeping your kitchen floor clean. Mum made such a great job of doing that, it made me utterly determined to have a different life. I want excitement, adventure, and all the fun she never had.

By the time we sweep up and lay a fresh towel on each chair ready for the morning, I've successfully shoved the watcher to the back of my mind, and I'm wondering what to wear tonight. Mary is yawning but ignores any barbed comments about her "little rest." I tidy the flowered coat hangers on the rack by the door, which reminds me of the glamorous wedding party.

"Eve, where is Glebe House?"

She tuts. "Glebe House for a wedding reception!"

"Is it very posh?" Mary asks, grabbing her bag and cardigan ready for our departure.

Catherine shrugs on her own sturdy, patched wool coat, and hands Eve an almost identical one. Outside the sunshine paves the street with gold and silver stripes, and the heat hits us every time a client opens the door. I wonder what they wear in winter.

"Glebe House is a ruin. It burnt down years ago, and the family that owned it never bothered to get it rebuilt. That's why Johnnie said they were having a picnic in the grounds." Catherine shoulders her bag, giving her hair another quick pat and pulling her pinny into the proper position.

Eve joins in. "Can't say as I'd ever have one of my kids get married up there. It's got a nasty history. The garden was built on an ancient burial pit, and there were a couple of other fires before the one that destroyed the place. Some people reckon it's cursed up there. Apparently some lord who used to own it believed all the local legends, decided his own wife was a witch, and burnt her to death in the garden."

The horrid story chills me, but I can see Mary almost succumbing to giggles as the pair grumble on about the ruins of Glebe House being a waste of good land that should be going to the new housing developers. They're more animated than I've ever seen them.

"But that isn't the worst of it," Catherine says. "Last year some poor girl was murdered up there. A local girl, I can't think . . . oh yes, Katie Something. She was killed on the Witch Stone, that's what they call the memorial stone that was put up for Lady Isabella. Shocking!"

The chills increase, so I'm shivering properly, and Mary has gone pale. "Really? Did they find who did it?"

Catherine is obviously pleased at the effect she's had. "She'd been seeing a new boyfriend, and her old one got jealous. The police brought him in for questioning, but then released him, and later he killed himself rather than be charged with her murder. A coward's way out, if you ask me!"

"Very sad, but it is in the past," Eve says firmly. "We'll see you tomorrow morning, girls."

At the top of Ship Street we take the opposite road to our colleagues, and wander towards Pearl's little bedsit in silence.

"That was horrible. The poor girl," Mary says eventually, twisting a strand of blonde hair in her fingers.

"I know. I see why you wouldn't want a wedding there. But things happen, don't they?"

Mary changes the subject. "It'll be weird when we move out next week, although it's lovely of Johnnie to get the room ready for us so quickly. We are so lucky to end up with him as an employer." She eyes an ice-cream stand longingly, but then claps a hand over her stomach, "I need to be careful about eating too much. I'm starving all the time at the moment. Maybe I'm having twins!"

"Cool. Although it might be more painful giving birth to two babies! I think I've got enough for a bag of chips each from my tips today," I tell her with a sigh. Then, because it has been niggling at me, I add, "I'm really sorry about before at the salon. I didn't mean to scare you. And I honestly can't think of anyone who would have followed us here." I deliberately don't mention my stepdad again. If I don't ever talk about it, maybe it will fade like a bad dream. Or wash away like that blood I stepped in the other night.

Another unwelcome thought strikes me. Could the watcher have killed the cat? If he really followed us from Croydon he must have been trailing us all day. But then why nothing for two weeks? Letting us settle into our new home perhaps, before he started to sneak into my life?

"S'okay. I know Derek won't come after me really. That's just how he is. While I was there I was convenient to punch, but now I'm not he'll just find someone else. It's not as if he cares about the baby or anything." Mary shoots me a look, "But you need to be careful. Someone's messing with you, Rubes. Maybe with both of us. This man you keep seeing, if he chucked your stepdad's ring over the wall, he came from Croydon. No question. It's like he's checking you out."

"You think I don't know that? I just can't get my head around how or who. He obviously doesn't want to confront us. He's just messing with us, like you say. I guess I wait to see what happens next." I hate the idea of being at the mercy of some lunatic but neither of us mention the police, for obvious reasons. I squeeze her arm, leaning my head on her shoulder.

The shop windows make us pause. They're decorated with spring flowers, and mannequins stand around in spotted bikinis, ruffled skirts, and red macs against a sky-blue background.

"I love that mac, but it'll take me months to save up in tips. By then I'll be all fat with the baby and it won't fit," Mary says mournfully.

"But when you've had the baby you'll be back to normal and you can buy the mac as a treat," I tell her, admiring the rows of suede boots and polished brogues.

"Do we tell Pearl about the ring?" Mary cups her stomach, smoothing the pink and grey fabric and fiddling with a loose button.

"No, I don't want to worry her. She's done enough for us. It'll work out okay, I'm sure. You'll be fine. We'll both be fine and the baby will be beautiful. Hey, what do you think about a picnic at Glebe House tomorrow after work? We could do with seeing somewhere new." I almost feel I need to lay the ghost, and the challenge of heading to the site of a previous murder — somewhere that makes me scared — might help. It's almost like I need to keep pushing myself, to keep punishing myself for what I've done. When a spark of happiness creeps in I have to stamp it out.

"What, at the 'cursed house'? Don't you think that might be pushing our luck?" She smiles, though. "Those London girls looked beautiful, didn't they? Imagine just heading off to the seaside to get married with flowers in your hair."

The evening sun glows over the older part of town, touching roofs and chimneys with gold and turning drifting seagulls into twisted shapes. I can hear the sea murmuring, and taste a whisper of salt on my lips. No dark watcher sullies the peaceful scene. The only people to pass us are giggling kids and workers on their way home. I stretch out a hand to dip into my purse, scraping out a few coins for chips, and my skin is pale and clean. No blood tonight, and the bruises are long gone.

Chapter Five

Back at Pearl's bedsit, we have the place to ourselves since she's got a late shift. It won't stop her coming out into town, though. She's promised to join us later. Mary and I scrabble to get changed out of our uniforms, and haul on our dresses.

I shove the signet ring into a little zip-up bag with the rest of my jewellery and hide the whole thing under a pile of knickers. It's a beautiful spring evening and we're heading out for some fun. I am not going to let any ghosts, real or imaginary, wreck my life again. "Can you throw my hairbrush over?"

I finish my outfit with some gorgeous, and outrageous, daffodil earrings. My dress is yellow as well — thigh-length, pleated, and nipped in at the waist with a wide white plastic belt. I brush my long dark hair carefully over one shoulder.

"Can I get away with this?" Mary holds up a huge netted skirt against a white peasant blouse. "Pearl tried to make me wear it last week, and she was a bit annoyed when I wouldn't."

"Only because my cousin sees us like dolls she can dress up. She's always been bossy, much as I love her." It looks amazing with her pale colouring, and I tell her so. I paint on my own pink eye-shadow, enough mascara to make my sooty lashes droop with the weight, and rose-coloured lipstick. Perfect!

Transformed into party girls once more, we head out arm in arm. It takes a good half hour of twisting our way down the now-familiar streets to get to the seafront. Johnnie and a couple of other girls are already leaning against the green railings with their cigarettes.

The beach sprawls behind them, and they look like a glamorous advert for Brighton in the summer. Tourists and day-trippers paddle and argue, dotting the sand in their gaudy swimming costumes, making the most of the early heatwave. A few cars whizz past. Mary takes my hand, giggling, and we totter across the road on our high heels in a rush, like kids let out of school.

A grey-haired man in a stately Bentley cruises along the seafront road, one arm casually resting on the window frame, enjoying the sun. He smiles at us and Mary giggles again.

"Very nice. Let's go and find the party!" Johnnie chucks his cigarette butt over into the sand.

"Johnnie! You can't do that, you might have hit someone!" Victoria tells him, stretching her arms skyward and yawning. The sun lights up her golden hair and her green eyes.

"Hope I did, and it was that dreadful girl in the green dress. Horrendous!" Johnnie leads us off down the promenade, dismissing the incident with a rude hand gesture.

"How was the wedding reception?" I ask. We trot along behind him towards the Regent. I suddenly remember my idea for tomorrow. "Why are you back so soon?"

He blows a kiss into the sun-streaked evening air. "It was divine and very relaxing. Guitars in the woods, garlands of flowers on the Witch Stone, baskets of purple hearts, and an infinite supply of champagne. I didn't stay long, because I had a prior engagement, but I'm sure they'll all still be there tomorrow morning. Rather them than me, darlings, with the history of that place."

"Eve was telling us about the Witch Stone. She said something about the girl that was murdered last year?" Mary gives him the dramatic opening he is so clearly looking for.

Johnnie purses his lips for a moment before his usual good humour returns. "Poor Katie. Yes, that was an awful thing. But to go back to the historical aspect, the Witch Stone was erected — yes, children, I said 'erected' — in memory of a rather beautiful and unfortunate young lady, whose husband decided she was a witch. He was obviously a bit insane, as so many of these toffs are." He waves off the laughter. "Anyway, the husband took his wife down to the end of the garden and burnt her at the stake. Technically it was recorded as murder, but actually, Lady Isabella Gordon might have been the last witch to be burnt at the stake."

"Eve and Catherine told us about that too. I think they were a bit shocked someone would have a wedding reception up there. I can sort of see their point, actually." Mary pulls a face. "But Rubes wants us to have a picnic there tomorrow evening."

Johnnie pauses for a split second, looking down with his cigarette halfway to his lips. Then he laughs. "Why not? It's a lovely spot for an evening out."

"Let's do it!" Victoria is enthusiastic, "I'll bring my cards if you like, and we can do some readings."

Okay. I wasn't expecting that. It turns out that nurse Victoria reads Tarot cards in her spare time. I may have to opt out of that. What with a fairly earthbound watcher who may or may not mean me harm, or the spirit of my stepdad lurking around somewhere, I reckon the dead can stay buried. But I do fancy following in the footsteps of the wedding party and their flower-strewn glamour.

* * *

"She looks like my sister Garnet." I point out a brunette spinning and twisting on the dance floor to a bit of Carole King.

"Pardon?" Mary leans in close to hear. "Oh. Yes, a bit. But Garnet's a bit younger, isn't she?" She snuggles back into the red velvet booth beside me and puts her hand briefly on my bare shoulder. "They'll be okay, Ruby."

I sip my Coca-Cola straight from the bottle, light another cigarette, and sigh. "I know. Just sometimes when we're having fun I feel guilty I couldn't bring them all with me."

"No regrets, remember. And . . . well, George is dead, so there is nobody to hit your sisters. They'll grow up safer than you ever did, sweetheart. Come on, you said we wouldn't talk about it while we're having fun!"

"Come and dance, Miss Pop-Lips!" Johnnie's in one of his crazy moods. He loves to call me this stupid nickname, and now some of the others have started copying him. But I laugh and get up to bop away to Elvis, enjoying the breathless, sweaty steps. I dance with Kenny and then with Ted. Ted seems to have got nowhere with Linda, but he seems quite happy to just watch her, and be granted the odd turn around the crowded floor. They'll probably end up getting married.

Finally, exhausted and sweaty, we grab a table and steal some more chairs from a very drunk group of older men. Kenny brings over a load of bottles and more glasses, and I gulp my gin and orange gratefully. I look round at the people round us.

I'm getting to grips with the different Brighton gangs now. Much as I admired the 'London girls' from the wedding party today, I stay away from the 'London boys' in dark suits flashing their cash at the seedier Brighton bars. I prefer the other tribes that gather on the seafront at the weekends. The suited-and-booted Mods and the leather-clad Rockers seem more like us. They seem less dangerous too, however often they clash with each other. I'm not sure where the university students fit in yet, but Pearl is always grumbling that most of the male students she has met already have girlfriends.

"Hey! You'll never guess what!" Victoria's pink shoes clatter over the floor.

"You got another new man?" Pearl appears on my left with a glass in one hand and a pretty gorgeous bloke in the other. She pulls him down next to her at our table, making the bottles and glasses chink and the whole structure wobble.

I hug her. "You made it!" Victoria pretends to cuff her friend's head (very gently in order not to ruin the elaborate hairdo).

"No! Gillian — you know, Peter's ex — she's got together with a London bloke and he only asked her to marry him! Maddie — she's part of Jack's crowd — told me just now. They are so shocked and *jealous*!" She laughs.

Pearl frowns over her drink. "But that's not good, surely?"

"Oh not one of the *London boys*. I mean a proper London chap like Johnnie. Apparently his family have a place in Chelsea, and an estate in Berkshire." Victoria, normally so cool and sophisticated, is practically hopping with excitement. "I reckon we might even nab a wedding invitation. Imagine little Gillian from Whitehawk becoming an actual lady!"

"Wow!" But actually my first thought is the Witch Stone story, and poor old Lady Isabella Something who got burnt at the stake by her rich husband. I must concentrate on the present, or that snippet of historical gossip alone is going to give me nightmares. And quite frankly I have enough of those. It makes a suitable challenge though, making myself go through with the picnic idea on the site of a couple of old murders.

"More drinks!" yells Pearl. "We've got to celebrate!"

"Oh, there's Leon!" Victoria squeezes my hand and looks apologetic before vanishing into the crowd with her new man. He looks an unlikely match for her, being tall, thin and rather bewildered, but then Victoria's men change week by week. I've yet to see a man strong enough to ward her off. It would be like resisting a tidal wave. She threads her way across the dance floor, dragging him along behind her.

Pearl yells after her, "I'll see you at the Starlight later. Oh, this is Chris, by the way. He's a medical student."

Mary and I smile at Chris. He has red hair, freckles, and a chunky body emphasised by a tight-fitting shirt. I can't help thinking what pretty babies he and Pearl would have, and get the giggles. I hide my amusement in my drink as they go off to the dance floor.

"Hey, Ruby. How are you doing?" It's Kenny, black hair all tousled and sweat glistening on his forehead. He slides into the seat next me.

"Good thanks. Want to dance?" He's such a sweet, undemanding companion and almost 'one of the girls,' so I never mind pairing up with him.

We join the crowded dance floor just as the band strikes up a smoochy Ella Fitzgerald number. Kenny's tried it on a couple of times, but he's quite happy when I pretend to ignore his whispered suggestions. I think he'd actually be surprised if a girl did let him kiss her. Sometimes I wonder if he's really still quite inexperienced, even though he never misses the chance to make suggestive remarks.

We spin round the far side of the floor. Suddenly, I get the all-too- familiar feeling I'm being watched. My scalp prickles, and a little electric shock of fear shoots through my body. Surely the watcher couldn't be here?

I dart a glance towards the London boys sitting in the smoky corner of the bar. Sure enough, one of them is staring right at me. I get a vague impression of blonde hair, before the other dancers hide my view. But not by any stretch of imagination is this man tall and dark, so he must be staring for a more basic reason. He's quite good-looking, actually, I have to admit.

The song ends, we break apart and Kenny heads off to get drinks. I can see the blond man pointing at me and laughing. A craggy, older man standing next to him is peeling off a wad of cash. My heart starts to thump painfully, and my fingers tingle. The craggy man *is* tall and thin, but he stoops, and his head is bald and shiny. He has a distinctive long nose, and bright beady eyes like a shrew.

Kenny returns from the bar, expertly balancing a bottle in each hand. "Your drink, Rubes! Hey, I saw Mary getting her coat, and she said to tell you they're all heading to the Starlight early. If you drink up, we can catch them at the door."

The band takes a break, and the little gang of London boys swaggers across the floor as if they own the place. A couple of suited members of the entourage are arguing loudly with the barman while their girlfriends titter and shriek encouragement. Two leather-clad blokes with greasy ponytails are getting in on the action, and I just know how this is going to end.

I slam my bottle of Coca-Cola down on the table and grab Kenny's hand, "Let's go now, before they start anything!" He nods, and we scoop our coats from the chairs.

It's very dark outside, and the light drizzle is a bit of a shock after almost three weeks of sunshine. But the streetlights light up the wet road, and I know the way.

We can hear shouting and breaking glass behind us. I speed up, and Kenny tells me that Brighton's getting rougher. "But don't worry, Ruby. It just pays to keep out of the way when something kicks off."

We dodge the passers-by and head briskly up the road, past the silent shuttered shops, the post office, and the row of dingy cafés. Someone's broken the butcher's window, and a couple of blokes are heaving a temporary wooden shutter over it.

"Hey! You're going the wrong way," Kenny tugs my arm. I keep on going down the side alley. "This is a short cut." Mary and I often come down here in the daytime. If Johnnie's in a good mood at the salon he lets us have a half-hour lunch break, and we let ourselves out of the courtyard door and charge down to Brenda's Café. It isn't the best place to eat, but she lets us have stuff on slate if we've spent too much the night before. We stuff ourselves with chicken and chips in a basket, washed down with Coca-Cola, and run back before the afternoon clients come in.

Shame I don't fancy Kenny in the slightest, because he would be a perfect boyfriend. I ignore his hand, and we march briskly on towards the Starlight Rooms. It's not like I've never been with a man. I keep that quiet though, and even Mary thinks I'm still a virgin. I'm not a slag, but for me all that kind of thing was just a way of growing up and proving to myself that I was different to Mum. There was never any love involved. I've never had any romantic dreams of white weddings and all that. Does that make me strange? Yes, I suppose it does, but it's up to me how I live my life really. Then I met Mary, and her relationship with her husband sort of confirmed what I already suspected — you have to get lucky with who you fall in love with or they'll just take advantage of your weakness.

A man runs past us and disappears into a crowd of laughing teenagers near the door of the Starlight, and I gasp. My heart beats a quick tattoo of fear. I wish I could stop being so jumpy.

"Rubes! That was quick. Did you run?" Mary's standing smoking on the steps with Ted.

"Hello, Ruby. Don't you all look amazing tonight?" Ted gestures to the other girls and at Linda in particular. She rolls her eyes but then winks at him.

"Of course we do, Ted. We spent long enough getting ready," I tease him. He's looking cool in black trousers and a red Coca-Cola T-shirt with a black jacket. He's about five inches shorter than the rest of us, but when you have a personality like Ted's it doesn't seem to matter.

Mary smiles at Ted too. In her purple skirt, with her hair in cascading waves and lips picked out in scarlet, you'd never guess she was pregnant. She taps one scarlet shoe impatiently while we stand in line to get in. I feel a warm rush of pride when I remember the mousy girl from teacher-training class. Come to think of it, if Ted wasn't mad about Linda, he'd be ideal for my best friend, with his mop of blonde hair and impish looks . . . Maybe in another life.

I take a quick glance but I can't see the blond man from the Regent. He's probably still smashing up the bar with the other London boys. We crowd into the smoky bar. A hand brushes my shoulder in the dark and I jump as I glimpse a blond head, but it turns out to be a younger boy entwined with a frizzy-haired girl. Probably a good thing. I don't need any more trouble at the moment.

The Starlight Rooms are in a basement. The walls and ceiling are painted black and the only light is an occasional strobe that flashes across the crowds. You have to hold onto your purse, but the music is great.

"How's your job going?" I ask Kenny, when we're eventually buried in a dark corner with a table full of drinks. Kenny's a junior reporter on the news desk at the *Herald.* He's only got eight months before he's up for promotion to another office, so he's determined to bag a big story before he goes.

"Not that good," he tells me dolefully. "I'm still trying to find that big story. Oh look, there's James! Hey, James, over here!"

He waves through the smoke. I look up to smile politely at the newcomer. "James is a junior reporter, like me," he tells me. "We're trying to hunt down that next big scoop." But I don't pay much attention, because James is gorgeous. For the second time in one evening I feel that dangerous jolt of attraction.

He's not classically good-looking, but he has a kind of world-weary charm. His features are a bit weathered, he has lines around his eyes and mouth, and his skin is slightly tanned as though he spends a lot of time outside. I try not to stare, and to sip my drink nonchalantly but I can feel myself blushing as an oblivious Kenny does the introductions. Thank heavens it's dark.

James nods at me. His eyes are almost turquoise and fringed with thick black lashes. "Kenny said you were new in town. Where are you from?"

Gorgeous he may be, but he's still a reporter looking for a story. So I fudge the answer. I say "Croydon" too quietly to be heard above the music and then move swiftly on to questions of my own.

"So when are you and Kenny going to get that front-page story?"

James slides into the booth opposite us and laughs. His teeth are very white and one of the front ones is slightly chipped. Up close I notice a scar on his cheek, running the length of his face from ear to chin.

"We're working on it, aren't we, Ken? I did get a great start last week on some old lady in London Road who'd been running a brothel, but then I gave it to Ben on the night desk and he signed it off under his name!" James is clearly disgusted.

"Told you *not* to tell that Ben anything, mate. Not ever. If he can nick a story he will — anything so he doesn't have to get off his fat arse and actually do some work." Kenny takes a swig of beer and gesticulates with a cigarette in his other hand.

"Watch it! You nearly set fire to that girl. I know, I know. I was just so chuffed to actually get a decent lead. Then I felt stupid for giving it to him in the first place."

"Well, you are a bit of a clod. I put it down to you being Irish."

James thumps him on the arm, "Half-Irish, and not as thick as you might think, mate! Wait till I get a front page and you'll be left reporting on the dog mess on the promenade."

They both collapse with laughter. They've obviously had quite a few drinks.

"Come and dance, both of you. Better luck tomorrow!" I tell them firmly, avoiding James's turquoise eyes. "I've told you anyway, Kenny, I bet I can find you a story. You have no idea what I hear while I'm ruining clients' hair!"

They both laugh, and we join the rest of the crowd in the heat and the bustle of the dance floor.

By eleven-thirty the nightlife is slowing down, and we head off home in a big bunch. Couples peel off to cars or the beach until it's just us strolling arm in arm up the road in the muggy night.

James and Kenny have disappeared to another party, this time at a flat in the rather grand Sussex Gardens, and nobody seems to have noticed that every time James speaks to me, I turn a silly shade of red. That is not sophisticated, but he's probably not interested anyway. Romance is the last thing I need on my plate.

The earlier rain has rinsed off a layer of dust and left a few puddles. The sea crashes on the pebbly beach, and I can see distant pinpricks of light that could be ships, or even France. It seems a long way. The hill feels steeper than usual, and we slow to a stroll. Mary is yawning, and Pearl hums 'A Hard Day's Night.'

At the top of the road, we turn down the familiar concrete path to the nursing accommodation. The building is pale in the moonlight, and I'm just thinking how lucky it is that Pearl's room is on the ground floor, with its own little front door. I don't think any of us have the energy to climb stairs just now. Oh . . .

We jerk to a halt.

The door of Pearl's bedsit is ajar. The lock hangs by two rusty screws, and swings gently in the breeze.

"No!" Pearl exclaims. I grip her arm with one hand and Mary's with the other. I can't breathe for a second. Then I force myself to move, certain that a tall figure is lurking in the shadows about to attack us.

"Bloody hell, someone's broken in. Look, you two stay right up there by the road. In fact start walking along it after me. I'll go ahead and get the night watchman and ring the police. Don't go near the door, okay? I mean it. They could still be in there! If anyone bothers you, scream bloody murder and wait for help." Pearl's off before we get a chance to answer, sprinting along the road towards the bright lights of the hospital main entrance.

My heart is battering my ribs. Mary and I cling to each other, huddled by the roadside and staring transfixed at the open door. Eventually I start to pull her towards the hospital entrance as Pearl told us.

"What if *is* Derek? Or that weirdo that keeps watching you? I'll feel so guilty if we came down to Brighton and ruined Pearl's life too," Mary wails suddenly.

I lick my lips. My voice is croaky. "It'll be okay, Mary. It probably doesn't have anything to do with us. And anyway we're moving out in soon. Look, let's walk down towards the hospital . . ."

We inch down the road, still clutching each other like a pair of Siamese twins. A few cars whizz past, and I keep turning my head like some demented owl, trying to look everywhere at once. There is no doubt in my mind that this is connected to me, and me alone. That warm feeling that my siblings and my best friend are all safe now has gone, leaving an icy stone of guilt in the pit of my stomach.

Bloody hell. Somebody else knows, and he's obviously going to keep reminding me.

Chapter Six

The night watchmen make us wait inside the hospital while they search the bedsit. We huddle together on a plastic bench, sipping disgusting weak tea. The smell of disinfectant prickles my nose, and a cleaning lady wheels a red bucket around, sloshing her mop close to our shoes. Mary fiddles with a packet of cigarettes, and Pearl keeps yawning.

The adrenalin and fear has dissipated, leaving us exhausted. I look at my hollow-eyed companions and feel that sick guilt again.

Pearl looks hard at me. "Ruby, I know how hard you two are trying, and I know it took a lot of guts to get out when you did." She pushes a strand of curly hair back, and takes a deep breath.

There's a 'but' coming so I speak quickly. "I really don't know if this is connected to anything in Croydon, or to our family. You have to believe me. But do you remember when I saw that man on the beach? At work today," I glance at Mary and she nods, "earlier today I was cleaning the salon windows and I saw him right opposite just watching me. It went on for so long I was going out to ask him what the hell he was doing, but then he just vanished."

Should I tell her about the ring? I bite my lip, racking my brain for anyone who would have followed us down here. The only sensible conclusion is that I *was* seen that night. But who would witness an attack like that and not call the police?

"It could be Derek," Mary says quietly. Her hand shakes and tea spills on her white blouse. She puts her cup down on the floor, and the cleaner coughs crossly in our direction.

I shake my head. "It isn't. I'm sure of it. Like I said, this man is tall, maybe even over six feet. Derek is shorter than me, and much fatter."

"Maybe he paid someone to follow us. Like a private detective."

"Do you really think he would have the money to do that? And like you said before, he doesn't care. He's far too lazy to try and find you."

She relaxes slightly. "You're right, and the only reason he'd hire someone to find me would be to . . . to hurt me again." Her bottom lip trembles.

"He can't and he won't!" I hug her tightly, almost crying myself.

Pearl's blue eyes flick from one of us to the other. A policeman appears at the hospital entrance, and my stomach lurches.

"Just one more thing," she says quickly. "I live there on my own, okay? You just came after work and got changed for a night out. These men will never realise that all the stuff isn't just mine. You give the salon as your home address, and we'll talk to Johnnie and get you moved out tomorrow. I shouldn't have had house guests for a couple of weeks. I could get in real trouble."

"Pearl, I'm so sorry." I touch her arm awkwardly. She doesn't look too upset, though, whatever calculating has been going on in her head, and she folds a gentle hand over mine.

"Ladies?" One of the navy-uniformed night watchmen beckons us into his drab, overheated little office. We file in like a posse of naughty schoolgirls, and he closes the door behind us.

"Did you find anyone inside?" Pearl demands.

"We have carried out a search of your property, Miss Smith, and of the surrounding area, but have no reason to believe that the perpetrator is still in this area. There have been a number of cash and jewellery thefts recently, up as far as Dyke Hill Road. I suggest you return to your accommodation and make a list of anything missing."

"Was there much damage?" I ask, tentatively.

He's a short, round little man with grey hair and a small beard, like a miniature Father Christmas. But he looks shrewd enough. "None at all. Just one more thing, Miss Smith. I suggest that your 'visitors' are logged in via the official channels next time."

To our huge relief, he winks at Pearl. She shakes his hand. I can see some of her sparkle returning.

"I will speak to the police and make sure all the paperwork is filled out. If you come by my office at some point tomorrow, I'll just need signatures and that list of missing items. If you have any worries, Miss Smith, please don't hesitate to come back up here tonight."

Slightly stunned by his efficiency, we're soon heading back down the concrete path with a new set of keys.

"Blimey, Pearl, they certainly look after you here!" Mary says in awe. The lock has already been mended, the door secured, and it doesn't look damaged at all.

Pearl says nothing, but grips my hand as we approach the building. A group of girls swishes past calling greetings, but we ignore them. It takes a moment to get the new key to work but then it scrapes around the lock and the door swings open.

I'm expecting the tiny room to be a devastation of upturned furniture and general chaos, but I let out a long, relieved breath. The sofa and bed are still strewn with our clothes and unwashed plates sit in a half-filled basin next to the utensils. It turns out that our combined makeup is still haphazardly arranged on a corner table, the shoes are lined up at the door, and my little zipped-up bag is hidden under the pile of clean knickers. You'd never know an intruder had been in here, except for the new lock. Weirdly, this worries me more than if we'd discovered a huge mess. Even when Pearl announces that the cash tin she hides under the sink is missing, I can't shake the feeling that this wasn't really about a burglary.

"God, we were so lucky!" Mary sinks down onto the bed. She massages her stomach gently and stretches out her legs with a sigh, kicking off her shoes.

Pearl drags out some enamel mugs, and sets her little pan to boil. As it starts to froth, she sniffs the contents of the milk jug, pours and adds a generous tot of gin to each mug.

"No way — gin and milk!"

"Well, I can't afford brandy. Not that I can afford gin either, but this was a Christmas present. I think we could all do with it. Even Mary."

Mary hesitates for a moment, then takes the drink. "It's okay. I think I'm past the sick stage. Even coffee is starting to smell normal now!" She leans back towards the table to push a lipstick lid back on with her finger. The whole table seems to be buckling under the weight of cosmetics. One accidental touch and the whole thing would go over.

I sneak a glance at Pearl over the rim of my mug. She frowns, checks through her sequin-covered jewellery box and shrugs.

"Honestly, nothing else is gone. There were only a few shillings in the tin, so I suppose there just wasn't the jewellery and money he was hoping for. All my stuff is just costume, even the bits Mum gave me — precious to me but you wouldn't get anything for it."

We sit in silence for a moment. Another group of student nurses clatters past.

"Do you want to speak to the police about this man that seems to be stalking you, Rubes? I'll tell that sweet night watchman about the cash, but if you want to report this man to the police, I'll come with you."

My stomach curls at the thought of speaking to the police, and my palms slip on the mug. I put it down firmly on the lino floor. "No. I mean, I'll sound like a loony, won't I? This man who *may* have been watching me swim, *might* have been spying on the salon, and then if I say I *think* he might have broken in here, what can they do?"

"Nothing," Mary agrees. "I think we should just tell Ted and Kenny and the others what happened, and see what happens next. It might even just be a coincidence. Sorry, Rubes, but I know what you went through with your stepdad, and it makes you look at men differently. You kind of see them as a threat, even when maybe they aren't."

Pearl takes our empty mugs. She dumps them in her washing-up basin, and starts to undress for bed. "Do you think Ruby is imagining this man following her?" she asks over her shoulder.

"No. I don't. But then I feel like every man I meet might knock me around. I expect Ruby feels the same," Mary says.

Unexpected tears gather in my eyes and I blink hard. "Yes. I suppose I do. I just — well, we can't do anything until this man actually does something illegal. If we'd seen him break in here that would be different." I take a deep, calming breath, rubbing my arms out of habit. The faded bruises seem to itch and sting.

I push my tears down and cough to clear the lump in my throat. "I think we should say nothing to the police and try to see the break-in as just a coincidence. Maybe, like Mary says, I'm just putting my own fear onto some random men." Pleased with this measured and practical approach, I unhook my bra and wriggle into a short nightdress.

It's only when I turn round that I notice neither of the other girls looks convinced.

Even though I'm exhausted, I can't sleep. When the sun rises and the room is washed with pale pink and silver, I'm still lying wide awake. My eyes are dry and sore and my heart is beating far too fast. The pink light of early morning streaks my hands with blood, and I sit up, sweating, pushing my hair back and ordering myself to calm down.

* * *

"Dare you!"

"I can't!" I put a hand protectively to my hair, but he doesn't give in. Johnnie's been nagging me since we started work today. Even though I told him about the break-in and the sleepless night, which he adored because it counts as 'scandalous gossip,' his mission is currently to make me model for some advertising photos he plans to stick up at the front of the salon, and add to our current style 'look book.'

"Of *course* you can. It'll take your mind off *things*!" Johnnie is wearing a candy-striped blazer and pink shirt today, and his blond hair flops neatly across his forehead. He looks like a naughty teenager who has sneaked away from one of those toff boarding schools. "I *really* need to update the styling books. You've seen those ancient pictures. I need colour and glamour and gorgeous girls! And believe me, this cut is quick and so easy to do so we'll get through more customers. Move over Vidal Sassoon!"

Catherine looks up sharply with her eyes narrowed at the *things* comment, but I meet her gaze innocently enough. She and Eve were furious that we turned up *after* nine this morning, but when I explained about the break-in, they had to lump it. It's not as if we've ever been late before. As I told Johnnie when we first met, we both need this job.

"I think you'd look great." Mary, the traitor, chimes in from where she's snipping at an old lady's grey bouffant under Catherine's watchful supervision. Amazingly, even when it's washed, the woman's hair sticks up like brittle candyfloss.

"I don't want to be blonde. I'll look stupid, like I'm pretending to be Marilyn Monroe or something!"

The old lady turns to look at me, narrowly avoiding losing an eye from Mary's scissors. "Really dear, you look more like that Liza Taylor girl, but of course your skin is darker." She smiles graciously, all wrinkles and powder. "Unusual around here, that skin tone. Is your family foreign?"

I roll my eyes, then hastily stop and smile sweetly. "London, actually." So there, you don't get much more English than that. Not that I care. Brighton is full of foreigners — there are Italians across the road towards the sea, two Portuguese women living right opposite, and that West Indian family who sell fruit at the market — but I do get the odd comment about my origins here.

"Oh come on, Ruby. Pleeeeease! I'll help you move into your new place tonight — oh damn, actually I won't because I have an appointment first — but I'll pick you up at nine *and* I'll order a food hamper from Russell's for our little picnic up at the Witch Stone later." Johnnie smiles as charmingly as he can.

Russell's is an exclusive little place down on North Street, with designs on being the Fortnum & Mason of Brighton. They have things like champagne truffles and French pastries loaded with chocolate and cream. It's way beyond the means of two hairdressing apprentices and a load of nursing students, but Johnnie shops there regularly with his rich friends.

"I don't really think . . . can't you get a real model to do it? Is this because of what that girl Anna said yesterday?" The bride with roses in her hair, who told me I looked like a model and needed a proper haircut.

"I don't want a pro, darling, I want you!" Johnnie folds his arms.

"Okay! I'll do it, but if I hate it, you have to dye it back." I give in, realising how much we rely on him. I can at least help him out this once.

"Excellent!"

After her client has been dispatched into the sunshine and Eve is washing the hair of a skinny woman dressed all in black (who appears to be called Miss Angelica-Rose Bottomside if the appointment book is to be believed), Mary is sent to mix the powder bleach for my transformation.

Catherine looks on disapprovingly. "That powder stuff doesn't get the same results as ammonia and peroxide," she mutters, frowning at us all.

Three clients cancel appointments, so it's a quiet half-morning in the salon. After lunch Johnnie sends Catherine on an extended break to pick up cough mixture for her youngest and then then sits me down in a chair and gets to work. I close my eyes, scrunching up my face and hardly daring to look. He laughs, snipping away.

An hour later, I stare at the new me. My hair is short, almost elfin, with stray tendrils curling across my forehead, and onto the nape of my neck. The brilliant whiteness of the new style highlights my dark blue eyes, my sharp cheekbones and pouty mouth.

"It looks amazing!" I look totally different. It's like having a new identity. Is it vain to really love my new hair?

"Wow!" Mary claps.

Johnnie looks like he's going to burst with pride.

"Damn, I knew I was good, but not that good. Especially considering the material I had to work with."

Mary giggles, but loyally adds, "She's always been beautiful. Go and get the camera, Johnnie. Mrs Collins-Hayward's due in at four."

I stand by the wall as he clicks away with the clunky black camera. "Turn your head this way a bit . . . good! Gorgeous, darling! Right, now undo a button or two—"

"Johnnie! She's supposed to be showing customers the amazing hair they can have, not posing for a pin-up calendar!" Mary clutches her stomach with laughter. I'm giggling too. "Take one of us together, please? So we can put it up in our new room?" We squeeze together while Eve sweeps the floor and starts dusting the cherub mirrors. Catherine rushes back in, out of breath, with a white paper bag under one arm and dark shadows under her eyes.

"You look very pretty, Ruby," Catherine says generously, as she stashes the medicine onto a back shelf and hangs up her bag. "Johnnie has always had an eye for a new cut. I'm sure we'll get lots of requests now."

"Such a shame you're a bit fat to be a model, because you're tall enough. Really, you should live on coffee and cigarettes like Anna. Then you could be on the cover of *Vogue*!" He slips out the back before we can retaliate.

A group of chattering girls bump through the doors. The majestic Mrs Collins-Hayward follows, dressed in a purple-and-pink blouse and a bright orange skirt, but punctual as ever for her four o'clock appointment. The girls all ask for cuts, which means soon we are busy washing and snipping. I do like hairdressing now I'm more used to it, and I manage the professional chatter as I lead the first client to the sinks. I shampoo her long blonde hair and I finish off with a quick head massage as Johnnie taught me. I remember to ask her if the water is too hot or cold several times, before applying the thick conditioner. Finally, I offer her a pink flannel for her face, and she carefully dabs away the drips, without ruining her makeup.

"I was thinking of going shorter with maybe a bonnet cut, but I really love *your* hair," she says, eyeing my new cut. "Do you think it would suit me? We're going to France for a holiday and I want to try something different."

She has really lovely honey-blonde hair, which hangs almost to her waist, but I'm paid to push Johnnie's services, and I guess his latest advertising idea is paying off already. I pass her a flannel to dry her face, and agree that we can change her look.

I start to comb out the wet hair, before calling Johnnie over for the cut and style.

As I work, I keep sneaking glances at myself in the mirror. I really don't recognise myself, and I get a shock every time I catch a glimpse of my reflection. If someone really is following me, this might throw them off the trail.

Despite a late afternoon rush — I must have shampooed at least five women, and carted a hundred dirty towels — we manage to finish up by six. We stop on the way back to the nursing accommodation, and I buy a bunch of carnations from a street seller. My tips from the chattering girls today just about cover the cost. The stems, still wet from the bucket, drip all over my uniform. Pearl's on a late shift so our plan is to get packed and out, leaving everything spotless, so she can come back in from work tomorrow morning and just enjoy her sleep.

"I'll wash the dishes if you do the floor," Mary offers, grabbing the cloth.

We tidy and haul out two bags of stuff to the doorway as quickly as we can. As a finishing touch, I arrange the carnations in a glass on the little corner table, and fold back the bedcovers, while Mary pops a neatly wrapped present on the pillow.

"I got one of the enamel flower pendants from the market in the end. Do you remember the ones she said she liked?"

"Perfect!" I agree.

At the top of the path, Kenny hoots and waves in his little red Austin Seven. Thank God for our lovely friends.

"Is this all your stuff? I thought you'd have loads more!" He focuses on my new look, pretending to do a double take. "Ace hair, Rubes! You look gorgeous. I might even fancy you for myself. How about a date?"

"Thanks, Kenny, you're such a hunk, I'll take that as a compliment," I grin at him, shyly pulling at the sides of my hair. It feels so odd to have short hair. And I'm blonde!

"Thanks so much for helping us out. Are you still coming to Glebe House later?" Mary smooths a proud hand over my 'do.' We chuck our bags in the car and settle down for the luxury of being driven down to the hairdressing salon.

"I'm still coming, but what time are we meeting and where? Because I have a story to file just before I leave tonight," Kenny says, pulling out. "Oh, I forgot to tell you, Ruby, you made an impression on our James. He keeps asking about you. I might have to fight him for you."

I laugh, but secretly my heart does a little handkerchief flutter, and I feel a smile tugging at my cheeks. "Asking about me in a good way, or a 'who is Pearl's crazy cousin?' way," I ask carefully. Mary giggles and nudges me.

I can see Kenny roll his eyes in the driving mirror. "James only asks about girls if he likes them. If he doesn't, they don't feature on his radar, and they would certainly never get in the way of a good story. Back to business — where and when tonight?"

"Victoria told Johnnie about nine would be best, and that suits us because we need to unpack. Johnnie's coming back to the salon to drive us up, so we don't get lost," Mary says, grinning away at my discomfort.

"And we're having the picnic actually next to the Witch Stone!" I tell him, still smiling at the thought of James, and hoping my cheeks aren't flushed bright red.

"Johnnie said to tell everyone to park in the usual place," I remember suddenly.

It feels weird to be arriving at work at this time of the evening, but we retrieve the keys from under one of Johnnie's fancy plant pots and let ourselves in by the side door. The bedsit is reached by a narrow staircase and when we open the second locked door, Mary bursts into tears.

"Oh wow! Oh *look*, Ruby!"

I almost feel like crying myself. The room is divided much like Pearl's bedsit, with a tiny kitchen area and a few mismatched chairs round a Formica table. There are two identical beds against the wall, with bundles of faded but clean linen dumped on them. The chipped mirror from the salon back room has been dusted and hung opposite the beds. The whole place is whitewashed and clean with huge, floor-to-ceiling windows. If I look left I can see the turquoise spread of the sea, and on my right I catch a glimpse of the green hills of the South Downs behind rows of new houses.

But the real reason Mary is sobbing her heart out is that right in the corner there's a little wooden baby crib, painted white to match the room and dressed with miniature bed linen.

"Oh Johnnie is just the sweetest . . . the most lovely man!" Mary eventually croaks out, blowing her nose hard.

I beam at her. "This is lovely!" I really can't believe our luck. Did we make this happen by running away?

Mary wraps her arms around me and we do a crazy celebratory dance, right there on the clean, faded wooden boards with the sunlight pouring through the windows, and all our worldly belongings scattered across the beds and floor. We spin round and round until we're both breathless and dizzy.

"I need to get organised tomorrow. I mean, I know we bought a few mugs and things but we need cleaning stuff, and a few bowls, towels for the baby. That sink needs scrubbing for a start and—" Mary starts a list but I pull her away.

"Tomorrow. Let's go out and celebrate tonight."

I spend longer than usual getting ready tonight. Mary is already dressed while I'm still gazing at the sun drifting over the sea. "Try pink lips, and really smoky eyes," she suggests. "Then you could wear the pink shift dress, and you'll look like a real live doll!" She giggles and runs her fingers carefully through her fringe, which is stiff with hairspray.

I blow on my pink nails to dry them. "Do you fancy trying that new coffee bar in East Street before we meet the others? What's it called?"

"The one with all the pink neon lights? Um . . . Baby D's, I think. I'm not sure if there's time—"

I stop dipping into makeup pots, and glance at my watch. "Uh-huh. You're right. We've only got ten minutes. Do you want to go down and wait at the front so he knows we're ready? I'll lock up, but I must finish my eyes!"

Mary laughs, "You might want to put some clothes on too. I'll see you in a minute."

Good point. I'm still in my bra and knickers, "I'll be quick, I promise!"

With a last blissful look around our new accommodation, Mary lets herself out of our new front door. Her footsteps echo down the hall and clatter quickly down the stairs.

When I'm sure she's gone, I pull on the pink shift dress, smudge some more black eyeliner around my lashes, and then slowly pick up my little zip-up bag. I only thought of this as today, but yesterday there were five pairs of white knickers in my pile ready for packing. Today, as I unpacked, there are four. We can't have mixed them up — Mary hasn't unpacked her underwear yet.

I really don't want to keep scaring my best friend. I want her to be as happy as she was today when she saw that crib, so I need to be alone to check. The careful intruder, the one who didn't move any of our belongings, and neatly screwed the lid back on the tin when he'd stolen the cash, could easily have searched the room. Pearl has a lot of clothes, and a proper jewellery case with tons of cheap stuff, but Mary and I only had a bag each. It wouldn't take long for a methodical person to find what they were looking for.

My fingers shake as I unzip my little bag and tip out the contents. A few bits of costume jewellery, my daffodil earrings, a little beaded bracelet, one of the only gifts Mum ever gave me, and a cheap brass locket with a photograph of me and two of my sisters. It was only taken last year, but I love it.

George's signet ring is in with the clutter, and totally at odds with the other pretty, sentimental pieces.

I'm just telling myself to stop being so silly when I touch a heavier piece of jewellery half caught in the lining of the bag. I pull out a man's heavy gold-coloured signet ring. It is identical to the one thrown into the salon courtyard. I hold it up to the light and even though the room is so warm, I feel as though someone just chucked a bucket of ice over me.

Chapter Seven

This ring is cleaner than its twin, but otherwise identical in every way, with the criss-cross markings and emblem of a lion's head.

What the hell is happening here? Before I can even try to think it out, Mary calls from downstairs.

"Hurry up, Ruby — Johnnie's here!"

I shove both rings and the rest of the mess into the bag, zip it up and chuck it under the bed. Then I step into shiny pink ballet pumps and catch a glimpse of the blonde girl in the mirror. She looks older and a bit tired, but she forces a smile. My finishing touch is the sweet white plastic purse with a yellow flower on it, which Pearl gave me last week. It matches my pastel outfit perfectly, but the sheen has gone from the evening. Only sick perverts steal girls' knickers.

I lock the front door securely behind me, and dash downstairs to where Johnnie is waiting impatiently with a carload of people. Mary climbs into the front, and Victoria and Ted pull me into the back.

"Wow, your hair!" Victoria exclaims. "You look stunning, sweetheart. I take it this was another magical Johnnie makeover?"

Johnnie laughs, "Of course. I'm pretty pleased with the results. I'm doing some new advertising boards for the front of the salon, and having some more styling books printed. Hopefully it will attract some gorgeously sophisticated clients."

"I thought you adored all those gossipy old ladies?" Ted takes my chin between thumb and forefinger and turns my head to survey my new hairdo from all angles. I swat him away, smiling, enjoying the cool breeze on my bare neck and shoulders.

"Oh, I do." Johnnie releases the brake and the car pulls smoothly away. "But they don't spend much money, bless them, because they don't have any. To take my business up a notch I need big spenders. These models and society girls are perfect."

"Hey, people! Want a hot tip for tomorrow's three o clock?"

Prince Monolulu keeps pace with us for a moment, patting the car admiringly. He's a real-life African prince, and a legend round here. He offers betting tips in exchange for cash, and I think he's often on the racecourse as a bookie in the summer.

"Can't today. I'm broke! Maybe next month," Johnnie smiles and waves as the car pulls away. Prince Monolulu smiles back, elegant and as strangely dressed as ever, with his huge feathery head-dress, rows of bangles and purple shirt. Rumour has it he does the rounds at all the markets offering his betting tips. I don't know anyone who's ever won anything based on his advice.

I twist my head round to watch him wander off across the road behind us, and raise a regal hand to acknowledge a bunch of yelling teenagers across the road.

"So how do you like your new place?" Johnnie shouts over the noise of the engine. This car, a rather too clean and sporty green 1955 MGA, suits Johnnie down to the ground but it's clearly not meant for so many passengers. Victoria's long legs are propped between the front seats, and I'm jammed in uncomfortably.

"We love it!" Mary says enthusiastically and I add my thanks, wedging an arm round Ted's shoulders to give Victoria more room.

"Great! I knew you would. Victoria, darling, move those gorgeous legs of yours a little to the left. I need to change gear."

She shifts one bare foot onto Mary's shoulder. I breathe in the scent of the sea and enjoy the ride.

As we make a right turn, I see lovers strolling on the pier. The old man who rents stripy deckchairs by the hour is yawning as he stacks them in giant mounds. The air smells of the seaweed, fish and chips, candyfloss, and rotting rubbish — proper scents of Brighton. The blue sea is as calm and unruffled as an oil painting.

It takes about half an hour to drive up to Glebe House and Ted gives us a running commentary of the Brighton sights until Victoria tells him to shut up. She rummages in her bag and produces a shiny box of cards.

"Oh no, not again!" Ted groans. "Last time the cards predicted I had to make a great choice and Johnnie had travel opportunities coming his way."

"It came true. You just need to look at it in a positive light," Victoria tells him with a steely green glare.

"Yes, I went up to London, and Ted had to choose which film to see at the Odeon!" Johnnie cackles from the front seat.

"Fine." Victoria pretends to be offended. "I bet Mary and Ruby want me to do their cards!"

"Yes, of course we do!" I tell her, smiling, and squinting in the low sun.

"Liar," Ted pokes me in the ribs. I squeal and poke him back. "In fact, we really *do* because maybe they'll say whether Mary is having a boy or girl," I point out.

Mary is much happier now everyone knows she's pregnant. In fact Kenny, Ted and Johnnie are always sweetly protective of her on party nights. The baby will have three doting uncles. She beams, and rubs her stomach.

"I bet it's a boy," says Victoria. Ted opens his mouth to disagree and she puts a hand over his lips.

"No fighting in the back!" Johnnie says.

We round a bend and come out of a new housing estate to a wooded area at the foot of the Downs. "We have arrived!"

The entrance to Glebe House is marked by two huge stone urns filled with weeds. The majestic impression is slightly ruined by the fact that one of the urns lies on its side, and the stone gateposts are just piles of rubble.

Despite this, the car crunches over stones and gravel, and creeps through a pale green oak wood. I take a deep gulp of the soft downland air, and feel myself relax a little. Rings and the mysterious watcher can wait. Mary and Pearl were right in a way. I can't do anything but wait for his next move. But I suppose that answers my own question about who's winning this freakish game. This weirdo holds all the cards at the moment and I don't like not being in control.

We pull up at the edge of the weed-strewn driveway, which is flanked by grassy lawns and towering oak trees. A few other cars are here already. It's clearly a popular spot. I can see a couple of other groups around picnic blankets, the girls in bright shift dresses, and boys in tight trousers and jeans. Further away there are couples wandering among the trees, and up ahead, on top of the Downs, a herd of cows is grazing on the green slopes. You'd never know that just round the corner behind us, you can also see those brand-new, box-fresh houses, and the beginning of the town.

I stagger out from the cramped back seat and take in the view. The whole place is carpeted with wildflowers —

a few I recognise, like buttercups and daisies, but lots I don't, including a purple flower that winds its way through the white daisies like velvet thread. Clearly this was once a formal garden but it has now grown wild. Time has blurred the edges of once neat lawns, and weeds creep across the gravel driveway.

Further away, a large, oblong ornamental lake lies in front of a younger, slimmer tree-line. The grey slabs that line its perimeter are covered in lichen and cracked with age. Despite the heat, the water looks dark and cool in the sunlight.

"Ouch, my legs aren't working now," complains Ted, uncurling from the seat in his turn. "Ooh, is that Victoria's new man? The one we aren't allowed to meet yet because he needs to think she's so studious and well-behaved?"

Victoria looks across, "Oh great, he's here already. Shut up, Ted, you're just jealous because nobody will go out with you. Leon!" She waves at a skinny man in spectacles who is leaning against an oak, smoking. The man waves back and wanders over. Johnnie grins and lights a cigarette of his own. "One look at her friends will tell him she's nothing of the sort."

Mary straightens her dress and tidies her hair with one purple-nailed hand. She takes a look at the gardens around us. "I suppose the ruins of the actual house are hidden behind those trees. Isn't it beautiful, though?"

I retrieve a picnic basket and hamper of food, which luckily seems to have survived the journey, and look around, "Where's the Witch Stone?"

"It's over on the other side of the driveway — see where the lawn is cropped short by the deer? I believe the original spot where Lady Isabella was murdered was nearer the house, but the stone was put up many years later. Sadly, the house was left in ruins after the last fire. People said it had supernatural causes." Leon's voice sounds educated, with just a hint of an accent. Welsh, maybe? He smiles at me as he and Victoria join us hand-in-hand.

"Everyone, this is Leon. Behave yourselves," Victoria says sternly. She glares at Johnnie, who is clearly delighted at the chance to stir things up.

"Let me take that for you." Leon leans down to take the picnic basket. "Is that where you want it — by the stone? It's a lovely spot, but blighted with bad history. In fact this whole area was once associated with witchcraft. Glebe House was originally built near its own church and village, but both were abandoned by the gentry who inherited it, and now all the buildings lie underneath that new estate you pass through at the end of the drive."

He's gangly and a bit clumsy, with hair that is just a bit too long, big brown eyes like a puppy-dog, and a slightly hooked nose. Not my type, but I can sort of see why Victoria is smitten. That voice could be talking about the most boring subject in the world, and you'd probably stop and listen. He's all gentle helplessness and old-fashioned charm.

I jerk out of my trance, and smile at Victoria to let her know I approve of her new man, even if Johnnic isn't looking that friendly. "Yes, please, just this side of the Witch Stone. Nice to meet you, Leon. Do you know a lot about the area?"

"Leon is writing a book on the history of Brighton," Victoria says proudly. She's obviously keen to show off her new boyfriend's academic credentials.

"Really? I do hope you're getting some of the interesting stuff in. Too many history books are just plain boring," Johnnie says.

Victoria gives him a cold glance, but Johnnie turns to unpack the hamper. There's a lot — sandwiches, biscuits, miniature pork pies, bottles of champagne, and some little meat pastries in a box of ice. Mary's in front of the stone, which is a bit like a gravestone, but taller. I drop my purse down next to a clump of buttercups, and wriggle over to read the inscription:

'In memory of Lady Isabella Gordon, aged 19, who lost her life in 1922, but is remembered forever.'

It's a bit bland, as memorials go, but I still feel a pang for the long- dead girl. What an awful way to die, in the flames and the smoke. There is no mention of the girl who died last year — was it Katie? It seems slightly distasteful to ask, like some kind of gossiping granny. My hand trembles slightly, and my cigarette drops ash onto the blanket. I brush it away and get a grip on myself, but when there is a lull in conversation I scan the crowds for the watcher.

"Are you interested in history?" Leon asks us, accepting a glass of champagne from Victoria.

I squint through the line of trees, picking out the blurred shapes of crumbling walls, and weed-strewn stones. "Sort of. I suppose I am if it's local. Did the family never try to rebuild the house after the fire?"

Leon shakes his head. "I believe there had been a couple of fires in the kitchens before, but this last one, during the war, took most of the main building, and I imagine it was just too much trouble, not to mention too expensive, to rebuild."

"I think the last of the family line was killed in the war, and with nobody to claim it, eventually it was handed over to the council," Victoria says. "I heard a rumour recently that they are going to sell the land for building. I'd love a house up here."

"Hello, you lot!" Kenny casts a shadow over our picnic blanket. "I hope you haven't eaten all the food, you greedy pigs."

Victoria introduces Leon, and adds pointedly that he is writing a book, but all I can see is James standing next to Kenny. He grins at me, turquoise eyes squinting in the sun, and Mary giggles just to annoy me.

Kenny has his usual plaid shirt half hanging out of his black work trousers, but James is in a fitted tweed jacket, worn over Levis, and his white T-shirt and tan skin make him look like a film star. It's a great look. He looks like a more masculine Johnnie, and has that same lazy grace. My heart starts to hammer at my rib cage like a lovesick schoolgirl. A few other girls further away give him flirty glances, but he doesn't pay any attention. "I like the new hair, Ruby."

Ted has found Linda and presents her with a bunch of wildflowers before ushering her over to our blanket. "Got room for another one?"

"Of course! Love the dress, Linda darling — red is so now. Is that necklace new?" Johnnie opens another bottle, and pushes the plates towards the newcomers. "So, Leon, tell us more about this book? Is it about Brighton or this area in general?"

"Well, it's more about this stretch of the South Downs, really. The mix of ancient historical fact and fiction is really fascinating—"

"Like this site. Wasn't Glebe House originally built on a burial site?" James asks.

"Not exactly, but there is evidence of human sacrifice and tribal activity through the centuries in this general area. It was perfect, you see. There's a natural spring — it actually feeds the ornamental water feature in this garden — there's grazing for animals, and a high point to watch out for approaching enemies. One of the most important burial sites in this area is Long Barrow on the next hill. You can access it from Dyke Hill Road and — sorry, I do go on when I'm interested in a subject, and I often forget how boring it is to everyone else."

Victoria smiles affectionately at her boyfriend, "He never stops working! We went out for a walk this morning and he started mapping out Roman remains, and picking up flints that might have been arrowheads or something."

It's one of those balmy, peaceful evenings with great company and delicious food that I hope I'll remember forever. If I could tuck the memory in my old locket, along with the photo of my sisters, I would take it out on a cold winter's day when I'm old and grey, and savour the warmth and sweet smells of summer. It doesn't do any harm that James and Kenny settle next to Mary and me.

Another group by the trees has a couple of musicians and soon the sound of jazz floats through the cigarette smoke.

"Have another drink, Ruby." James upends the bottle and passes me a glass.

"I've already had too much, and that isn't my glass," I look hazily around. I'm well on my way to a champagne hangover tomorrow morning. I really need to slow down, but I'm having a good time. Maybe just a couple more. After all it isn't often that we have champagne on tap.

"James, Eve at the salon was telling us about the history of this place. She said that a girl was murdered up here last year." He's a reporter so he must know all about it, and despite my reservations I want to know what happened. Not just gossip, but hard facts.

"Hmm . . . it was a big story for us, but in a really lousy way. You always want to get the news first, but then it turns out to be someone you hung around with. That's not good. You don't exactly get hero status for writing about something like that," He sighs, and screws up his eyes against the last rays of spring sunshine.

"You *knew* her?" Now I feel really bad.

"Oh not well, but she was seeing a friend of mine for a while. You know how it is when we all go out. You know everyone, but you sort of don't." James smiles and then his expression changes. "It was a difficult situation, but some men turn to violence when they can't get what they want, and that's what happened with Katie. It was very sad, but a simple case for the police. Awful for the family though obviously, having the police and then us hanging around when they just wanted to shut themselves away."

Somebody shrieks from the ornamental lake, and then we hear a couple of splashes. Inevitably, most of our little group wants to join the swimming party.

James takes my hand to pull me up, and holds on for a bit longer than he needs to. He slides his fingers up my wrist and rests them lightly on my arm. I get that flash of attraction again, and wander with him towards the lake. The grass is sweetly scratchy under my bare feet as my pink dress floats out in the lazy evening breeze. Mary's laughing at my side, Victoria drags Leon along, and Johnnie strolls at the rear with his cigarette. A few ducks fly off in alarm, as we collapse on the daisy-scattered lawns that surround the oblong of dark water. At three corners there's a mouldering stone statue, but the fourth corner is bare.

"Someone stole Narcissus," James explains, seeing me looking. "The statues in the garden are all gods and nymphs and curvaceous naked girls. Clearly the family who owned this place always had good taste." He grins.

"No way am I jumping in a stinky lake. What is with you lot and swimming at night?" Ted asks, plonking himself down on the grass, and lighting a cigarette.

"Nor me!" Victoria is clutching a bottle of champagne. She's drinking straight from the bottle, sharing with Leon who smiles benevolently at us all. But James is still looking at me and Kenny is pulling off his shirt and trousers.

"I'm going in!" I announce, quickly before I can change my mind. I stand up and the garden spins round in a haze of gold. The dip will sober me up.

Kenny dips an experimental foot into the lake. "Freezing!" he tells us cheerfully and jumps straight in. A diamond rainbow of drops scatters across bathers and watchers. Some of the people in the water are starting a rough game of water polo with a football.

"Come on, Ruby!" yells Kenny, "James, you big girl, get in here!"

"I'm staying here!" says Mary, stretching out on the grass. Her slim legs look nut-brown against the greenery, and her hair is white-gold in the evening sun.

James hauls off his shirt, and I try to look at the laughing, chattering crowd of partygoers instead. Everyone is stripping off, the jazz trio has settled on an old jetty area, and bottles and cigarettes are passing from hand to hand.

"Come on, Ruby." James grasps my fingers, but I wriggle free and unzip my pink dress, looking straight at him. Then I grab his hand and we take a running jump into the teeming mass of wet bodies. The water is icy cold, and I surface laughing and gasping for breath, spitting mud and water weeds. There's even a bulrush crowning my new short hair.

Someone pulls James into the water polo game, and I swim over to Ted's crush Linda, who's standing near the side, waist deep in her bra and knickers. She's shivering, but she's gamely cheering on the teams in the water.

"Oh hi, Rubes! That your new chap? Isn't he one of Kenny's friends?" Her pretty little freckled face is almost hidden by her mass of curly nut-brown hair. "I love your new hair, by the way!"

"Tidal waaaaaave!" Three teenage boys launch themselves, and a whole lot of water, towards us, and Linda scowls at them.

"Ruby, meet the most badly-behaved brothers anyone ever had. John, Larry and Chris, meet the gorgeous Ruby."

I spit out more sour lake water, and grin at the noisy threesome. They look like their sister, with loads of freckles, and cheeky round faces.

For a while, I just stand there enjoying the cheering, the crowds and the romantic setting against the backdrop of the rolling green Downs. I catch a glimpse of James in the mass of half-naked bodies, and his muscular, slightly tanned torso doesn't disappoint, but it comes second to a lot of things. This is what I came for. To belong somewhere and be part of something that isn't domestic drudgery, or that grey half-life of barely scraping through the days. I feel alive.

I also feel pretty cold. "I'm getting out now," I tell Linda, and she nods enthusiastically. We crawl onto the warm paving slabs and Johnnie hands us another bottle. "Although it should be brandy after that dip!"

I look up at him lounging on the bank, immaculate as ever, and wipe some mud off my face, "Thanks!" The scene has stopped spinning but I'm still woozy and thick-headed.

Little Ted winks at us both, "Good thing you two wore matching underwear!" I throw a clump of muddy water-weed at him and he laughs and chucks it back among the swimmers. There's too much screaming from the lake to talk, so I stretch out next to Mary, enjoying the heat of the night. Linda accepts Ted's jacket, but makes no effort to get dressed. He watches her adoringly, and then gently crowns her wild hair with a daisy chain.

More cars have arrived. Other more elegant couples are sitting on the grass, in the soft glow of the sunset, oblivious to our riotous behaviour. Even the Witch Stone is a thing of beauty now. The evening light turns the grey stone white-gold and throws a long thin shadow towards the woods, like an arrow aiming for the moon.

"Hey, Victoria, you never did our Tarot cards," Mary says suddenly.

Johnnie groans and Victoria turns reluctantly from Leon to poke about in her bag. Finally she drags the shiny box out and spills a set of colourful cards onto the grass, "Okay, Mary and Ruby pick five cards each—"

"Don't forget me," Linda squeaks, finally pulling on a pleated dress and abandoning Ted. She peers over my shoulder, and then shrieks as someone flings their arms around her neck.

"Oh not those weird fortune-telling cards again. You're as bad as that stupid Carla!"

"Shove off, Larry. Go back in the lake or something or you can walk home." She's laughing, but her brother obediently wanders off.

"Okay, just the three of you then. But you must take it seriously or the cards won't predict anything," Victoria tells us sternly.

"I'll shuffle the pack before they pick to make sure nobody cheats." Leon winks at us.

I'm fighting the floating, slightly sick feeling that goes with too much alcohol and dreamily choose my cards without thinking about them. My best friend picks hers carefully.

To my uneducated eye, they just look like odd playing cards, but Victoria waxes enthusiastically about cups, pentacles and swords. She tells both Mary and me that our futures are going to be challenging but bright. I get a hermit, which also apparently means I have a solitary quest to complete. There is nothing about Mary's baby. Oh, but I have to make a life choice soon. I can't help wondering if she's quite as good at this as she thinks, and Johnnie laughs so much he almost falls into the lake.

"My turn now," says Linda, displaying her cards on the grass, "Oh I got Death. That's not good!" But she giggles.

"It doesn't mean actual death," Victoria explains, as Mary and I abandon our less interesting choices, and lean in to examine Linda's card. Whereas we got away with saint this, and the two brothers that, and my bent old hermit man, hers depicts a skeletal Death riding on a white horse, wearing a suit of armour. He holds a banner showing a white rose on a black background.

"It means you are choosing a new path, or you're about to enter a new phase of your life. Maybe you are going to be an actress after all?"

"Really? How do you figure that out?" Linda asks, taking another cigarette from Ted.

"Well, Death is ruled by Scorpio, the sign of desire, taxes — and yes, death — but as I said, picking the card signifies beginnings, ends, and a possible transformation or transition in your life." Victoria looks expectantly at Linda, who frowns and pulls at her brown curls.

"It means you need to visit me, darling, and let me do your hair!" Johnnie is laughing again, "If Ruby had done the cards a week ago she would have picked Death too, but now it's too late because I've transformed her look!"

"Or it could just mean you're going to die if you don't get your brothers out of that lake and deliver them home to your mum!" James suggests. He's still damp in his T-shirt and jeans, hair all tousled, and he towers above us.

Victoria throws a handful of grass at him. "Reporters, what do they know?"

As the sun slides away, and the noise lessens, the final shivering figures emerge from the water. The musicians accept everyone's praise and a few tips, and everyone starts to wander back to the cars. Two colourful groups of girls are strung out along the gravel driveway, ready for a long walk home, and lovers loiter among the trees. The night is cool and smells of grass and roses, and I drink in the beauty of this tangled Sleeping Beauty garden. I think where I was last month. How much can change in a few weeks. One choice can change your life, but I suppose there's always a price, just like in the fairy tales.

The stories of witchcraft and spells seem far away, but there is definitely an air of sadness about the whole place now, which suits my mood.

Our group splits at the cars, and I take one last glimpse of the now almost deserted gardens. The lake has a menacing black sheen, and the shadows of the ruined house beyond the spiky young trees give a hint of the place's tragedy. I stand for a second, revelling in the beauty of the night and the gentle drama of the soft moonlight.

"Are you out tomorrow night?" James asks me as he turns towards Kenny's car.

"I think we're going to the Roller Rink," I offer, looking round for Mary, who's off chatting with Leon and Victoria. "You?"

He grins, "I might see you up there. If that's okay, of course?"

Somehow our hands link again, and I find myself half-sitting on the bonnet of the car. He leans closer, and presses his lips on mine for a quick kiss, before jumping in beside Kenny. I wave them off, laughing.

All the way back to the salon, Ted teases me about my new boyfriend, and Johnnie is only too happy to join in. I'm quite glad when we pull up on the side of the road, next to the shadowy pots of flowers, and the neatly-stacked furniture padlocked to the railings.

"Thanks for the lift, Johnnie. And for our lovely new home." Mary is clearly halfway to tears again. I add slurred thanks, and we clatter cheerfully through the first door and up the stairs. Despite my slightly drunken dizzy feeling, I get a catch of fear in my stomach as we reach the second door. Pearl's broken lock and the stealthy intruder are still fresh in my mind.

But the door is as solid as when we left, and the paintwork gleams in the half-light and blurred shadows. Mary pulls out her key and we stagger inside and begin the usual after-party routine.

Tonight, despite our tiredness, it takes longer than usual to get ready for bed, as we stumble round making the beds — something we really should have done *before* we went out. Mary is still cooing over the baby crib, and I lay out my uniform for tomorrow while she chatters on about the picnic.

"So what's really going on with you and James?"

I pause, hairbrush in one hand, "I'm not sure. I mean, he is gorgeous, obviously, but I don't need anything extra right now." I can't bring myself to ruin the evening by mentioning the watcher, or his little extra 'gift' from the break-in at Pearl's.

Mary sits on the bed next to me. Her pale hair is neatly plaited for the night, and her pink nightdress hides the now slightly rounded belly. "You are allowed to have fun, Rubes. You don't have to marry anyone! Hell, I certainly wouldn't advise that, but if you want to have a boyfriend, then do." She smiles. "Especially when he's as good-looking as James!"

I'm just drifting off, soothed by the moonlight swirling through the bare windows, and by Mary's gentle snores in the next bed, when I get a niggling feeling that something is wrong. I rack my alcohol-fuddled brain, but draw a blank. The feeling persists, but eventually I drop off.

By the time the morning light blazes through the room I know exactly what's wrong. The sick numb feeling hits me like a fist in the stomach. How could I be so stupid? After everything that has happened?

Chapter Eight

"Mary?"

"Mmmm?" She rolls over, pushing her hair out of one eye, peering at me through the sunshine. "What time is it?"

"Just gone five. Mary, I left my white purse at the picnic last night. I need to go and get it!" Panic rises in my throat. I kick the twisted bedsheet, sit up abruptly and hit a wall of nausea so solid I nearly vomit onto the floorboards. I take a huge breath and focus on the windows until the room stops spinning and then turn back to Mary.

"You what? Okay. Don't worry, I expect one of the others picked it up. Was it on the picnic blanket?"

"Yes, I think so . . . I mean I don't remember . . . but it has my house key in it!"

"Oh, bloody hell!" Mary snaps into alertness, swinging her legs out of bed. "You think that watcher might have got it. Are you sure you just lost it? *He* could have been there last night and stolen it."

She sounds panicked, and I get that hot rush of guilt. "I don't think he was there. I think I was just stupid and left it on the picnic blanket, when I was talking to James. But I need to find it."

"I . . . well, okay. I suppose if he had the key he would have followed us back home anyway . . . and . . ." she stutters to a halt. I can tell she still believes the worst.

"*Mary!* I'll get dressed and go straight up there. I'm sure the bus stops outside Green Ridges. It's only a five minute walk from there." I start hauling my clothes on, ignoring another wave of nausea that makes my head spin again. "I should be back in time for work, but if I'm late can you tell Eve or Catherine what happened? It would be today that Johnnie's gone up to London, wouldn't it."

"Wait, I'll come with you!" Mary looks round for her own clothes.

"No, you get ready for work. If it's there I'll find it and if not — well, we can do what you said and ask around, see if someone picked it up," I'm driven by a frenzied need for action, and still furious with myself for being so careless. I put us all in danger just by drinking a bit more than usual. I'm a fool.

"Okay, and don't worry. I'm sure you'll find it." Mary sounds calm again now, but her eyes are anxious. She roots around in her own purse and hands me some coins, "Here, take enough for the bus fare at least!"

I give her a quick hug and head straight down the stairs in my old checked cotton dress and flat shoes. I hurtle down towards the sea in the early morning silence, leaping round the few workers dotting the streets, and ignoring for once the friendly deckchair man setting out his wares. I have to dodge a red delivery van, but I arrive at the bus stop seconds before the big cream bus pulls up.

It's only a few stops, but the noise of grinding gears and stench of diesel seem to go on for an age. At last the bus pulls into the side of the road and the driver makes the doors open with a bang. I leap out almost before the gap is wide enough, and start running through the new houses. The road winds steeply upwards, and I'm soon gasping and clutching a painful stitch in my side. My usually comfortable flat shoes weren't made for running, and have rubbed blisters in both heels by the time I slow to a walk at the entrance to Glebe House.

The panic has lessened, but even when I slow down it's still hard to breathe. My feet crunch on the stones, crushing the flowering weeds. The early morning air is crisp and sweet, with a promise of warmth to come.

I follow the tyre tracks from last night and when I see the bend in the driveway I start to run. The Witch Stone was where we first laid our picnic stuff, so I decide to start my search there. Plenty of long grass that could hide a little purse, surely.

My first thought is that Linda looks very uncomfortable, sitting propped against the stone like a wild-haired doll. My second is, "How odd. She must have been there all night. Is she asleep or just drunk?"

Her red dress is arranged neatly around her knees, and although her hair is tangled with grass and leaves, it is pulled back off her face. She's not asleep — she's looking right at me.

Except of course she isn't.

Linda is roped securely to the Witch Stone, staring sightlessly down the driveway. At her throat, instead of that pretty white-and-gold necklace, there is a deep dark slash. Her chest and arms are covered in blood. My eyes travel down her body to her scratched legs, and the one shoe dangling from the tip of her toes. The other foot is bare and twisted at a sickening angle.

"Linda?" Despite the fact she is obviously dead, I creep forward, one hand outstretched as though to a potentially vicious wild animal. My whole body is shaking so much I can hardly move, and my jaw is rigid with pain in the attempt to stop my teeth from chattering. Lovely, happy, round-faced Linda is dead. Not just accidentally dead either, but sadistically, carefully killed, like that poor cat on my first night in Brighton. I withdraw my trembling fingers and rub my arms furiously. The long-healed bruises

throb and I rub harder, staring at the body, tears coursing down my hot cheeks.

There is nobody else to disturb the early morning magic of the garden, and the woods sway gently in the light breeze. A flock of crows flies up squawking, their ragged feathers harsh against the blue. They jolt me back to reality and I turn to run back down the drive, faster than I've ever run before. I stumble and fall hard on the gravel and stones, grazing my knees and palms and sprawling like a little child. I scramble to my feet and stagger to the end of the driveway.

Blood. So much blood everywhere. As I turn down the road the horrors are spinning through my mind, blurring past and present.

* * *

I'm back in Croydon the night we left . . .

"Ruby?"

My mum's soft, whimpering voice barely reaches me as the door bangs behind my stepdad. I want to shut her out, push away that pathetic person who should be strong enough to protect her kids, strong enough to walk away.

"Ruby, don't be angry with me. I'm trying my best . . ." She gives a little sob that as usual catches my heart and tears it to tiny shreds.

She is trying, but she just doesn't have the courage to break away. My mum is worn down by the years of motherhood, of ill-treatment from various men. She's weaker than I ever imagined. I swing between pity and disdain.

I wriggle upright. There's sticky blood on my hand. My head still throbs and my stomach aches. I get up and run a bowl of water and get towels. It's what I always do. The house smells of sweat and beer, but my little siblings are blessedly silent. Quite often George's shouting wakes them, and after he's gone I have to deal with the screaming babies first, before I tend to Mum's and my own wounds.

Mum is still lying on the floor, her eyes dull, face closed, and I slip an arm round her shoulders, urging her to sit up. Her cheek is purple already, and the cut above her left eye should probably have stitches.

"You need to leave him," I tell her, as I have a thousand million times before.

Her answer surprises me. "I think . . . I think I've found a way, Ruby. It will be better for all of us — Aunt Jackie will take the babies, and you and Garnet, you're big enough to take care of yourselves."

Her blue eyes, so like my own, search my face. I shift awkwardly, dipping the towel and dabbing her cuts.

"What do you mean? You're going to run away but leave your kids with that monster?" She can hear the contempt in my voice. I sit back on my haunches, staring right at her, daring her to confirm it.

"No, Ruby, I'm not running away, but I am leaving." Her voice is still soft but there's a new note of tired resolution.

"What do you mean?" I check my watch again. The seconds are ticking loudly by. I was supposed to be out of here long ago.

Like a child displaying a prize, my mum slips a hand into her grubby apron pocket, and pulls out the object. She winces, and slides up to sit against the wall. It's a knife — a small penknife, the kind of thing the kids play with down the market. Mum flicks the handle and the blade opens, sharp and shiny against the dirty lino.

"Mum?" Like an idiot, I still don't get it.

"I know you don't understand but I can't go on like this, and the only way out for me is—"

"But, Mum, you're pregnant!"

"It will be better in the long run. I can't look after another child, Ruby."

My mind is spinning. I look at the bump where the baby is, and imagine it wriggling around, breathing, growing inside Mum's belly — until she decides to end both their lives before it's even born.

"You can't do this," I tell her. Does she know I'm running away with Mary tonight? But she's clearly thinking only of her own selfish path to freedom. I make a quick decision and grab her by the shoulders "If George left you, would you have the baby? Would you

let Aunt Jackie help out with the other kids, and maybe go back to your job at the laundry?"

Her eyes are blank holes, and her mouth moves like a mechanical doll. It's like she's already gone. "But George won't go, and he won't let me work at the laundry. He says the other women are . . ." she stutters to a halt.

"Sluts. He says it about every woman he meets. He's got a problem. But we've got a bigger one. Come on, Mum, think hard. If he just vanished into thin air on the way home from the pub tonight, would you be okay?"

While I talk, I'm edging my hand towards her penknife, but she pulls it away protectively, finger nails scrabbling on the floor, "Mum?"

A tiny spark has caught right at the back of her eyes. She knows what I am saying, what I am offering. "Yes. If he was gone, I could be happy again."

We both know that isn't quite true, but she'd certainly be better off. "And you'll have the baby?"

"I will. I promise! Oh, Ruby, I can feel the baby moving!" She takes my hand and puts it gently on her bump as something inside pokes out, an elbow or a knee, and squirms from one side to the other.

Can I trust her? Can I do it? My own bruises are throbbing, and with time marching on, Mary and I only have a small time slot to get out of here. I can't let my best friend down.

* * *

Running down the hill from Glebe House, half blinded by my tears, I'm almost surprised to find my hands are wet with sweat alone. No bloodstains or bruises today. But my arms still hurt.

I'm sure there's a telephone box at the end of the road but before I can reach it I turn a corner and run headlong into tall man in office clothes. He catches me by the elbows.

"What's wrong, love? Has someone hurt you? Do you need help?"

After a brief moment of panic, I realise the slightly alarmed, middle- aged face staring down at me is not the watcher, or my stepdad resurrected.

"Someone — my friend has been murdered by the Witch Stone — I need to call the police!"

The man studies me for a second and then yells towards the house, "Angela! Come here, love. Quickly!"

I blink rapidly, dragging an arm across my snotty, teary face. I've clearly ambushed this poor man outside his gate. A woman who must be Angela appears at the door and exclaims at the sight of me.

"Girl says there's been a murder up at the old house. She just found the body. You look after her and I'll call the police." He runs in while Angela —blonde with lots of makeup — storms out of the gate, and gathers me up into her arms like a child. "A murder! You poor thing. Can you tell me what happened?"

Other curious neighbours turn up and Angela tells them there's been a murder. I don't see any harm in telling them, and their little community closes around me, safe and reassuring.

"I lost my purse last night at a picnic up by the Witch Stone. Linda . . ." I struggle to say her name. Angela and the other women make sympathetic noises and push a cup of tea into my cold hands. "Linda, my friend, was there too. This morning I came up before work to look for my purse, and I saw her . . ."Fresh tears spill over and Angela puts an arm around my shoulders.

"What a horrid thing to happen! Look, love, you're safe now. Wait with us until the police get here. Albert and Terry have gone up to make sure nobody else goes near that poor dead girl." An older woman with tight curls and a green apron takes charge of the neighbours.

"This is just like what happened last year. Another poor girl was killed up there, but the man that did it is dead. He couldn't deal with what he'd done so he hanged himself," a young man is a brown suit tells the assembled crowd. "It was a love triangle."

"So who killed this poor girl, then? Did you see anyone up there?" The aproned woman has a deep whisky-and-cigarettes voice and looks a bit like an ageing movie star. She gives the young man a withering look that makes him blush.

I blink at her in the sunlight. I can't speak. I can't think of anything except Linda's blind stare and red throat.

"That's enough. She's still shocked and no wonder. I'll look after her until the police come." Angela ushers me into her smart little house, one gentle arm still firmly around my shoulders. "What's your name?"

"Ruby." Suddenly words gush out along with my tears. "I just can't believe she's dead. Why would anyone kill Linda? She was so sweet and funny—" Ted's going to be devastated, I think numbly, and her lovely, naughty brothers. Her parents. I don't know what they look like but I imagine her mum to be a freckled copy of Linda, and the dad — large and homely with a brown beard.

"Such a terrible thing to happen. We only moved in last month when the houses were finished. This is a lovely area. To think something like this could happen right under our noses." Angela purses her mouth. "I'll get you some more tea, and you can use the phone if you like. Maybe call a friend, or your mum, or your work? Such a good thing we've got one."

I sit on her sofa and try hard to get my thoughts in order. First, I'm worried the watcher is responsible for Linda's death. Should I tell the police about him? If I do, I'll have to add my suspicions that he followed us from Croydon.

And that leads back to George, and a nasty little blood trail. Oh God, what if they find out about George and think I killed Linda too? I can't prove that she was dead when I got there. I start panicking again, breathing faster as my heart thunders in my chest, echoing in my ears.

Angela returns with a mug of tea and a plate of toast on a wooden tray. She whips a white scalloped cloth out from the table drawer to pop the whole lot in front of me, and then waits expectantly.

"Thank you, Angela," I say, making a huge effort to smile at her. My stomach is churning, and I couldn't possibly eat anything, but I sip the hot drink gratefully. "Do you mind if I telephone work now? They'll be worried about me."

She indicates the telephone, and rather to my surprise she leaves the room tactfully while I dial the salon number.

"Ruby! Where are you? Are you okay? Did you find your purse?" Mary fires anxious questions at me, while I try to find a way to tell her.

"Mary, are Eve and Catherine listening?"

"Sort of, but we're really busy at the moment."

I listen to the buzz of interference on the line and wish I was there, working through the clatter and chatter of the salon on a normal day. "Mary, I went to look for my purse, but — Mary, Linda's been murdered. She was tied to the Witch Stone. Some really sweet people in the new development at the top of Green Ridges let me call the police." I can hear the sharp intake of breath, and really wish I didn't have to keep shocking her like this.

"*Linda?* Someone *killed* her?"

Before she can start asking any more questions, I see two police cars pull up outside, and lower my voice. "Mary, this is important." I glance round, but I can already hear Angela at the front door. "This is not to do with anything else in our lives. We are Linda's friends and we want to help find out what happened, but I can't think of anything that would help at the moment." I pause for a moment, then add, "Can you?"

There's silence. I can almost feel Mary's frantic thoughts through the telephone line. Eventually she whispers that she can't think of anything either, and I sag with relief.

"Mary, I've got to go, but ring Johnnie. Okay?"

As I put the receiver down, Angela ushers the police into the room. She insists on seating us all at her polished wood table and providing never-ending supplies of tea.

I don't know why I'm surprised that one of them should be a woman, but I am. She is probably in her early thirties, and her uniform is very smart. The dark material of the jacket and skirt contrast with her pale face. Her white shirt and dark tie seem to highlight her authority, and the metal on her belt and buttons sparkles. When she removes her hat and sets it smartly down on the table, her hair is shiny, dark, and caught back into a severe pleat. In short, she looks amazing.

If someone had told me I could get a job in the police force instead of teacher-training, getting married, or being a secretary, I think I'd have signed up pretty quickly. But nobody did. In fact, of all the women I know, none of them are in the police force. I wonder if she likes her job.

The man with her is older, broad-shouldered, and wears crumpled black trousers with a slightly less pristine shirt. His jacket is slung over the chair and his tie is askew, as though he got dressed in a hurry.

They introduce themselves as WPC Eileen Stanton and Inspector Hammond. Even in my panic I note she gets a first name, but he is clearly too important. They drag out notebooks and settle themselves on the opposite side of the polished table — the inspector folds his big body awkwardly into the polished chair. Then they stare at me as though I'm the most spectacularly interesting person on the planet. My guilty brain scrabbles frantically. I'm squirming like an animal caught in a trap, or flailing under the gaze of a predator. We run through the basics, and I even stumble on my own name.

"So, Ruby, can you just tell us exactly what happened this morning, and we'll go from there?" The inspector smiles at me, but his slate-grey eyes are cold. "Don't worry,

Eileen will just be taking down what you say so we get the key details right."

I concentrate hard on my answers, explaining about the picnic, my purse, my worry because my house keys were in it, my horror at discovering Linda's body, and the fact that I saw nobody else up at Glebe House this morning.

"Did you meet anyone else on your way up from the bus stop?" he asks quietly, lighting a cigarette and pushing the packet across to me.

Do they think I'm protecting someone, or do they suspect me after all? "No. I don't think so. I mean, there were people on the bus, and some in the road, but nobody I really noticed." I clear my throat, and take a gulp of tea.

"Let me take you back to the activities of last night. Just take us through who was with you, and when you last saw Linda."

Eileen scribbles away, flipping onto the next page, and I try to recall the events of last night as accurately as possible. My mind scrabbles for names, facts, and even car details. Who went home with whom? Linda was with Ted most of the time. Her brothers were there too. What else?

"Inspector, someone told me about the murder last year . . . a girl called Katie was killed at the Witch Stone, wasn't she?"

He studies me. I can't read his expression. "Who told you about the case?"

"Eve and Catherine. They work in the salon, and then Johnnie mentioned it . . ." Hell, I really hope I haven't got him into trouble. I bite my lip. "James, he's a reporter at the *Brighton Herald*, told me she was a local girl, and we talked about it — the case, I mean — last night."

"Did anyone seem especially knowledgeable about Katie's case, or take care to see that you knew all the details?" Inspector Hammond leans forward, stubbing his cigarette out in Angela's pink saucer.

"Noooo. Not really. Everyone knows about it, but Mary and I didn't because we only moved here a month ago." I can't believe I just said that, and cover my confusion by draining the last of the tea, putting the cup down with a clatter.

"Where did you move from?" It's an idle question. Surely it is?

"Croydon. We were enrolled in a teacher-training course, but then we decided to move down to Brighton to try hairdressing. My cousin Pearl's doing her nurse's training at Brighton General," I say. I try to speak slowly and carefully, acutely aware of the WPC taking down the details in her little notebook.

"And you weren't aware of the case before you moved down here?"

"I . . . no, of course not. I told you, we'd already been here a month and nobody mentioned it. Not until we started talking about Glebe House. There was a wedding party, you see." I go through the whole thing, emphasising that it was my idea to have the picnic at the Witch Stone. I really don't want to land any more of our new friends in trouble.

The shock of finding Linda is wearing off. A sort of cold horror is replacing the numbness and the tears. My fingers are icy and my limbs are heavy. What if it is the watcher and the killing is connected to me? I'm not sure I can go down that road right now. Not while Linda dances in my brain, alternating between happiness and the tragedy of her sightless stare, with her red dress neatly arranged over her bare legs.

"Why would he do that? The killer, I mean," I ask the police officers. "If she was dead . . . her dress was quite short, but had big pleats from the waist. Even though one shoe was missing, whoever killed her took the time to fold each one of those pleats so the skirt was laid out like a fashion page in a magazine."

Inspector Hammond doesn't get it, but Eileen does, and she looks up from her notebook. She glances quickly at her superior before speaking, "You mean some care was taken on one particular element of her body? Or clothing, in this case? We haven't been up to the scene yet. But we have officers at Glebe House already, so if you can tell us anything else that struck you as strange or different, that would be very helpful." It's the first time she's spoken since they arrived. I was starting to think maybe she wasn't allowed to take part in the interview, and was only here to take notes. Her voice is sharp and quick.

The inspector nods at her approvingly but quickly adds, "In answer to your question, a murder will often be personal, so Linda may have known her attacker. Perhaps the red dress is of significance to both victim and perpetrator?" He ponders, rubbing his sideburns, and I see a little nick of scarlet where he has obviously shaved in a hurry. He shifts again on the hard chair, and he rubs a hand through his bushy hair.

"I can't think of anything else that I particularly noticed. She — well, this morning when I got to the garden, at first I thought she was just sitting there, and had maybe fallen asleep after the picnic." I lean forward. "You know when you don't want to admit what's staring you in the face?"

Eileen nods, and the inspector gives me a slight smile. "I think we have enough now, Miss Baker. We'll come down to Johnnie's later and have a chat with Mary, who you say was also at the party last night. If you can make a list of anyone else you remember seeing at the picnic, that would be very helpful," His smile becomes wider, but the eyes are still wintery. "My wife spends a fortune at that salon. I just don't understand it — ladies and their hair, bless them!"

Eileen quickly shuts her notebook and picks up her hat. Her colleague is still smiling at me, and I decide he can't possibly be as bumbling as he appears. His looks like one of the porters down at the market, slightly too big for his suit. But his eyes belie this genial impression.

"My husband will run you home, Ruby love," Angela announces, returning with a pink plate of iced biscuits. "Are you sure you won't have more tea?"

The police decline. I follow them to the door, catching a scratchy crackle of the radios. There are more uniformed policemen with notebooks talking to the neighbours.

"Are you sure your husband doesn't mind, Angela?" I ask timidly, "All this must have made him late for work. I can easily get the bus."

"Indeed, you will not, my love. After what you've been through! And don't worry, he took the day off. They're good like that at the bank, and I think this most definitely counts as an emergency." She wipes away a tear and folds me into another bosomy hug. "If you need anything, you know where to find me."

Soon I'm sitting on the back seat of Albert's slightly grubby Ford Anglia, anxiously rubbing my arms at the thought of seeing Mary and having more coded conversations. What about the others at the picnic? I can list Kenny, Ted, James, Johnnie, Victoria and Leon, but will it get them into trouble? I'm sure I'm not the only one with secrets to hide.

As I finally bid Albert farewell, I feel a surge of affection for him and his wife. Some people are just good, just as others are just bad. Most of us are somewhere in between.

"Oh, Ruby?" Albert leans out of the car window, subdued and a shade paler than he was when I first ran into him. "I want you to know me and Terry — well, we stayed with her until the policemen got there. Just, you know, so she wasn't alone."

Tears threaten again, and I nod, understanding, "Thank you for doing that. And please thank Angela again for me."

"She was happy to help. We both were. Good luck, love, and God bless!"

I watch the little white car travel all the way back up the hill, before trudging into the salon.

"Ruby's back!" Catherine calls into the back room. She's busy trimming the fringe of a tall woman with bushy black hair.

Mary and Eve both emerge with fresh towels, and Mary dumps her towels and grabs my hand. "Come on. Eve said that when you got back we could both have a ten-minute break upstairs. Instead of a lunch break," she adds, rolling her eyes in the direction of our colleagues.

"Sorry to hear the news, Ruby!" Catherine calls. Eve just picks up a brush and starts sweeping.

Mary whirls me outside, round the side and upstairs. As usual, she unlocks and relocks the door carefully. We always do.

"Right. Tell me quickly what happened, because I can't quite believe it. You must be sick to your stomach." Mary folds her hands over her belly and sits up straight, like a child waiting to recite a spelling test.

I sit right opposite her on my bed. I'm so relieved to be home that I start crying again, and Mary leans over and hugs me, scrabbling for a handkerchief and eventually producing a clean pair of knickers.

"It was awful. Poor Linda." I describe the scene, and Mary watches, biting her thumbnail the way she does when she's anxious. It's not easy for her, I can see. But having already gone through this with the police, I'm starting to get a grip on my emotions.

"I can't believe you found her. That's the worst thing, Rubes, seeing her like that." Mary snatches back the knickers and blows her own nose, wiping away tears with her fingertips. "When are they coming to see the rest of us? I don't know anyone's home addresses, and most of them will be working until tonight. Is Pearl still on the night shift at the hospital? Because she's the only person I can think of who knows everyone."

"Later today, I think. Did you phone Johnnie? He must have all the phone numbers too."

"I left a message at his house. The woman said she would give it to him as soon as he got in, but she didn't know when that would be or where he was." Mary stands up and rummages at the bedside for my uniform. "Come on, get dressed as we talk or that ten-minute break is going to be up, and the stingy cow will probably dock our pay or something. Although I have to say, they both seemed quite concerned about you when I told them about the murder. Just, you know, for half a second. Are you still saying nothing about . . . well, anything else?"

I pause, halfway into my tunic, and then haul it quickly into place. The little zip-up bag with the two signet rings seems to be flashing a neon sign over my bed, but I keep quiet. "Nothing. I said we moved down here to be with my cousin and gave our address as the salon. In fact, they didn't seem that interested in where we had come from." I give my short blonde hair a quick brush and wash my face from the bowl of water on the table. A dab of mascara and some red lipstick, and I'm good to go. Well, actually the mirror shows a ghostly pale reflection, with red eyes and greasy hair, but it'll have to do. I force a smile.

"Right. If you're sure. I don't want Derek involved in any of this, and certainly don't want him finding out where we are. Which is bound to happen if the police start poking around." Mary unlocks the door again. "We'll get through this, Ruby. We've dealt with worse."

I feel uncomfortable under her direct gaze, but I follow her back down the stairs. Sunlight pours through a little fan window above my head. The window is positioned high above the bare staircase and the coloured glass is predominantly red. To me, the light shining through spreads bloodstains on the wooden stairs.

I take a breath and run through the blood, chasing after Mary into the blinding heat of the day.

Chapter Nine

"You feeling alright then, Ruby?" Eve asks when we get back down to the salon.

"Fine, thanks," I say, lightly.

"Good. I'm so sorry about what happened. It seems awful we were just talking about poor Katie the other day and then . . ." She sighs heavily. "Go and do the towels for me then, and Mary, you can get on the reception desk."

Later, as I take over shampooing duty, some of our regulars begin to bring in the latest gossip from Glebe House. I'm surprised it's taken all morning to reach the lower end of town. Ancient Mrs Marchfield (short white hair) tells me that she's heard two girls were murdered last night, Mrs Grey (tight brown curls and red nail polish) is sure that the murderer was caught this morning, and Mrs Acton (blonde and pretty) says she heard it on good authority, from her brother-in-law's second cousin, that some poor girl was burnt at the stake last night, just like poor Lady Isabella.

I hadn't realised what hard going it must be for the police — all these conflicting stories, and none of them with more than the teeniest bit of truth. I rub up a soapy lather and then rinse through Mrs Acton's long hair. She's pretty old but loves to tell us she's never had one single grey hair. Johnnie says she uses a bit of yellowing bleach or dye at home to keep any spouting signs of ageing under control, but surely it's weird to lie to your hairdresser? A bit like lying to your doctor. There's no point.

When I finally leave the basins and start the inevitable floor sweeping, I hear the door ping. It must be the police. I grip my brush tighter, and exchange glances with Mary, who's polishing the mirrors. But instead of the policemen I was expecting, a dark-haired teenager in baggy purple trousers rushes in. "Here you go! These are for Johnnie. Mads said you wanted them in a hurry!"

"I'll sign for them." Eve carefully prints her name on the delivery note, and studies the package without opening it.

"Oh, those must be the photos Johnnie took for the window adverts and the style books. Can we have a look, Eve?" Mary has been pretty subdued all day but she finally manages a smile.

"Weeelllll . . ." Eve looks at Catherine, and I think she's going to say no, just for the sake of it, but she surprises both of us. "You've had a bad day, so why not?"

She rips open the package and glossy prints tumble out. I stare at the huge pictures. The blow-ups of our fun afternoon are massive, at least five feet square. Every detail's magnified. I don't look like me, but some huge-eyed model, all cheekbones, lips and naughtiness. The last print is hidden underneath, carefully wrapped in brown paper.

Eve lifts it out, and almost smiles. This picture is smaller, and already framed in white wood. Me, laughing with Mary, with the cherub mirrors in the background.

Linda was still alive then. The thought hits me so hard, it almost physically winds me. She should still be finishing work and thinking about what to wear, about whether she should actually date Ted, or how to do her hair.

"What a lovely memento for our new home. Our first picture." Mary winks at me. But her face is lined with exhaustion and worry.

The police appear just as we are closing up, and it isn't Inspector Hammond and WPC Eileen Stanton, but two younger men, who are clearly excited to be working a murder case. They could be twins — both fair-haired, blue-eyed and around my age — and introduce themselves as Constables Billings and Benton, which makes me blink in confusion. I silently christen them Bill and Ben.

Mary sits with Ben while Eve and Catherine make tea and hang around "finishing up."

"I did think of one more thing after I spoke to Inspector Hammond," I tell Bill. He is busy scribbling in his notebook and looks up, all eager and over-keen, like a dog ready for a walk. "I know it sounds crazy, but one of our friends had a box of Tarot cards, and when Linda picked her cards one of them was Death."

I feel stupid for mentioning it, but the man nods, slightly patronisingly. "I think it's unlikely that a Tarot card has any influence over your friend's life or death, but I'll note it down anyway."

I can tell he's disappointed that I haven't come up with anything more exciting, but I can't help but feel a bit resentful that this man is so excited that Linda is dead. It feels personal, even though I know it isn't. He's doing his job, like I'm doing mine.

"Thank you, ladies, that was very useful, and if you could drop that list of names in as soon as possible, it would help us to eliminate suspects," Ben tells us. Their polished black boots clomp off down the hill.

To my surprise, Eve is unimpressed with the law. "Those two young idiots have got about as much chance of solving a murder case as they have of running the country. One of them is Sarah's nephew — you know her, don't you, Catherine, from Eastern Road? I haven't seen him since he was in shorts, but he hasn't changed a bit. Bet he's still got grubby knees too." She pushes us all outside and locks the salon securely, dropping the keys into her vast brown handbag.

For some reason this is wildly funny and when I start laughing, I can't stop. I lean against the railings doubled up with hysterics. Mary giggles. Eve and Catherine look at us with more sympathy than usual.

"Tell you what, girls, why don't you go and get yourselves some dinner and then get an early night? It'll all look better in the morning," Eve presses some coins into Mary's hand and brushes aside our thanks.

They head off up the hill into the dusty evening. "Was she just nice to us?" I ask.

Mary uncurls her hand. "She was, and she gave us food money, which means we can feast tonight."

We head to Brenda's Café for a comforting cup of tea and fish and chips drenched in salt and vinegar. Brenda, a huge cosy woman, bustles over, coos over my new hairstyle and then leaves us to it, clearly delighted we can actually pay this time.

I lick my fingers and dig into the flaky fish, while Mary devours chips at a great rate. At last, feeling pleasantly full for once, I lean back in my chair. The sunshine warms my shoulders, and I dip my finger into stray grains of salt, idly making swirling patterns on the grey Formica table.

Eventually, Mary too finishes her feast, and starts playing with the dirty salt and pepper pots in a little plastic cage at the centre of the table. "So what do we do now?" she asks.

I suck a salty finger, squinting along the promenade at the blue horizon. The heat haze swirls above the road, and a man is walking along the front with great frothy mounds of pink candyfloss. The A-board on the pavement next to us reads 'Best Brighton Rock,' and I have a sudden craving for the sickly candy. Instead, I light a cigarette and push the half-empty packet across the table to Mary.

"My poor darlings!" Johnnie descends in a whirl of tweed and expensive aftershave, disturbing quieter customers. "I got your message, but the line was permanently engaged at the salon, so I called Kenny. So useful to have a friend in the newspaper business. Anyway he said that Linda was—" he drags out a plastic chair and sinks down at our table, fanning himself with a paper napkin. "Christ, it's hot today — he said Linda was murdered this morning at the Witch Stone, and her body was found by a local girl. So Mary's rather confusingly cryptic message saying that Ruby had been involved in an accident finally made perfect sense. Sort of."

"Well, I could hardly have left a message with your housekeeper saying one of your friends had been murdered and another of your friends, who is also an employee at your salon, had discovered the body, could I?"

"Good point." Johnnie nods at Brenda and orders a cup of tea and some chips. "I can't believe it. I don't believe it." Despite his usual bounce and affectations, his face is pale under the tan.

"Johnnie, can I ask you something?" Mary asks suddenly.

"You want to know why I run a hairdressing salon but have a housekeeper in London?"

She stirs her tea, clinking the spoon against the chipped mug, adding more milk from the blue jug. "Sort of."

"Darling, I may be posh but I'm a bit broke. Everyone in my family is. We all do the King's Road and Claridges thing, but I don't think my father even owns the house anymore. The bank will do very well when he finally hands in his chips. But we all accept that." A shadow crosses his face. "Apart from my brother, of course, but that's another story."

I wonder for a moment what Johnnie's house is like. I imagine one of those grand terrace affairs. A perfect slice of iced cake with swirly decorations across the plasterwork outside. The hallway would be vast and chequered with black-and-white tiles, and the housekeeper would answer the door in a black dress and white apron.

"Do you really have a housekeeper?" Mary sighs enviously. She's clearly imagining her own life of luxury, and it's my turn to giggle.

"I do. Well, my parents do actually. But shall I tell you a secret, angel? My family don't actually have *any* money at all. Lots of us don't, but we still have the trappings. All those old-school glamour-pusses, pretending like mad everything's still like it was before the war, and life is just one big, gay whirl. Most of them are mortgaged up to the eyeballs, down to their last pound. Can one get away with that in the same sentence? Because it describes us exactly."

I've never heard him so serious, but I have to admire his courage. It must take guts to break out of a family like that, especially to run a hairdressing salon in Brighton. I imagine he's not the favourite son.

As though he follows my thoughts Johnnie finishes, "That's why I had to get away, because times are changing and families like mine are not. We're a dinosaur breed and unless we adapt we'll die."

It's clearly time for a subject change, and to stop dancing around the main topic, I think. "So what are we going to do now? The police told us to make a list of everyone who was at the picnic last night so they can 'eliminate them from their enquiries,' but we don't have all the addresses and phone numbers." I look expectantly at Johnnie and he nods briskly.

"I've got hold of all our usual gang, and we'll meet on the beach tonight at eight to talk it out. Between us someone may remember something useful." Johnnie looks serious for once. "I don't trust the police so we'll do this our way. Linda didn't deserve this, any more than you deserved to find her body."

"I keep seeing her at the back of my mind," I admit. "The policeman kept asking about who was at the picnic last night, like it could have been one of us who killed her. But there were loads of people there that I don't know, and surely it's just as likely to be some random loony."

The other two digest this in silence, and Johnnie merely repeats that he doesn't want to say more than we have to around the police, because he "doesn't trust them."

We leave a good tip for Brenda, and wander back up to the salon. It's nice to feel a cool breeze. I kick a dropped chip towards one of the seagulls you get everywhere here. "Vile creatures. Don't encourage vermin, Ruby! I'll make some telephone calls, and see you down from the Palace Pier, opposite the hotdog stands, at eight," Johnnie says. A quick kiss each, and he's off.

We watch his car race off up the hill, threading through the traffic, dodging vans, and straggling pedestrians.

Mary takes my hand. "So where does Johnnie live when he's in Brighton, if he has a grand family home in London?" she asks.

I shrug. "I don't know. I suppose with a boyfriend or something?"

She nods slowly, eyes wide. "Really? Do you think he's, you know, *queer*?"

"I don't know. Would that be so bad? Pearl said something ages go, and I was a bit shocked, but now I've had time to think about it. . . why shouldn't he have a private life?"

Mary's gone bright red. It's clearly even more of a shock for her. "But that's illegal."

"But it's up to him, isn't it?"

"It still seems wrong."

"Come on, let's get changed," I give her a gentle push so she stops staring at me, and open our door.

Halfway up the stairs she stops, and puts a hand to her stomach. "Mary? Are you alright?" But she looks glowing and excited when she turns round.

"Rubes, I think I just felt the baby move! It was a sort of fluttering, like it just turned over or something."

"Wow! How exciting. Really? Isn't it a bit early, although maybe you're further along than you think? We should ask Pearl."

Mary's thin face is radiant. "Well, it was either the baby moving or wind after all those chips — heavens, I still can't believe I'm going to be a mum!"

Out of habit we pull on our party clothes, adding little pastel cardigans against the chill of the sea breeze. I fish around in my bag for a long fake pearl necklace. My fingers touch the two signet rings. Two rings and two dead bodies. I slam the door shut on that one for the moment. Am I afraid of the police thinking I'm insane or is it really that I'm terrified of finding myself arrested for murder?

"Ruby, I said 'are you ready?'"

I'm about to answer when I hear loud knocking on our outer door, and freeze.

Mary cranes out of the window but shakes her head. "I can't see far enough round the corner. But it's broad daylight with loads of people walking up and down the street."

"Okay. We'll both go down."

The knocking is louder now, and we go out together, locking our inner door securely before we walk down the stairs. "Who is it?" I shout.

"Police!"

"Well, they could have bloody well said so before. I feel sick, I'm so scared!" Mary hisses in my ear.

I swing the door open, trying to smile and to quiet my thundering heartbeat. It's one of the young officers from earlier. "Miss Baker? We found a purse near to the murder scene that matches the description of the one you lost. Can we ask you to come down to the station and identify it?"

"Couldn't you just drop it off here?" Mary asks.

"No, miss. You see, Miss Baker needs to formally identify the item, and sign for it." The officer beams at us. "I have the car parked out the front, so would you like to accompany me now?"

The police car smells of sweat and cigarettes. It feels odd to be sitting in the back, but we're not under arrest or anything. The driver eventually pulls neatly in at the police station, an imposing and deceptively elegant building which looks more like the kind of grand old residence that Johnnie's parents would live in.

We are asked to wait, and sit down on a couple of grey plastic chairs. My nerves are jangling, but Mary seems as serene as ever, humming a little tune, and glancing at her watch.

"I hope they hurry up. We're going to be late meeting Johnnie." She lowers her voice. "Do you think that's why he doesn't like the police? You know, because he's queer?"

I hug my cardigan around me, and rub my arms, "Probably. I mean like you said, it's illegal, so the last thing he would want is any trouble. Or maybe it's because he just wants to figure it out himself. It's personal, isn't it? Linda was one of our friends."

"I wonder if he knew Katie — you know, the girl from last year?"

"Probably. Brighton is smaller than people think. James knew her." I keep my voice low.

"*Did* he?"

"He said so at the picnic."

Some drunk men yell from the cells. The desk sergeant stomps down the corridor and bangs on their doors, telling them to be quiet. It works for about ten minutes, before they start up the racket again. A headache is nudging at the base of my skull, and after being all fired up from Johnnie's pep-talk about finding Linda's killer,

I'm now just totally exhausted. It takes half an hour till a beady-looking woman takes us through to a narrow grey room which stinks of urine and has scuffed floors.

My white plastic purse with the flower on the front is in a clear bag. I sign for it as quickly as I can.

"Just one more thing, Miss Baker. You need to sign for the contents as well," the policewoman tells me. She empties a plastic bag onto the table.

I poke around in the little pile. A couple of lipsticks, including my favourite, a pound, and a few pennies. My brass house keys. I breathe a sigh of relief and Mary smiles at me. My house keys are safe. But there's something else. A cheap silver coloured locket, a bit like the one I have with the picture of my sisters and me hidden inside.

My fingers withdraw from the table, and I shiver. "Um . . . this locket isn't mine. Sorry."

"Really?" The woman consults her list and frowns. "It was found in your purse. Are you sure?" Before I can stop her she picks the object up from the table, and flicks it open.

Mary and I peer inside, half expecting a photograph, but instead it's a plaited lock of hair. Or rather, three locks. Two dark and one fair, intertwined like a Victorian sweetheart's trinket. The fair hair is baby-fine, but the others are dark and coarse. The locket is strung on a thin silver- coloured chain, with no clue about the owner.

"This isn't yours?"

"No!" I say louder than I need to. Mary shoots me a warning look.

"Perhaps it was found near the purse and someone picked up thinking it had fallen out," Mary suggests, because of course she knows exactly what I'm thinking.

This is another gift from the watcher. Which means he was there last night, as we drank and swam and relaxed with our friends, feeling safe in the crowd. Maybe I spoke to him. Maybe he killed Linda.

Chapter Ten

We're late to meet Johnnie, and almost everyone is there already. Our group is just one of many enjoying an evening on the beach, just like we did at Glebe House last night.

But tonight it's different. There are bottles of beer, but I reject them in favour of a Coca-Cola, and Victoria has brought some candles in a cardboard box.

"I thought, you know, it might be nice to light the candles for Linda and just remember her for a bit . . ." Victoria sniffs, rubbing her nose. Her white blouse and dark skirt could pass for mourning clothes, and her hair is up in the usual high ponytail. Leon discreetly passes her a very white handkerchief. I meet James's eyes and he smiles gently at me.

We fall silent for a few minutes after the candles are lit. It feels as if we're the only people on the beach, sealed in our own little bubble, watching the flickering flames burn out and the waves rising and falling.

At last we settle into two smaller groups, sprawled on blankets with our bare feet stretched out on the pebbles. It's obvious that everyone wants to talk about it, but that they don't want to upset me.

"I think that Johnnie's right," I say eventually, clutching my cola bottle like a weapon. "He said earlier that we should try to find Linda's killer and I agree with him. Most of you know by now that I found her body. It was so horrible to see her like that. Nobody deserves to die, but she was one of us, and it makes us partly responsible for finding out what happened."

Most people murmur their agreement but Ted, who has been sitting slumped on the outskirts of the group, shakes his head. His face is in shadow and his pale hair is the only light on his body. "I can't. I'm sorry but I just can't. I was interviewed by the police today. Being suspected of murdering the girl I loved is one of the most horrendous experiences of my life." He pauses. His normally chirpy voice is low and dull with pain. "I was going to ask her to marry me, you know."

There's a crunch on the stones, and a familiar redhead flings herself into our group, grabbing me tightly. "What the hell is going on? I leave you all alone for one night, and this happens! Oh, Rubes, thank God you're okay."

Under cover of Pearl's dramatic entrance, Ted creeps away across the beach. Kenny makes a move to go after him but Victoria pulls him back, murmuring, "See him tomorrow, Ken. He needs to grieve on his own for a bit first."

The seagulls float above, and a flock of starlings line up on the pier struts. The sky is dotted with grey streaks of cloud, and the beach is still warm. I run my hand over the pebbles, then pick at a piece of seaweed, bursting the seed pods with a fingernail.

Pearl embraces everyone, lights a cigarette, and sinks down with a bottle of beer. Her white shorts show off golden limbs, and the mass of red curls is held back from her face with an emerald flower clip.

"How did you escape from Matron?" Victoria calls from her blanket.

"Oh, I told her what had happened. She was even quite nice about it, and suggested I take a couple of days to get over it." Pearl rolls her eyes. "As if it's that easy. But she was trying, and that was the first time she's smiled at me all year."

"They found my purse. The police said it was just the other side of the stone. I must have left it there when we moved over by the lake. That's why I went up to Glebe House so early," I say, to everyone and nobody. I need to shove aside my worries about the purse. Mary tried to ask about the locket as we walked down here (no free police taxi ride home), but I hedged the answers. I know she's dying to grill me when we get home.

But Pearl has other ideas, "Bring me right up to date. Who took Linda home? Who was last to see her, and all that? Was that Ted I saw by the pier?"

"I think you missed your calling, darling. You should be leading the police force!" Johnnie tells her. He's drawing patterns in a patch of sand with a sea-bleached piece of driftwood, but I can tell he misses nothing. "Kenny," he asks suddenly, "What are the papers saying tomorrow about Linda?"

Kenny and James look awkward and I can hardly blame them. This is a great story and they are right in the thick of the action. No more wasting their time on little local stories. This is a front-pager, and we all know it.

"We'd never hurt Linda or any of our friends," James says firmly. "But we do have to write to order, and if we don't produce some decent stuff the boss is going to wonder why."

"So?" says Pearl impatiently. "What have you written for tomorrow, boys?"

Kenny licks his lips, pushing his dark hair out of his eyes. Beads of sweat are gathered along his forehead. "Someone leaked the story of Victoria's Tarot cards, and the fact that Linda picked Death. We're leading with a witchcraft theory, which is mostly padded out with lots of historical mumbo-jumbo — sorry Leon — and very little fact."

Leon looks uncomfortable, no doubt at the 'mumbo-jumbo' remark. Victoria scowls. "If you mention my name in your—"

"Hey, we have a job to do. But of course we won't mention you by name, and before you ask, it wasn't either of us who leaked the story," Kenny says defensively, lighting a cigarette and chucking the match onto the pebbles next to his knee. "In fact, before anyone says anything else, we have to mention Katie too. Sorry, Johnnie, but the editor has already dug out her files from last year."

I look up from the seaweed, and screw up my eyes in the evening light to study our little group. Johnnie's face is set and pale. "The police messed up the investigation into Katie's death, and because of them Terence got the easy way out. He should be rotting in prison. But it's okay, Ken, it wasn't your lot that botched it."

"You know what I think?" Pearl says, and we all stop bickering because when my cousin has an opinion, she likes to be heard. "I think whoever killed Linda is someone she knew. She wasn't an idiot, and she was streetwise. Rubes said that Linda was going to drive her brothers home, so she must have gone out afterwards. It would have been pretty late by then because we left at what? Elevenish? A bloody lonely drive if she came back to Glebe House. Why would she do that?"

"She wouldn't, I suppose," I say doubtfully. "She wouldn't have come all the way back for any reason, even if she found out she'd left something behind. She'd have waited until morning like I did. For daylight."

"Right. And she would do this because, like you, and like the rest of us, she wasn't stupid. So we agree she was killed somewhere else and the body moved to the Witch Stone? Katie was killed at the Witch Stone because she met Terence there to try and smooth things over.

Different circumstances, same place. Perhaps someone is playing with us. Not just us, but this whole town."

I'm pondering her words and hearing echoes of her last sentence in something Mary said to me the other day, when I get that feeling again. Someone's watching me. I glance up at the pier, more annoyed than fearful this time. Even if the watcher is a murderer I have my friends around me. Right at the sea end on our side, apparently enjoying a spot of evening fishing, I can see a tall dark man. He might be fishing, but he's staring right at me.

"Were there any other suspects in Katie's murder?" Leon asks, flicking his cigarette into the shingle and lighting another.

"I don't remember really. Her ex-boyfriend was questioned, I think. And me, of course," Johnnie says.

"You?" Mary isn't the only one is who is shocked.

"I was one of the last people to be seen with her the night she was killed. She asked for a cigarette at the door of the Starlight Rooms, and I gave her one and lit it for her. I'd seen her around, probably even talked to her on previous nights out. Her friends mentioned it to the police after her death, and suddenly I became a suspect." He pulls at his shirt collar with a shaky hand.

Kenny asks a few questions about other people I don't know, and Pearl adds a few more names. I tune out for a moment, glancing back over to the pier.

"Ruby?" Mary prods me. "You still with us?" She looks in the direction of the pier-end, but apparently sees nothing more threatening than a fisherman out late.

I gulp down the sick feeling and compose myself, smiling blandly under Pearl's blue gaze and Victoria's green one. "Just a bit tired, I guess."

Let him watch, the crazy bastard. If it makes him happy, let him leave his stupid gifts or stare at me from so far away that I can't tell whether he's really looking or I'm going mad. He can carry on with his little games, but if I get one shred of evidence that he killed Linda, I'll tell the police everything. Even it means leading a trail right back to a man bleeding to death in a dark alley.

"We've got to go," James says, glancing at his watch and nudging Kenny. "If we get anything, we'll ring you or drop in at Johnnie's."

It's still early by our standards, but as the sun sinks beneath the waves in a mirror-flash of burning gold, Mary and I also wander slowly back up the beach. Before we turn for home, I swing round and stare deliberately at the dark figure still sitting on the end of the pier. He stares back. At least I think he does. The promenade is warm and still humming with people. The odd bus rumbles past, and I lick salt from my lips.

"We're going for a coffee, if you want to come?" Pearl says, as we pause by the pier. "Oh, I forgot—" she glances quickly at Leon, then passes me a slip of paper.

"What's this?"

"Doctor Kale's on Church Road. I meant to give you this *ages* ago."

I must still be looking blank because she hisses impatiently, "*The pill*, Ruby! You know, birth control? And when Mary has had her baby I suggest she also pays him a visit. It's okay, he won't ask questions. He's one of *those* doctors."

Oh. No wonder she lowered her voice. Anyway, Leon seems to be totally absorbed in conversation with Victoria. "Thanks, Pearl! Actually I think we'll get an early night, it's been a hell of a day."

"No worries, I'll play gooseberry to these two lovebirds before I head back myself. I might use the telephone box and do some ringing round — maybe see if I can get hold of some other friends who might be able to help." She shakes her head. "You know, I still can't quite believe it. When I turn around I expect to see Linda following along behind, nattering to Ted. It was bad enough last year, when Katie was murdered, but it was only Johnnie that was involved properly. I hate to think this is some sort of copycat killing."

Pearl kisses us both and we wave at the lovers before wandering slowly across the road, ignoring the lure of hotdogs from O'Hagens.

"So what do you think about Linda, then?" Mary asks eventually.

"I don't know," I tell her, "And before you ask about the locket, I honestly don't know about that either. It probably is totally innocent, and as you suggested, it got shoved in my purse by accident."

I hoped my sleep would be untroubled, but of course the ghosts crowd my dreams. George is back, but he's joined by Linda, and they're both running down an endless dark alley.

* * *

I knew what Mum wanted, and I knew I had less than two hours to get away with it. George was a creature of habit. I pulled out the biggest kitchen knife I could find, and hid it under my old coat while Mum watched. Then I made her give me the penknife.

"God bless, Ruby, and thank you," she called from the doorway as I set off into the night.

When I thought about it later, it seemed a kind of funny thing to tell her daughter as she sets off to commit murder.

The night was heavy with clouds, and the pavements were wet from rain earlier in the day. I sloshed my way to the alley that my stepdad would come down from the King's Head and slipped into a doorway. I knew the backroads, the warehouses, and alleys round there as well as I did my own living-room.

It was over an hour later when George staggered back after his "quick one." I was half-frozen, and almost ready to give up. I was also panicking about meeting Mary and catching the bus. Finally, I heard his heavy, lumbering walk and his thumping nailed boots echoing in the alley. I glanced out quickly to check that yes, it was my stepdad, and whipped back, crouching low. He walked right past without seeing me. I screwed up my courage, leapt forward and plunged the knife into his back with both hands.

Blood spurted warm and metallic into my face, all over my old coat. I spat it out while I went on clinging to the knife, twisting the blade for good measure driving it further in. It got stuck. I pulled frantically to withdraw it, and then stabbed him again. My heart pounded and my breath came in short terrified gasps.

He seemed to take ages to fall, but when he did, he toppled like an oak tree in a winter storm, and fell with a thud I was sure must have been heard by anyone who lived over the alley. He was still groaning when I drew the blade out for the third time. I wondered whether I needed to stab him again. I swallowed my nausea and clenched my hands around the knife handle in case he moved to get up. He didn't move. I wiped blood off my hands onto my coat while I waited for him to draw his last breath.

Chapter Eleven

Blood pooled across the alley, seeping into the cracked concrete, lapping at the rubbish piles like some vile scarlet sea. But the body still gave out slow gasping sighs. The rough fingers clawed at the ground, and after a while he still wasn't dead. I took a breath, told myself to think of my siblings and especially the unborn baby, and shut my eyes, driving the knife into the back of his exposed neck. Something snapped under the force of my blow, and the stench of his last bowel movement made me gag.

His body was finally limp as I withdrew the knife for the last time. I forced myself to lean close, looking for signs of life. I couldn't find any, and I stepped away shaking with relief and fear. I looked away from my victim, checking the alley for danger. It was always going to be a risk doing it here, but there was nowhere else, and no time to plan. The risk had been worth it. There was nobody there.

I felt so cold and so in control that I wondered if I was evil. If I could take a life so easily and not care, what else could I do? Perhaps all murderers felt the same, and now I had joined their ranks. It wasn't till I scrubbed myself in the river near the furniture warehouse and dumped the coat and the knife into a convenient skip that I began to shake.

My jaw started to rattle with the shock, and I had to stop and vomit twice on the way to the place where I was due to meet Mary. I kept feeling his blood on my arms, on my face, like a million tiny red bugs creeping across my skin. My skin looked clean, but I could still see blood.

The bus had already rattled past me on the way to the main road as Mary crept out of hiding from behind a pile of industrial rubbish. Her thin face was wet with tears, and she was shivering. "Ruby! I thought you weren't coming!"

I put my arms round her. I knew, as I had that day we first met at the college, that I had finally found someone who would never let me down. Soon after Aunt Jackie telephoned with news of the death, she guessed the truth, and I knew I had also found someone who loved me enough to let me get away with murder.

* * *

"Ruuuuby, wake up! We can't be late today. Not when Eve and Catherine have actually started to be nice to us." Mary is shaking my shoulder, with her fine hair tickling my face as she leans closer. *"Ruby!"*

I roll over, confused and exhausted by my dreams, rubbing my sore eyes. The banging headache seems unfair after a teetotal night, but at least the weather seems set to match my mood. After a month of beach weather, today our windows look out over a dull palette of soft greys as clouds roll in from the Channel, and the heavy sea fog hangs thickly in the street outside. The glass is covered in tiny water drops, and the light is muted and cosy in our bare little room. It's a day for staying in bed.

"Coming. But why do you care if Catherine and Eve like us anyway? It doesn't matter. We work hard and they work hard." I move my hand automatically to push my hair over my shoulder. I'd forgotten for the umpteenth time that it's short now. I do like it, especially being blonde, but I feel a bit naked without a mass of hair to hide behind.

Mary is making up her face, brushing extra blush across her skin to hide the few spots sprinkled on her forehead. She shrugs and turns, gesticulating with her mascara brush, "Future babysitters? No, not really, I just think we need all the *good* people, on our side. You know, the people we can really trust. Especially now."

I force my legs over the side of the bed, wincing as my bare feet hit the wooden boards, and forage among the piles for clean clothes. I really need to do some more washing.

"You mean that one of our friends could have murdered Linda? Come on, you can't think that Kenny or Ted, or anyone, could do that?" I'm quite shocked, but more shocked by her answer.

"I don't suspect anyone. I'm just saying that you can be nice and normal and just like everyone else, but you can be a murderer underneath." She catches my expression. "Ruby, I don't mean you. That was different and we both know it."

I stare at her, wondering — half hoping, I suppose — if she is going to talk about George. I want to tell her all of it, and what drove me to do it. I want to say that it wasn't just because of the regular beatings, it was to save my unborn sister's life. But her blue gaze slides away, and she makes a big fuss about choosing a necklace. Eventually she settles on a rope of coloured glass which she twists twice around her neck. I remember Linda's pretty white-and-gold necklace. And then, although I try not to, her red slashed throat.

"I'm ready, and it's still early. Have you got some coins for the paper? I want to know what Kenny and James wrote about this crazy witchcraft theory."

I retrieve my plastic purse. I left the locket at the police station, of course, but my money is all there. "Here."

Mary takes the coins, and picks up her key and coat, "See you in ten minutes!"

* * *

A couple of hours later, Johnnie's is packed. The throng includes customers, a few other reporters who have heard I found the body, and friends dropping in to "check we're okay." Thursday is also delivery day for boxes of styling lotions, chemicals, soap, and industrial detergents.

Johnnie evicts the reporters angrily, and gets straight on the phone to the *Brighton Herald* to complain that they are harassing his staff and annoying his clients. When he finds out that one came from the *News of the World*, he even makes another call to shout at their news editor.

Even though we were a bit shocked to have the reporters sidle up with notebooks at the ready, the clients are loving the drama. Half the regulars seem to have suddenly rebooked for "a quick trim." Today's paper sits well-thumbed and slightly damp on the table next to the 'waiting area' (actually just a line of chairs in front of the window).

Three more women clatter through the door, grumbling about the weather, and shaking out umbrellas, raincoats and headscarves onto the rain-spattered dirty floor. The place is covered in wet footprints and hair, but with all of us working on clients there's no time to clear up.

The phone rings again and I apologise to my client before leaning over to the reception desk.

"Good morning. Johnnie's! Ruby speaking, how may I help you?"

"Hello, Ruby." An unfamiliar male voice, with a northern accent.

"Hello? Sorry, can I take your name please?" I say breezily, ready to brush off another reporter.

"Why did you leave my locket at the police station, Ruby? It was a gift, and it really isn't good manners to reject a present. But then I don't expect your mam taught you any manners, did she?"

I hold my breath. The room's chat and bustle seems a hundred miles away. The rain rushes down the windows, and I could be sealed in a glass box with this unseen man. Everything is spinning, and the blood drains from my face making me dizzy and faint. The watcher. I hold onto sanity, gripping the telephone receiver with one clenched fist, and the reception desk with the other.

"Was it you?" I manage. I mean of course, *Was it you who killed Linda?* but there are far too many people within earshot.

I can feel the blood pumping through my veins, far too fast. I feel as if my heart were powered by a faulty pump. I force myself to think. I can't work out his age from his voice. The northern accent is unmistakable, though. I'd say Manchester, but only because my stepdad had friends up there. They were a rowdy bunch of roaming men, picking up work on the docks and railways. They only came to visit a couple of times, nodded approval at Mum and her tiny house, and disappeared down the pub with my stepdad.

I open my mouth, but nothing comes out. I hear the click and buzz as he puts the phone down. The invisible bubble vanishes, and the roar and heat of the salon swirl around me. In her chair next to the reception desk, my client smiles politely at me, and then glances pointedly at her watch.

From his place near the back, Johnnie is flashing a hand mirror for client approval, Mary is busy snipping away at the indomitable Mrs Green, and Eve and Catherine are trowelling chemicals onto two regulars.

"Sorry, I'll just be a moment," I tell my own client.

"You've already been more than that. Are you alright, love? It's just that I've got to be back at work at half past so if you could get a move on . . ."

"Yes! I will. Sorry." I force my legs into action. My whole body is weak and my limbs move stiffly. It was *him,* calling me *here.* "It was — I just need to—"

I pick up the phone, and dial.

"Exchange."

"Hello. Sorry, someone just called a minute ago. Can you tell me where they were calling from please?" I hold my breath and bite down hard on my lower lip. I grab a pencil to scribble down the location.

I hear the fingernails clacking on a keyboard, and then the telephone exchange girl says, "No, sorry, we can't do that. Can I put you through to anyone else?"

Making "just coming" noises to my poor wet-haired client, I drop the pencil. "No. Thank you anyway," I tell the girl on the other end of the phone. What next? He comes into the salon for a chat?

I give the client a super-quick trim (with Eve watching beadily to make sure I don't do any wonky lines). I feel guilty enough to offer a few nuggets of news — yes, I have heard about the murder, and yes she was a friend of ours and a very beautiful, sweet girl who didn't deserve to be killed. She leaves happy, with a bit of gossip for her own workmates, while I ponder on her comments. Everyone says that when someone is killed or dies before old age. They say, "Oh, he didn't deserve to die," or "she didn't deserve to die like *that*" but does anyone *deserve* to die? I already know the answer to that one . . .

"Ruby, have you got some scissors? I can't find mine!"

I dry a selection of combs and scissors carefully on a towel and pass them to Mary, who is combing a head of long wet hair. Catherine is watching over her, eagle-eyed and ready to tell her what she's doing wrong.

"Next, please!" Wearily, I paste on a smile and usher a thin blonde in a pink mini-dress towards the basins.

Finally, when we've waved the last of them back out into the rain, the six of us heave a sigh of relief and take in the chaos of the salon.

"Right. Tea all round, girls, a quick break and then we'll get on with the clearing up. I must say — and don't take this the wrong way because you know how much I want this bastard found — but murder is excellent for business." Johnnie, down to his pale blue shirtsleeves for once, starts shuffling papers on the reception desk, cashing up the till, and flicking through the appointment list for tomorrow.

Eve stomps out to the back room to make tea and get the milk from the cold little nook that was once the entrance to the cellar. It's been boarded up, but you can leave the hatch open and go a few steps down to the cool gloomy space. Perfect cold storage, especially in the recent hot weather.

"I'll nip over to Dick's and get some biscuits, shall I?" Catherine offers, delving in her handbag.

"You're an angel. Custard creams if they have them. Here, I'll pay." She beams at him in her usual devoted fashion.

"Thanks for all your hard work today, girls," Johnnie tells us. Then he looks at me closely. "What was that telephone call about earlier, Rubes?"

"I . . . which one?"

"The one where you looked like you'd seen a whole room of ghosts afterwards. Don't tell me it was Mrs Richards-Bateman, because I already know she has that effect on people. Wait until you meet her in person!" Johnnie's face crinkles into a smile.

"It was—" Mary interrupts herself at the sight of my face. "Another reporter. I didn't get what paper he was from but he had a northern accent."

"Mmmm, nosy bastards. Like those idiots who came in earlier. At least James and Kenny have the decency to keep us updated, and their story is pretty good — if total rubbish."

I inch over and pick up the paper to reread the article, smoothing the crumpled front page. The ink is smudged and someone has torn a little piece from the bottom corner.

CURSED HOUSE GAINS LATEST VICTIM

Local girl Linda Beeston has become the latest victim of the so-called curse of Glebe House. Her battered body was discovered early this morning tied to the Witch Stone. Although police have made an extensive search of the area, the killer remains at large, and Brighton residents are asked to take special care when out and about.

A source tells us, "Linda was looking at Tarot cards as she picnicked with her friends at Glebe House last night. She picked the card marked Death and everyone laughed."

Last August eighteen-year-old Katie Simmons was murdered at the Witch Stone, by ex-boyfriend Terence Jacks. The police have denied they are looking for a copycat killer and insist the cases are being treated an entirely separate entities.

Glebe House, originally owned by the Gordon family, and its lands have always been known for strange and often gruesome happenings. When the original house was constructed, it took far longer than predicted due to a high number of accidents to the workmen.

The Gordon family history was also punctuated by tragic happenings. In 1910, a younger son, Alexander, drowned in the newly constructed ornamental lake. The elder sons were killed in WWI, and a cousin, Henry, inherited the property. Lord Henry was known for his eccentric and often controversial views on witchcraft. In 1922, his wife Lady Isabella was found burnt at the stake in the gardens, not far from where the Witch Stone memorial stands today. Rumours that Lord Henry himself had murdered Lady Isabella, were widely accepted as true, but he escaped trial by boarding ship to Australia at Southampton.

Most recently, Glebe House has passed into the ownership of Brighton Council, who have sold much of the surrounding farmland for development. Green Ridges is the latest of the new housing estates, but construction work was blighted by several incidents and a serious fire, which delayed work for several months.

If anyone has any information that may help the police investigation, please call Brighton Police Station.

"No wonder nobody rebuilt the house. After all that tragedy, and what's happened recently, I'd say it probably is cursed. The sooner the council get permission to clear the site and build new houses the better." Mary gives a little shiver. She's biting a thumbnail again.

"Would that help, though?" Johnnie says thoughtfully, "If a place is cursed, isn't it cursed forever? I wouldn't like to be living on top of an old burial site or whatever it is. Those ancient ghosts might be causing all of this. It might be ley lines or whatever they're called, attracting bad energy. It's like luck, isn't it?"

"You sound like Victoria," I tell him, "You can change your luck. Some people do." I shoot a glance at Mary, but she's still attacking her nails.

If you want something badly enough, you'll always find a way.

Chapter Twelve

"So who is the mysterious source, then, Ken?" I ask, sipping my drink. I lean over to flick ash off my cigarette into the grubby white bowl in the centre of the table.

He shrugs and shifts in his chair. "I can't tell you a name, but I promise it wasn't any of our crowd. It was just someone who overheard us by the lake."

"Male or female?" Pearl taps a pink-painted nail on the table between us.

We've gathered at the Milk Bar in Queen's Road for a quick meeting before heading off to the ice rink. Johnnie got the word out while we cleared up, and a surprising number have turned up. Like threatened animals gathering in a herd, I suppose. We want to be close to our friends. But Johnnie's and Mary's words haunt me. How far can we trust these friends now?

Mary didn't ask anything about the phone call, but I told her anyway.

"You're still not telling the police about this?"

"No. He hasn't actually done anything." My words sounded weak even to me.

"Ruby, sweetheart, he's following you! If he's from one of your stepdad's crowd, those men are hard. You need protection."

"And if that protection led back to our lives in Croydon?"

She shook her head. "I don't want Derek to find me, but if anything happens to you—"

I grabbed her hands, "Or if anything happens to you. But don't you see? We're stuck with the lesser of two evils. The watcher is weird, and yes, he must be something to do with my stepdad, though I can't see why or how at the moment."

"How can you say that, when the locket was obviously from someone up at Glebe House? Of course I don't think someone accidentally put it in your purse. He was *there!*"

"So were we, but that was the night before. Say he was in the crowd, saw me lose my purse, or took it from our picnic blanket. I was too drunk to notice. That doesn't mean he was back later with Linda's body."

We agreed to disagree, but I know she won't let it rest.

The Milk Bar fills up as the rain starts to drift inland. More girls run in off the street shaking out umbrellas and laughing, a few scooters are lined up outside, and the jukebox plays all the latest hits. The seagulls over the old town swoop and soar over the jumble of houses. A few birds land only a few yards from us to peck energetically at discarded wrappers and chips.

Victoria is missing from our gang tonight because it's her turn for the dreaded night shift at the hospital. Pearl's working early tomorrow morning, but has slipped out "for a quick one."

I stand up and prise a shilling out of my purse, "Who wants what?"

The jukebox is great at the Milk Bar, and you get five plays for a shilling, so it's a bargain too. My current favourite is 'The Loco-Motion.' It seems to suit the party beach atmosphere of Brighton. Kenny and Johnnie both want some Dee Dee Sharp, and Mary goes for the Contours' 'Do You Love Me?'

James is missing tonight too. In a way, I'm glad. I have way too much to think about at the moment anyway. I remember him handing me another glass of champagne at the picnic, and the way his eyes lingered on my body when I stripped off by the lake. Which reminds me, I really must fit in a trip to Doctor Kales and pick up the birth control pill. One baby in our bedsit is going to be quite enough.

I'm back at the table, sucking the last of my strawberry milkshake, squeezed between Mary and Pearl, when a familiar face appears at the door.

"Ted!"

His eyes are still red, he's got two days' worth of stubble and his T-shirt is grubby. Even his curly blonde hair is drooping. "I thought . . . I wondered if you'd had any ideas yet. You know, about who killed Linda? Because if you do, I want to help find whoever did this and hunt him down."

Johnnie leans over and claps him on the back, and Pearl gives him a hug.

"We haven't found anything, mate, but the police interviewed me and James, and a couple of girls who work on the subs desk who were up there that night," Kenny offers. He leans back and crosses his legs, scraping a hand through his hair and making it bristle up on end. His hair is shorter, I realise suddenly, and he looks better for it. The chunky face and misshapen boxer's nose look younger and cheekier. Not that he's being cheeky at the moment.

"They spoke to me last night," Johnnie admits, lighting a cigarette.

"You didn't say!" Mary frowns. "But anyway, the police don't seem to have any idea. There must have been over fifty people out at Glebe House that night, and it doesn't even have to be someone who was there. It could be someone who saw Linda on her way home."

"I wanted to ask her brothers if she went out again that night, but I don't know where they hang out, and I can't just ring her house. What if her mum answers?" Pearl says.

"The police will have done all that." Ted's voice cracks again. He pulls the remains of Pearl's milkshake towards him and swigs it like beer, giving himself a white moustache.

The jukebox has just finished the last of our songs, so we start a move towards the SS Brighton. Ted trails along, and Pearl and I link arms with him, leaning our heads on his shoulders. He sniffs a bit, but that's all.

Normally the indoor ice rink is buzzing with chat and the crash of unfortunate skaters hitting barriers, but today there is only one topic of conversation, and everyone is subdued. People whisper in corners and huddle close to their friends. Still, I manage to forget about everything for a little while. I stay upright with the help of Kenny's hand, and I wave at Mary as we scrape over the ice. The skates give us blisters, but we soon pick up speed before scrambling breathlessly into the side barrier.

"That wasn't bad, Ruby!" Kenny says, though he can't help laughing at my struggles to stay upright. "You know, James wants to ask you out on a date, but I said to wait a bit." He peers closely at me. "Was that right?"

"I . . ." I'm surprised by his intuition. "Yes. I just couldn't after Linda, but . . . I have some other things to sort out too. Things that I need to deal with before I start seeing anyone."

"Well, just so you know. James doesn't let go, if he likes a girl. Takes a lot to distract him from work, and you seem to have done that."

I grin at him, trying not to blush. "Let's go around one more time!"

Later we grab a booth, rest our aching legs, and order hot blackcurrant in tiny glass mugs. Mary doesn't skate because she's worried about falling over and hurting the baby. She fiddles with her glass necklace, looking worried.

"What's up?" Johnnie asks.

"I just overheard some girls in the next booth talking about Linda's—" She stops and glances at Ted smoking and staring into space. "They were talking about Linda, and they're meeting at Glebe House tonight to do a séance! One of them was really keen on the whole witchcraft idea, but her friend seemed a bit edgy."

Johnnie narrows his eyes. "Stupid, and risky too, with that bastard still out there. I suppose they got excited after that article in the paper this morning — no, Ken, I'm not blaming you."

"I seriously doubt if they'll get anywhere near Glebe House. When we went up this morning with the photographer, the police had cordoned off the entire garden and half the wood," Kenny tells us. "But you're right, some people are just idiots."

"I wonder what the people living in Green Ridges think of all this? I mean, if I'd just spent loads of money on a new home, I wouldn't be that happy to find out it was bang in the middle of a murder scene and some centuries-old witchcraft curse," Mary says.

I yawn. "They were nice. At least Angela and Albert were — the ones who let me use their telephone. I'm sure you're right, though. They can't be sleeping well at the moment."

Kenny rustles in his pocket and flips through his battered blue notebook. "It won't stop the developers, though. We got a press release through today from Ridgeway's. That's the firm that built Green Ridges. They just confirmed they're starting work next week on another fifty houses the other side of the wood at Glebe House. Let's see . . . there is also a small development of ten houses due for release today. And guess what it's called? Glebe Farm. How hypocritical is that?"

"Well, I wouldn't buy a house up there." Pearl shakes her red head. "I don't believe in witches, but I do think some places just have bad luck. Don't tell Victoria I said that though, or she'll want to do my cards again."

"You don't think the Tarot cards really predict the future, do you?" Ted says suddenly.

Pearl pulls him close. "No, sweetheart, I don't. Victoria just likes to think they give her guidance, but really they're so vague, they just confirm what she's going to do anyway. For Christ's sake, don't start thinking this was anything to do with the cards."

We leave early, and I make sure I give little Ted a hug. My throat swells with emotion every time I think of him proposing to Linda, and the way she teased him whenever we were all together. Did she have deeper feelings for him, or maybe even loved him? Sometimes not knowing is worse.

"Did you see him tonight?" Mary asks as we undress, shivering slightly.

"The watcher? No. I was looking out for him, but if he isn't staring right at me, I could walk past him in the street without noticing."

I really hope the heatwave is back tomorrow, because I really don't have the money to go and buy warmer clothes. Mary and I are still wearing some of Pearl's. We should give them back, even though she assures us she won't miss them.

* * *

My wish seems to have been granted when I wake up. The sun is out and the windows show nothing but a rectangle of blue sky. As we're both up early, I make toast on the rusty grill under the stove. It's a bit burnt but tastes fine with butter and the last scraping of jam.

"Let's go down and wait for Eve to unlock the salon. We can get the chairs and tables out, and sit in the sun for five minutes."

In the street, the fresh sweetness that comes with sun after rain is marred by the stench of the dustbins in the alley outside our front door, and the heap of rubbish stacked on the pavement. But the warmth of the golden rays makes me sleepy, and as we sit, smoking, I can feel my shoulders droop.

"Wake up, sleepyhead!" Eve marches past us in her heavy wool coat and bulging handbag. She starts fiddling with the keys.

Mary waves at someone in the street. I turn, blinking in the brightness, to see Johnnie striding down the hill. No car today. I wonder again where he lives when he's in Brighton? If any of us ask he just dodges the question and tells us he has "accommodation" sorted, thank you very much. I think he probably has a "friend" down here, and stays with him. Still, as I said to Mary, that's really his business.

"Morning, ladies! Another busy one today, so let's get cracking. Eve, can you set up in the salon, Mary, the back room and Ruby, you can start by getting us all a cup of tea." He grins, brushing a piece of dirt from his tailored tweed jacket. A lemon yellow shirt and dark grey trousers complete the look.

The telephone rings as I head off to make the tea and I pause as Johnnie picks up the receiver. He looks at me and makes a "wait a minute" gesture with his hand. I freeze.

"Ruby, it's Pearl for you." I almost run to grab the phone. "Pearl? Are you okay?"

"Fine, sweetheart, but I thought you'd like to know that I had a telephone call from Mum and she said Aunt Eve had a baby girl."

"Oh! That's great. Is she okay? Is the baby alright?" I stammer. Relief floods through my body, leaving me weak and limp. I hadn't realised how much I still cared, but it was there, locked in the back of my mind. It was worth it, that terrible trade-off.

"Wonderful, and they're both doing really well. Mum said she hasn't seen your mum so happy in ages. Apparently she's looking after Garnet and Emerald, and a neighbour's got the younger ones so Aunt Eve can get a bit of rest. And guess what she's called the baby?"

"Not Diamond, I hope?" I'm beaming into the receiver now.

"No! Amethyst. Poor child will just have to be Amy or something when she's bigger. You and I got off easy, sweetheart — what?" Pearl says something I can't catch. "I've got to go. Someone else is waiting to use the phone. I'll see you later. Love you!"

"You too!"

"Good news, angel?" Johnnie is folding the style books back at the new photos, putting one on each chair.

"Yes! My mum had a baby girl." Everything else fades into the background, and when Mary comes out with more towels I almost shout the news.

She hugs me, with tears in her eyes. "Oh Ruby, that's amazing! What's she called?"

"Um . . . well, that's the bad news. Amethyst." I grin.

"Really?" Johnnie is wide-eyed with interest, "You never talk about your family, Ruby, but I think I'm in love with your mum already. Amethyst. Destined to be a famous actress or artist, obviously. Gorgeous! Now get on with that tea."

I'm just pouring boiling water when I hear the bang of the salon door and raised voices. I kick open the door, and take the tray out into the corridor.

"Here, I'll take that." Catherine has arrived, heavy-eyed and yawning. She scoops the heavy tray away from me. "Can't believe the night I've had. Tom and Laura have got some tummy bug, poor loves, and I think I might have snatched about two hours sleep."

I tell her about the new baby and she smiles. "Lovely. Can you take in a new bottle of conditioner?"

I break open one of the stacked cardboard boxes, and drag out about a gallon of Estolan, following Catherine into the salon.

Kenny's there, talking to Johnnie. His tie is askew, his white shirt is untucked, and he has mud on his shoes. Both men turn and stare at me.

"Kenny? What are you doing here?" My heart does an uncomfortable flip.

"Oh God, Rubes, sorry but I thought you'd rather hear it from me," Kenny is pale, and his eyes are shadowed with purple. "There's been another murder."

Chapter Thirteen

Before I can respond Mary's body hits the lino with a loud bang.

"Mary?" I crouch over her, frantically tapping her white face.

"Here's some water." Catherine is right beside me. To my surprise, she takes hold of Mary's hand and gives it a rub. Johnnie proffers his handkerchief. I wipe her face — at least she seems to be breathing okay. Kenny grabs a towel and wedges it under her side. Her small bump is now cushioned from the hard floor, but her face is still milk-white.

"Has she fainted before?" Eve asks.

I shake my head, "Not since we've been here. She stopped feeling sick about two weeks ago. But she won't go and register with a doctor or have a check-up." I stop, feeling I've said too much, and I can feel the others exchanging glances.

"Should we telephone for an ambulance?" Johnnie says, but Mary starts to stir, muttering something under her breath.

"Mary! How are you feeling? Do you have any pains?" I demand. "No, don't get up, just stay leaning against me for a bit." I hold her as she props herself up on one elbow, and then slowly eases into sitting position.

"I'm okay. Sorry, I just felt so light-headed and dizzy and then everything went dark."

"You'll be fine, love. I expect it's your blood pressure. Mine was sky high with both my last two, and it does make you keel over." Eve smiles at her. "I even fainted in the Co-op on London Road once. Right by the fruit and veg!"

For some reason this makes us all giggle, until we snap back to reality when Mary asks about the murder. I almost black out myself.

Kenny frowns. "Someone called it in to the police at five this morning. No idea who the victim is but it's another girl." He holds up a hand as we burst out again. "Don't worry. I rang all of our lot, and got an answer from everyone except Pearl, who was already on the wards — I rang the matron to check — and Victoria, who I think is staying at Leon's. I don't know where his place is, but she was on the night shift last night, so I rang the hospital to check what time she left. She was caught up in an emergency on the ward, and didn't clock off until seven thirty." He pauses, and takes a deep breath, grabbing a random mug of tea.

"Go on. I'm impressed by your organisation, and thank God all our lot are safe, but there's more, isn't there?" Johnnie grabs a mug of his own, He's clearly glad to hold something hot, wrapping his long fingers around the drink, even though the sun blasts in at the salon windows.

"I'm afraid so. It turns out the police took the cordons down yesterday evening about six. Apparently they had just been waiting for the team searching the wood to finish up. Nobody was guarding the area, and why should they? Then this morning a man out walking his dog discovered a girl tied to the Witch Stone." Kenny looks sick to his stomach, and blinks rapidly.

"Not another one!" Catherine exclaims.

The phone rings, making us all jump, and Kenny gulps down the rest of his tea, "I've got to go. I'll keep you in the loop. I'm supposed to be up at Green Ridges tracking down this dog walker who found the body. Everyone on that estate is going to be frantic, so I should get some good quotes — I mean — oh dear, look, I'll see you later. Take care, Mary!"

We watch Kenny rush out of the door with his shirt-tails flying.

"Bloody hell!" Johnnie exclaims. "What's going on? Right, first I'll run Mary up to the hospital for a quick check-up. It's okay," he adds, seeing her scared look. "You can just say you're my sister or something. Use my surname."

She nods, and I see Catherine and Eve exchange a brief look. Johnnie knows the reason we ran away — well, the part of it we can tell anyone — but we agreed not to tell anyone else yet.

"Johnnie, do you remember those girls at the ice rink last night? The ones who said they were going to do a séance?" I say, suddenly remembering what Mary said.

He looks grim. "You can't help people if they are going to walk right into danger, but it might not be them. Too much of a coincidence. As we said with Linda, just because he leaves the bodies at the Witch Stone that doesn't mean they were killed there. Come on, Mary, I've parked the car in Middle Street to avoid the delivery vans. Can you walk just round the block or shall I drive it round to the front?"

Mary stands slowly with Eve's help, and Catherine bustles back with another mug of tea.

"Here you go. That one's got sugar in. Johnnie, you run round and get your car, love, and we'll have her out front in a minute!"

As soon as Johnnie whisks Mary away — after promising to ring us when she's seen the midwife — the three of us start preparing for the day ahead. I almost can't make myself behave normally, and I have to force my stiff limbs to carry towels, measure out little plastic bowls of thickening cream, arrange the magazines and today's paper on the table, and wash up the tea mugs ready for clients.

"Right, Ruby, you take Miss Appleton. I can see her getting off the bus now. She only needs a quick wash and trim. Catherine and I will do the colours, and I'll watch you for the cut. With any luck Mary and Johnnie will be back soon. Oh, can you do a couple of manicures later too?"

By mid-morning, the news of another murder has spread across town and all our clients are talking about it, wanting details, asking each other who the poor girl was, and anything else they can think of. A number of them notice that Mary isn't here, and ask us if she was the victim.

Johnnie telephones, with lots to tell us. "Her blood pressure *is* a bit high, so she'll have to take it a bit easier from now on. But the big news is that they think she's nearer full term than twelve weeks! The midwife said that the baby has turned, all ready to be born and the doctor said some people just don't ever show that big baby belly at all." He's laughing, and I hear Mary say something in the background. "Mary says stop worrying, you've got about four days to prepare!"

It's a relief and a shock at once. I give Eve and Catherine a 'thumbs up' signal and glance once again at the busy street.

There are people lingering in the sunshine, smoking or gossiping, and some younger children have their noses pressed to the windows of the ice-cream shop. But no tall stranger with his gaze fixed firmly on the salon. Is that good or bad? Every time the phone rings I wonder if it will be him. Even with the distraction of these murders, I constantly check for tall thin men when I'm out.

* * *

Kenny pops back in just as we're closing, and starts to update us, but the door pings and this time it is the police after all. He pops back out again as quickly as he can, muttering he'll see us later. I stay where I am, feeling braver with the reception desk between myself and the law.

Inspector Hammond is sweating, and has shed his suit jacket. His grey hair is wet with perspiration, and I resist the urge to offer to give it a quick cut. But his grey eyes show their usual fierce intelligence, belying his shambolic appearance. Eileen, the WPC, looks as crisp and cool as ever. Even her light but perfect makeup is firmly in place.

"Miss Baker? Can we have a quick word, please?" He is polite, I'll give him that. He moves carefully out of the way of Eve's furious sweeping, sneezing as a cloud of hair flies up.

"Would you like some tea?" Catherine offers.

"Just a glass of water, if you have one," Inspector Hammond nods his thanks. "Are Miss Evans and Mr Barton-Shaw also here today? We need a quick chat with them as well."

I bite my lip, thinking quickly. "Mary, that's Miss Evans, is in hospital. She's a bit worried about her baby. This morning she fainted with the shock of hearing about the other murder. And John — Mr Barton-Shaw is with her. They should be back soon."

"Thank you. Just a few questions. As you will have already heard, from your customers if not from your friends at the *Herald*—" He pauses as Catherine returns with the glass of water. "Thank you. As I was saying, this morning another body was discovered at Glebe House."

"Who was it?" I know I would have heard by now if it was someone in our circle of friends, or even someone local, but part of me still freezes, expecting to hear a familiar name, until he answers.

"Her name was Carla Wilkinson. She was nineteen, and worked in a fish and chip shop in Hastings. She was out last night with a group of friends in Brighton. Do you know Carla, or have you ever heard her name mentioned?" He slides the photograph of a pretty girl with long blonde hair across the desk.

I shake my head. I might have danced with her, shared a cigarette in a sweaty bar, or bumped into her at the ice rink. She looks like all of us, just another party girl in her short blue dress. Even though nobody is accusing me of anything, and I'm safe in the hot salon, dog-tired and sweaty from the long day, my secrets rattle through my exhausted brain. To me, the internal noise is so loud that I'm shocked the police can't hear it.

Catherine and Eve are still clearing up, but they both pause at the name, and when I swing round hopefully, both shake their heads. No connection there, and Catherine seems to know everyone in Brighton.

"Do you have any idea who is doing this?" I ask, fiddling with the cuff of my uniform. I tug at a loose thread hanging out from the end.

"Not at the moment. Do you?"

I meet his gaze steadily, "No. I've thought so hard about the night before Linda's death, who was there and why anyone would want to kill her — but I can't think of anything at all." I swallow hard. The threat of tears makes my eyes hot and sore. "I do know one thing, though. It isn't witchcraft, and I don't believe in spells or ghosts." Well, not anymore, but I'm not sharing that little nugget. I haul my thoughts into order. "And it isn't bad luck, because you make your own luck."

I never thought I'd be quoting Mum in an interview with the police, but she's drifting around at the front of my mind at the moment. Part of me is just so relieved that she and the baby are okay, and another part is just waiting for the news that she's hooked up with another man.

Eileen latches onto my statement like a terrier grabbing a rat. "You mean Linda and Carla are in some way responsible for their own deaths, by 'making their own bad luck?'" Her eyes widen. She scribbles quickly as I answer.

"No! That wasn't what I meant all. The paper, and everyone in town, is starting to say that the whole area around Glebe House is unlucky, and bad things happen. I just meant it isn't luck. People make bad things happen, not ancient curses." Okay, that doesn't make sense even to me. I know what I mean, I think, but it's come out wrong.

"That's fine. Just for the record, we don't believe the site is cursed either." Inspector Hammond smiles and gets to his feet rather quickly as Johnnie's car pulls up outside. "If you do think of anything, any old boyfriends Linda may have mentioned, or even the slightest link to Carla, then let us know."

"What about Katie?"

"Sorry?"

"You know Katie who was murdered last year . . ." My voice trails away.

"We're not looking for anyone else in connection with Katie's murder, but we are possibly looking for someone who was aware of the details of her case." He looks and sounds as bland as ever. "Don't forget, if you think of anything, get in touch."

I nod, managing to force out a strained smile. We watch Johnnie carefully help Mary out of the car and see her to the door before rushing off again.

"He's gone to park the car," Mary says, flicking an anxious glance towards Eileen and Inspector Hammond. She's carrying a handful of hospital notes and a white paper bag with a bottle of pills poking out the top. Her hair is tied in an untidy topknot, and her eyes are rimmed with shadow.

I fling my arms around her, forgetting the police for a second. "I'm so glad you're fine. But are you really that far along? That means the baby will be here in a few days!"

"I know! I was so shocked after the examination, but one of the nurses said her cousin didn't even know she was pregnant until she went into labour! I mean, they said they can't be exactly sure of the date, but it could any time from now really, and the baby is a big one," Mary is still pale, but bubbling with excitement. "We need to get organised — apart from the crib I don't have anything ready."

"No wonder you said it was moving around!" I'm not sure it's a good thing the baby is big. Doesn't that mean more pain pushing it out?

The phone rings. Eve and Catherine are clustered round Mary, wanting all the medical details, so I grab the receiver, "Hello, Johnnie's, Ruby speaking. How may I help you?"

The caller is there because I can hear breathing, and as my heart starts to thud, louder and harder, I repeat *"Hello?."* I try to sound bored, drumming my fingers on the reception desk and pretending to look idly from the window. Just another phone call on just another busy day. The breathing on the other end of the line is slow, controlled, and clearly belongs to someone a whole lot calmer than me.

"Not having a good day are you, Ruby?" a voice says finally. The strong northern accent grates on my already shredded nerves. "Be careful, but remember I'm watching you too."

I'm acutely aware of the police in the corner, Johnnie just about to burst through the door, and my own possible mistakes in the interview earlier. I chirp into the receiver, "Oh don't worry, Miss Parkinson, the line can be terrible sometimes. I'll wait for your call next week to rebook you!"

Done. Luckily Johnnie's entrance gives me a second to haul myself together. I'm angry now, furious that the watcher, who clearly knows more about my life than I do, and probably knows the police are here, that he can get away with doing this, and that I can't do a thing about it.

If it wasn't for the rings, I would tell the police some man is following me around, making horrid phone calls, but I can still see the bloodied signet ring on my stepdad's left hand as I flee from the darkened alley, knife in hand, shaking and crying. The watcher was there somehow. And now he is here.

Chapter Fourteen

Tonight we're gathering at Black Rock. We meet late, after seven. The kids have gone home, but a few teenage groups are still lounging in deckchairs outside the café, and some athletic old men are swimming lengths.

The two swimming pools are set on the edge of the sea, and the changing rooms are always freezing, even after the heat of the day. Although I opt to swim in the hope it'll take my mind off things, I'm still shaken by today's events.

The police clearly think they have a killer on their patch. They must have some idea who did it. Perhaps an old boyfriend like Katie's? Or . . . I don't know . . . a dodgy family member? Before their murders, nothing seems to tie Linda and Carla, except their party-girl lifestyles. I run my hands through my short hair in an effort to clear my brain, and drag on a pink bikini. It will be good to get in the cool water, and I feel safer around our little group than on my own, or even just with Mary.

The top and bottoms of my spotted C&A bikini are pleated and the fabric is pretty flimsy, but I'm pleased with the general effect. I may not be as skinny as I'd like, but

Pearl has shown me that it isn't a bad thing to show off a few curves. Mary sticks with her lime green swimsuit, and surveys herself in the long mirror near the showers.

"I just can't believe that—"

"That you'll have a baby soon!" I beam at her, "I wonder if it's a boy or a girl? You have such a neat little bump. It looks great in that swimsuit."

"It's going to be hard saving for all the baby things, and then the hospital said to make sure and rest at midday." Mary frowns. Her glow is fading. She takes an elastic band from her wrist and quickly plaits her blonde hair into a neat braid, coiling the ends under to keep them out of the water.

"We'll be okay. Johnnie said he'd still pay you for full days, didn't he? And I'll ask Pearl if you can apply for some sort of allowance. You can just keep using your maiden name for any official paperwork until you decide about the divorce. I know that's going to be difficult so we should just leave things as they are until you have the baby. Don't you think?"

She nods, smiling now at her reflection.

"Don't you two look gorgeous!" Pearl and Victoria finish rummaging in their bags for towels and join us next to the door.

"Wow, so do you," I tell them.

Victoria is showing off her long legs in a cream bikini. Her blonde hair is swept up and pinned on top of her head. She's still in full makeup and pretty jewellery — a thin brown leather and gold bracelet, and a little gold chain around her neck.

"Oh, I hate these stupid metal disc things," she mutters, fumbling as she tries to pin the number disc on her towel.

"You won't get the right pile of clothes back if you lose that, and you don't want to lose that skirt," warns Pearl. She has plaited her own red mane, and is displaying impressive cleavage in a brown one-piece. She grins at

Mary. "I'm glad you're okay. Ruby was so excited on the phone! Can we all be godmothers? My God — just three days, do they think? Although you know, the dates might still be a bit wrong. And I think the first baby is supposed to always be late! Are you ready for the birth now?"

"Nooooo. Not ready and I'm a bit scared now. I thought I had ages to go," Mary admits, rubbing her belly gently. "They asked me to count through from when my periods started going funny, and when I did the dates made sense. I was really regular before that so I suppose we can be pretty sure the dates *are* correct. I suppose I wasn't really thinking properly with all the stuff going on at home," A shadow crosses her face, but vanishes almost instantly, and the glow returns. "I want to be the best mum I can!"

"You'll be a great mum, sweetheart," Victoria tells her. "And what a load of doting aunties and uncles this baby will have."

Mary looks surprised, and a little wary, but I laugh. "Lots of great babysitters waiting and ready for action!"

My best friend beams again. "I thought you meant . . . but you're right, this baby is lucky."

We head out into the main pool area. Victoria waves at Leon and Johnnie on the deckchairs along the side with their drinks.

Mary giggles, "He really is sweet, your Leon."

"He does have a sort of naughty professor look about him, I suppose," Pearl muses, with a wicked grin. "What's he like at . . . well, you know?"

Victoria rolls her eyes and gasps with the cold as we sit down and slide our legs into the water. She takes a sharp breath and pushes out across the pool, before spinning round and gliding back to us. "For the record, he's very imaginative," she says pertly, green eyes sparkling. Then she looks serious. "Actually he's as perfect as you could wish, but I wish he didn't take so many pills.

Not just party pills but something nearly every day. Still, he doesn't need much sleep!"

"Is that a good thing? The lack of sleep, not the pills. I know a few of the medical students pop quite a few to stay awake while they're studying, so I wouldn't worry too much." Pearl inches into the pool, visibly holding her breath as water reaches her stomach. "Hell! How can it be this cold? Maybe I should just sit in the café with the boys."

"Weaklings! Come on, you lazy lot, we've only got an hour before they close!" Victoria solves her friend's dilemma by sending a small tidal wave over all three of us and kicking her legs until we're soaked and shouting at her to stop. I dive underwater to avoid the chaos, holding my breath for as long as I can. It's nice to be alone with the muffled thump of my own heart, and the weightless feeling surrounding my tired body.

After a few half-hearted lengths and lots of chat, we lounge, waist deep, trying to warm our shoulders and backs. The sun sinks low in the sky, a last spark burning a trail across the darkening sea. The café staff have started clearing away.

I'm on my last length, sliding through the water with one eye out for James and Kenny who promised to join us but have failed to show, when I spot him.

He's behind the diving board, in the shadows next to the concrete changing block. He is smoking again, and watching me with a kind of lazy appreciation. I stop in the deep end, treading water. I look back at my friends laughing and shivering. Friends who I could call on at any second. Johnnie and Leon haven't undressed. They could just jump over the low wall and find out who this lunatic is . . .

But I don't call out, despite an almost paralysing terror at seeing my tormentor so close. Because this time I can make out features — familiar dark eyes, narrowed against the blue twist of cigarette smoke, tousled dark hair, and pale skin with a shadow of stubble along his sharp jawbone.

* * *

"You okay, Ruby?" Johnnie asks as we wander back along the seafront, enjoying that beautiful twilight time between sun and stars.

"Fine. Yes, sorry."

"Well, I have news about Linda," Johnnie says.

Leon looks up from murmuring to Victoria. "You have? Something that might help find her killer?"

"Maybe. I ran into her brother Larry at the ice-cream shop earlier, and he said she had started seeing someone fairly recently. Not only that, but when they all got home after the picnic, she said she'd left something at Glebe House and was going to try and find out if anyone had picked it up. Harry couldn't remember what but he thought she might have said it was her necklace." Johnnie pauses. He looks like a cat ready to pounce.

"But I was the one who forgot something! My purse!" I exclaim, jolted and confused by this new information. "The police handed mine back. They never said they found anything else — oh!"

"They found a locket," Mary says quietly. She looks at me, but I nod and she continues. "When they gave Ruby's purse back, it had a locket inside. We told them it wasn't ours, but they were sure it had been found inside her purse. We thought maybe it was found in the grass, and one of the other girls picked it up and thought it was Ruby's."

Johnnie nods grimly, "But Linda had that new gold-and-white thing on, didn't she? It wasn't a locket."

"She never said anything about a new man. In fact I was sure that Ted was actually getting somewhere at long last." Victoria takes a last puff of her cigarette before grinding the butt neatly under her heel.

"I didn't really know her of course, but surely as your friend Linda would have told you about a new love interest? I mean—" Leon looks slightly embarrassed — "Girls love to gossip about that kind of thing, don't they?"

Victoria hits him on the arm, "You make us sound like we have nothing else to think about!"

"Sorry, darling, you know unless it died at least a hundred years ago it doesn't figure on my radar!"

"He's right, though. She would have done. Great gossip, was our Linda. Oh, anyone fancy a hotdog?" Pearl rummages in her bag for change. We can never resist the glass counter at O'Hagen's. As we stand in the queue, I consider this new information. It makes sense that Linda went back out on purpose, that she sneaked out to see some new boyfriend. Maybe he was married. That's the only reason I wouldn't tell the others about a new love interest. But then I hope I wouldn't be stupid enough to fall for a married man in the first place.

"So Victoria tells me the baby is due in a couple of days? How exciting. I'm sure there will be lots of competition among the godparents." Leon beams at Mary. "I have five sisters, and the youngest was born when I was fifteen, so I have excellent childminding credentials if you ever need help."

"Thank you, that is so kind of you. I'll hold you to that! And well . . . if the dates are right, yes, much sooner than expected." Mary smiles back at him. Her short dress skims her tiny bump and shows off long tanned legs.

The lost necklace? The lost locket? I'm not sure how that fits in at all. I can tell Mary wants to share the watcher with our friends, but I'm still reluctant. It's too close to Croydon, and to our past.

The queues shuffle forwards under the brightly painted boards. There's blue writing for the fish and chips, red swirly letters for cockles and mussels, or yellow for Lyons ice cream. I see my stepdad's brown eyes in everyone lining up to get their dinner, both men and women. His face was usually red, and scrunched with fury, but occasionally — when he was in a good mood, or there were other people around — he put on a show. His brown pupils had an amber ring round them, making him look quite like a jungle-cat, and he had very dark lashes. The combination was both attractive and disturbing.

I can see why Mum fell for him, but not why she didn't have the guts to pack up and go when she discovered what he was really like. I suppose he'd been chipping away for years at whatever little confidence she'd once possessed. I can sort of remember that every time he said something nice, he'd follow it with something nasty, just so she'd glow with happiness for a minute, then sag like a pricked balloon the next.

A couple of motorbikes roar past. The riders wear studded leather, and the girls ride pillion on the back with their long hair streaming out behind them. They make a couple of rude hand gestures. A group of suited Mods queuing for fish and chips at the next counter start yelling insults back.

Eventually, clutching our dinner in folds of newspaper, we split up. Mary and I are going to obey her doctor's orders for an early night, Victoria and Leon are going to the Starlight Rooms, and Pearl is taking Johnnie to a house party near the Bedford.

"Hey, Kenny and James never showed up!" Mary says suddenly, as we reach our little side door on Ship Street.

"I expect they're busy writing the story for tomorrow. I wonder if they know about the secret boyfriend theory." I lock the door behind us when we're safely though.

Mary walks slowly up the stairs. "I'd rather it was some love triangle than the witchcraft idea. That really spooks me."

"It seems to have spooked everyone in new houses as well. Mrs Shorton was telling me today that her husband works for Ridgeway's — you know, the developer who's building the new estates near Glebe House. Apparently they had waiting lists for properties up there, and now people are ringing up and asking to go on the list for an estate in Hastings!"

I heat up some milk for Mary and make tea for me, "How many of those pills do you have to take?"

She pulls a face. "Two at night, and then two pink ones and one white one in the morning. With milk or water."

"Well, I can't see the doctor saying wash it down with a glass of beer," I point out cheerfully. "You're a responsible expectant mother now. Hell, you could have the baby tonight!"

"Shut up!" Mary props herself up on her bed with her pillow behind her back. "I'm so excited. Scared, but really excited."

"It's going to be amazing," I tell her, scoffing the last of my chips and dipping a greasy finger into the corner of my paper cone to get the last of the salt grains.

Our windows frame the velvety black of the night sky, and show a little half-moon hanging out over the sea. It should be the best feeling ever, to be safe in the little white-painted bedsit with my best friend. But I don't feel safe anymore. I know he's out there among the shadows, and I know now that I was right. It's personal.

Add that to a killer with a penchant for party girls, and the city by the sea becomes a dangerous place to live.

Chapter Fifteen

BRIGHTON KILLER STRIKES AGAIN

Carla Wilkinson, aged 19, from Hillsdown Road in Hastings, may have become the third victim of the man police are terming 'a possible serial killer.' Miss Wilkinson's body was found at Glebe House yesterday morning by local dog walker Andrew Jackson.

Mr Jackson told our reporter that he found Miss Wilkinson tied to the infamous Witch Stone, which locals are now dubbing, 'The Killing Stone,' at around 5am. "At first I thought she was still alive, but then I realised she was tied to the stone, and it looked like she was sitting upright. I did see a couple of other men out walking, but nobody near the body. It was shocking, and my heart goes out to her family."

A source tells us that police are investigating several leads, including the possibility that both victims were members of a local group of girls with an interest in witchcraft, in particular the life and death of Lady Isabella Gordon. The case of Katie Simmons, whose battered body was discovered in the same location last year, has been reopened after new evidence suggests that suicide victim Terence Jacks was not the perpetrator of the crime. Local girl Linda Beeston was also found murdered last week in exactly the same spot.

Green Ridges resident Sarah Tomes told us she had recently moved to the area, but is now, "living in fear" after the recent spate of murders. Her neighbours, who prefer not to be named, added, "We don't let our girls go out at night now. It must be obvious to the police that there is a serial killer on the loose, but we haven't seen any more of them around town. Everyone is scared."

While the council is likely to make a final decision on the redevelopment of the remaining land at Glebe House next week, developers Ridgeway's declined to comment on reports that buyers are staying away from the area.

Detectives have been drafted in from neighbouring counties to form a larger investigation team.

"Grim," Johnnie says, studying the front page of the *Brighton Herald.* "I assume Kenny and James had a hand in this, so where's the mention of Linda's secret assignation, or the fact that Carla's father was arrested last night?"

Mary and I look up from the newspaper, and Eve abandons her sweeping.

"How do you know that?" Catherine calls from the far corner, where she has just finished shampooing Mrs Green.

"I have my sources."

Mrs Green wipes her face with a towel and joins the conversation, her little pointed face alight with curiosity, "My husband works in the butcher's down Main Street, and Carla's dad is in the meat business, so we knew, of course."

I'm about to take an instant dislike to this woman — I know everyone loves to gossip but this is taking it a bit far — when she adds firmly, "But he didn't do it! Carla's dad loves his girls, and I won't hear a word said against that family. I know what people are saying, that young girls out at parties, taking drugs and drinking, deserve everything they get. Well, I say why shouldn't they all have a bit of fun? Life's short enough, without some killer stalking the streets."

"I agree with you there, Iris. Even though my older lot are all married, I still worry about any of them out after dark now." Catherine begins to tease out Mrs Green's tangles with a wide-toothed comb.

Mrs Green twists round to face Johnnie for a moment. "You said there was some sort of love affair going on with the first girl, though?"

I interrupt quickly. "I asked the police yesterday if they thought the deaths were connected, and they more or less said they weren't."

The client nods, as if I have confirmed her suspicions, "What do they know anyway? Looks like the police blamed Terence Jacks for Katie's murder and the poor man was innocent. Think of his family too!"

Johnnie frowns at her. His blue eyes look tired and slightly bloodshot, "I personally think that the more people who work on this, the better chance we have of catching the killer. We all need to be part of the investigation. Someone may well have a vital piece of information, but they don't know it."

Mrs Green nods so frantically that Catherine sighs, and puts the comb down. Mary opens the door to another client, and Johnnie brings her into the conversation too.

And so it continues all day, until a dozen theories are flying around, and every one of our tables outside is full of gossiping clients. Some have a full head of rollers, others are set up with a towel around wet hair waiting for a cut, and even the ones under the three shiny dryers are exchanging ideas and putting forward possible suspects. Nobody looks at the magazines, but everyone paws over today's newspaper and the mountain of dirty teacups grows.

At lunchtime, Mary tidies her work area and pops upstairs for her afternoon rest. "Are you sure you'll be okay? I feel fine today, and we're so busy," she says, surveying the chaos.

"You need to rest now, because we're going shopping for baby stuff later. It's the evening market in The Laines. I bet we can pick up everything for a few pence — well, maybe a few shillings!" I grin at her, and then glance down again quickly. I'm carefully painting a client's nails in shocking scarlet, and it will look pretty unprofessional if I get the nail polish on her skin.

"Go!" Johnnie shoos Mary out, before starting to pin rollers into another client's hair. "So, Annabel, did you know Linda?"

"You did that on purpose," I tell Johnnie, as I make a dash to the back for more towels an hour later, and find him calmly smoking on the stairs, a little notebook and pencil balanced on his knee. "You've turned the salon into — into an investigation bureau!"

"Well, not quite, angel, but I like the name. We are a gossip station for locals anyway, despite my efforts to bring in a few more high-enders. And we need them. The police are pursuing two pointless leads if you include that ridiculous witchcraft theory. God knows where they got it, but apparently it comes from a reliable source."

I can hear Eve calling me from out the front, but before I go I ask, "And the other lead?"

He shrugs. "Carla's dad was indeed a family man, who loved his kids, but he was also prone to starting affairs with girls half his age. Inspector Hammond is looking at the possibility he was seeing Linda, and Carla found out."

"No way! Linda wouldn't — not with a married man! Would she?" I think about how little I actually knew about the freckled-faced girl with the wild brown hair, "Besides Victoria is sure she was starting to think seriously about Ted. Wait, how do you know all this stuff anyway? Have you seen Inspector Hammond again?"

Johnnie flicks me a bland blue stare. "Get those towels, Miss Pop-Lips. I can hear poor Eve calling again." He goes back to his cigarette and notebook.

The last client finally leaves at six thirty, and I make the usual tray of tea. My feet are hurting, my legs and back aching, and my throat's sore from so much chat, but I'm still not in a hurry to finish up. In fact, I've been so focused on the 'investigation bureau' that the watcher has barely crossed my mind. Just, you know every hour or so, which is an improvement.

Does it help knowing who he is? Not really, because he has such a massive motive for revenge, and I can't do a thing about it. If he wanted to go to the police he could. Or if he wanted a confrontation he could follow me one night to a coffee bar, a party, or even the beach.

Johnnie sits on a client chair and flicks open the notebook.

"Wait!" I tell him. "We need to get Mary, and then have a proper meeting at the end of each day until the case is solved."

Catherine smiles. "I always thought I'd make a great detective. Missed my calling, but it's never too late! Go on then, Ruby, but make it quick, I've got to pick up Laura and Tom." She and Eve pull out chairs and stretch their legs out, with only a quick glance at their watches. Johnnie's like Pearl, carrying a whole raft of people with him on a tidal wave of enthusiasm for whatever project takes his fancy.

I pop outside, take a couple of deep breaths of blue sky and golden sun, and swing round past the dustbins to our little front door. The door is open. Not fully, just ajar. Just enough to let a slash of light stripe the floorboards inside.

"Mary!"

I stop for one frozen second. Then I run through the hallway calling her name. My feet slip and my fingers scrabble at the rough-painted walls. The noise echoes through the silence. My breath comes in painful gasps, and everything seems to blur into a kaleidoscope of shaken colour.

The second door is ajar too, and inside the room is painfully empty. The motionless baby crib in the corner seems to mock me, and my throat constricts with tears. Mary would never go out and leave both doors open. She would have stuck her head in and told us if she needed to get some more milk for her tea, or she wasn't feeling well.

I take a quick look around. We're more organised now, after a lunchtime shopping spree last week, and a generous loan from Johnnie. We have acquired a couple of old rails for our clothes, some wooden boxes for knickknacks, and a long skinny table for the neat rows of makeup and toiletries. The old make-do pieces are dressed with colourful scarves, and a string of fake pearls hangs over the battered mirror. Even the kitchen area is clean and neat, with a cluster of white mugs, plates, and bowls stacked in the corner.

All except for one mug, which lies smashed on the floorboards. Shards of white litter the scrubbed wood, and an ugly brown stain spreads towards Mary's bed. Her sheet and pillows are ruffled, but no more than I would expect if she'd had a lie-down. The mug of tea would have been on the box next to her bedside. A magazine lies face-down, pages bent, in the space between our beds.

No note, no other disturbance. Her blue purse and new fake leather shoulder bag from the market are still on one of the mismatched chairs. I force myself to check the contents. Money, makeup, a hairbrush, house keys and her little phonebook are all still intact.

I stand for perhaps half a minute, gathering my thoughts. No other signs of a struggle, and no blood. She would have screamed, surely, if someone tried to take her by force. She'd have been shocked to see the door opening.

The door.

As I run back down I quickly check both doors, running shaky fingers over the wood to check for splinters. I have a vivid memory of Pearl's broken lock. Nothing, which means either Mary opened the door and let someone in, or they have their own key. I start running again, pelting past the bins, dodging people on the pavement.

"Slow down! Where's Mary?" Johnnie says sharply, as I hurtle in at the salon door.

I almost can't bring myself to speak, but manage to tell them, in a high, shaky little voice, what I think has happened, before a few tears leak down my cheeks. I brush them away angrily and I force myself to focus.

"No! Are you sure she hasn't just popped out for some fresh air or something?" Catherine asks.

I'm already dialling the number for Brighton Police Station. I bite my lip as the phone rings for ages. If I dial 999 I'll have to navigate my way through to Inspector Hammond, and it seems more sensible to go straight through to the man in charge. I drum my fingers on the desk.

Johnnie flicks quickly through his notebook, muttering to the other two. I half listen, trying not to scream with frustration, waiting for someone to answer the bloody phone.

Finally a desk sergeant picks up the phone, and I don't waste any time. "I need to speak to Inspector Hammond. It's Ruby Baker, and my friend Mary Evans has been abducted."

* * *

By the time the sun sinks to a red gold ball flaming over the sea, Johnnie's has become headquarters for our search, and is buzzing with people. I used the call box down the road, Johnnie the telephone in the salon, and Catherine set off with Eve to alert the neighbours, with strict instructions from our employer.

"Knock on every bloody door in your road, and tell all the people you know. We need everyone out searching for Mary. With luck, the interest on the streets will put this bastard off doing anything until we find out where he's keeping her," Johnnie told them.

I called the *Brighton Herald* and said I had the story on a local abduction but would only speak to Kenny or James. They were both out, but the girl on the news desk promised to let them know. Now I'm ringing around my half of the list of those friends who have phones, repeating my questions again and again.

Inspector Hammond appears briefly to get the details, minus Eileen, but with the interchangeable Bill and Ben constables that I remember from a couple of days ago. They scribble notes as we talk.

"Can you describe the day? Tell me exactly what happened." Inspector Hammond is clearly feeling the pressure now. His shirt shows sweat patches spreading under his arms and across his chest. The damp material clings to his large body. He rubs his stubble with a rough hand, grey eyes flicking slowly around the room as I talk.

I tell him how Mary went upstairs for a rest, and four hours later I found she'd disappeared.

"The doors were both open?"

"Yes. Just ajar, you know, not pushed right open." I know what he's going to ask next — the question I have been dreading.

"Can you think of anyone who would want to harm Miss Evans?"

"She has a husband, Derek Brooks. That's why we came to Brighton, to get her away from him. He used to hit her, and she was worried he would harm the baby, so I suggested we came down and stayed with my cousin, Pearl."

"I see. It does rather sound like this is more like a misunderstanding than anything linked to the recent murders, so try not to worry," he smiles reassuringly, in a 'kind uncle' way that makes me want to scream. "Is it possible that her husband could have discovered the whereabouts of his estranged wife? Could he have maybe made contact with your cousin?"

"No. She would have told us," I say firmly, "There have been a couple of weird phone calls, though, and we thought maybe someone was watching us on the beach." I give them an edited version of events, making it seem more like we thought the watcher could be a friend of Derek's or even a private detective. "Derek is just too lazy, and he's not a very intelligent man. Mary and I talked about it. He had convinced himself the baby wasn't even his."

"Right. Well, you've been very helpful. As I say, try not to worry too much. If you could just leave addresses and names with Constable Billington here—"

The salon door bangs open. A bald man with a thin mouth and sparse grey eyebrows introduces himself brusquely as Detective Inspector Cobbler. The atmosphere between him and Hammond is clearly strained — as the newcomer fires more questions, the inspector assures me we are finished for now. They both jump on my answers, making me jittery so that I'm stammering like the prime suspect. After ten minutes, they finally stand, making a big deal out of telling Bill and Ben to make sure the notes are on their respective desks in an hour.

"Thank you, Miss Baker, we'll be in touch as soon as we hear anything," Inspector Hammond says over his shoulder, as the four men file uncomfortably through the narrow doorway.

Johnnie shakes his head. "Inspector Plod has got about as much chance of solving this case as I have of starring in a Hollywood movie."

I'm shaking so much my jaw hurts with the effort of keeping it clenched, but I hardly dare open my mouth in case I start screaming. I need to find her now, not talk about who might hurt her or who might have taken her.

A client has made me a cup of tea, and when I look up I see more clients behind the reception desk. We are definitely closed and the big pink clock on the wall is showing ten minutes past nine, yet I recognise Mrs Acton, ancient Mrs Marchfield with her cloud of white hair, and the equally elderly Mrs Carpenter.

"Don't worry, love," Mrs Acton reassures me. "The reinforcements have arrived. Johnnie knows he can rely on us in a crisis. We didn't go through the war to get beaten by some lunatic who thinks he can just take our girls off the streets."

I thank her and sink into a chair. I close my eyes and ignore the bustle.

When I open them again, James is sitting opposite me, tipping his chair back against the cherubs on the wall. Kenny is perched on one of the shelves under the mirror, till Johnnie yells at him to get off.

"I'm so sorry, Ruby, I came as soon as I got the message," James says. "Look, we'll find her, okay? Tell us what you want us to write."

"Thanks." I finish the tea, wishing it was something stronger, and give him the details. "So what do you need first?" I'm going to get through this by being as organised as possible. We will find my best friend and she will be safe.

"Well, I suggest we go with whatever you think will help us find her. Gut instinct — do you think this is connected to the murders? Or do you want us to name her husband and say anything about that? I know you told us in confidence, but if there is the slightest chance he could be involved—" James's blue eyes are vivid against his tan, and his dark hair is tousled. He shoves back a handful of fringe from his sweaty forehead. Lines of fierce concentration net around his mouth. "I want to help, Ruby."

While I run quickly through the basics, watching their faces as I briefly mention wife-beaters and being followed by a stranger, I consider this carefully. It has been very important to ensure the police know as much I can tell them about Derek and the watcher, but the press are another matter. "No, I really don't think her husband is involved. But maybe just mention they aren't together any more. We need to keep everyone focused on the fact that the murderer is probably local, not have them thinking it's some revenge act by her husband. Honestly, I think this is to do with the other cases."

"The bastard. Whoever's got her, Ruby, we'll find him," Kenny says. His normally sweet face looks almost brutal for once. "We'll emphasise that she's local, pregnant, and works here. Just that will get half the people in Brighton looking for her. In many ways this place is still a village, and we look after our own!"

"We did discuss Derek, because of course she was worried he would come after her, but in the end we decided he wouldn't bother. He's a lazy git, and probably found someone else to beat up by now. The police will hopefully sort that one out. I think they said they would send someone to question him anyway." I glance over at Johnnie, who is busily flicking through his notebook, and he rolls his eyes, shaking his head at the notion that the police will do anything useful.

"What about this other man who has been following you? Seems like you and Mary have had more than your fair share of trouble, Rubes. Do you want him mentioned?" James studies my face intently, standing very close.

"I don't think so." I meet James's eyes and I can tell he knows there is more.

"Are you sure? If not, then anything else we can use?" Kenny snaps a pencil, swears, apologises, and drags another out of his jacket pocket.

My instinct says no, I don't want the watcher in the papers. Not because of who I think he is, or even because of where it takes me, but just . . . I don't think he took Mary. I think about our last meeting. I was close enough to look straight into his eyes, and although they were steady under my gaze, some of the fire was gone. If I didn't know better I'd say he looked amused, even affectionate. If it saved Mary's life and her baby, I'd happily go down for murder, but for now I hang onto what I know.

"Brighton isn't that big, and for a man to be getting away with killing all these girls he must be somebody we all know. Not well, maybe, but a man who maybe hangs around when we party. Linda was going out to meet a new boyfriend. Katie had ex-boyfriend problems — and we know her new boyfriend was cleared, but did she have someone else? Carla might have had an interest in witchcraft, but equally she might have fallen for the same mystery man. Focus on the fact that the murderer has Mary." I wobble slightly, but clear my throat defiantly. It won't help her if I panic, dissolve into frustrated tears, or do what I really want to — which is to run down to the sea screaming to the waves about the unfairness. Why didn't he take me?

"You say that he either had a key to your place, or Mary opened the door?"

"Yes, which again all points to someone we know. She wouldn't just let anyone in. We're both really careful." I take a quick look around the packed salon. "Pearl and Victoria are working, but the police have already been up to the hospital and interviewed them."

"Who else? Ted's out with the seafront search party and Leon's over there going through all the notes from today and collating them. We know at least twenty more people we see regularly when we go out, but who would Mary trust to open the door to?" Kenny trails off, interrupted by the cheerful departure of the "home guard," those indomitable old ladies, who call that they will be back tomorrow to "help out."

"Wonderful people." Johnnie beams after them. "Did you know Joyce was a ferry pilot? She used to take the planes between RAF bases in the war. Amazing lady."

"*Mrs Carpenter*? I thought she was a hairdresser?"

"Oh, she was. She was only a pilot during the war. While I think of it, Ruby sweetheart, have your own set of keys for the salon. I was going to give them to you and Mary tonight anyway, but it makes so much more sense for you to open up since you're living here."

"Thanks Johnnie," For some reason silly tears are making my eyes all shiny, and I blink hard, pretending to be groping for my cigarette packet in my pinny pocket.

"Ken?" James gives him a shove, "Do you have something?"

"Not sure . . . I know he's Victoria's boyfriend, but how much to we know about 'Professor' Leon?"

"*Leon?*" I almost laugh at the suggestion. "The police interviewed him after Linda's murder, but only because he was with us at the picnic."

James jumps on it. "Yes, but has he been questioned about the other murders? Does he have alibis for all of them?"

"I don't know . . . oh, yes, Victoria said he was questioned again after Carla's death because they wanted an expert view on the witchcraft aspect. I suppose with the Lady Isabella connection they needed an historical point of view. But Johnnie has been interviewed more than any of us, and nobody thinks he's the murderer, do they?" My head feels dull and heavy, hardly able to contain my spinning thoughts. Just when I think I can see a clear path through the chaos, my roadway shatters and reforms, leading somewhere entirely different.

I can hear Johnnie laughing as he comes back with the brush. "Like I have time to nip off and murder people! I think we'll have a proper clean- up tomorrow, Ruby. We should have Mary back by then. In fact, I'm sure of it."

Kenny shrugs. "I hope so. We'll all do our best tonight, but meanwhile, Rubes, you be careful," He claps James on the back. "We'll find Mary. Try not to worry. James, I'll go and file the story if you want, mate."

Something passes between them, a quick look like the flicker of a shadow, and James nods. "Thanks, Ken. See you later. We'll go down to Baby D's and catch up on the news."

James and I are left staring at each other in the brightly lit salon, as Johnnie locks up. "Are we really going to Baby D's? Because I don't really feel like talking to anyone. But I don't want to sleep while Mary's missing. I just can't." I feel like as long as I'm awake, I'm willing her to stay alive. If I sleep, I lose our invisible connection. She isn't dead. I would know.

Chapter Sixteen

"I'm going to leave you to it. Don't do anything you shouldn't — and James, please be careful with her." Johnnie snaps off the lights. "Where are you going anyway? In case I get any news?"

"I think we'll skip the coffee bars and go down to the sea. I won't let you fall asleep, Ruby."

The road is quiet now. We watch Johnnie walk down the alley to his car, then wander in silence through the balmy twilight to the dark mass of water swirling gently beneath the summer night sky.

A few other late night beach-goers are hunkered down on the west side of the pier, and a group of ten or so have dragged sleeping bags under the shadowy, weed-covered structure.

I hesitate, but James takes my hand and pulls me on past Black Rock to where the shingle meets the dusty white chalk cliffs. A car flashes past, and a bus grumbles its way down the seafront. I can see the passengers in the brightly lit interior hanging onto leather straps and swaying.

"Down here." James gives me a hand. The beach crunches under our feet as we jump down. It's low tide and this end is dotted with little coves.

We settle on a warm patch of sand, high above the waves, sheltered by the sea wall. I'm exhausted and on the verge of tears, but James starts to talk. He tells me about his childhood in Whitehawk, his Irish mum and Portuguese dad, and his burning desire to get away from Brighton, to make a name for himself as a reporter.

"So these murders are good for your career?" I say lightly. I haven't talked about myself. I have no family memories I want to share, or fond stories of childhood. That time belonged to someone else.

James is a silhouette on the beach beside me. His face is in darkness. All I can see is his eyes on my face. "I wouldn't commit murder to get a good story, Rubes. If you thought it was me, you wouldn't be sitting on a lonely beach in the middle of the night, would you?"

He sounds like he's teasing, but I do get a prickle of unease. Not because I think James is a murderer, but because he might want something I can't provide. I lie back and close my eyes. Mary's terrified white face looks back at me and I snap them open them again.

"Tell me about Mary," James says, propped up on one elbow. I can feel his breath warm on my neck and his body along the length of mine.

"She's brave and smart, and I love her more than anyone." Too late, I've revealed rather more than I meant to about my own life. "But more than that. She has this kind of sweetness. It's genuine and quiet and —oh, I don't know. The other day she was sitting outside the salon and just staring at the sun and the sea, with one hand on her belly. That is what she's like. She sees happiness, I suppose. And really feels it."

"And you don't?"

"Sometimes, but not with that kind of pure certainty. It's like a child's view of the world, and even after everything she's been through with Derek hitting her, she still has it." Exhaustion is coming in waves now, beating me back against the sand. My eyelids are heavy and gritty. "Don't let me sleep."

James pauses for a moment, so close, then pulls out a tiny bag of pills, "Have one of these. They keep you awake forever."

I study the bag uncertainly. "Are they drugs?"

"Purple hearts. I have a couple when I'm working the night desk, and need to keep alert. It's fine as long as you can sleep it off a couple of days later. It makes you feel . . . great." He tips a couple of pills into one hand and I wriggle over onto my side to see properly.

The pills are actually little blue triangles. I'm about to refuse when another wave of exhaustion hits, and I feel sick with the effort of staying awake. I can't let Mary down. "Don't we need water to swallow them?"

"Ideally yes, but they're so small they go down okay with nothing. Here!" He tips one into my hand.

"I won't go mad or anything?"

"Not any more than you already are." He grins in the darkness, his eyes steady on mine. "Look, Rubes, you don't have to take them, but it will help you stay awake if that's what you want."

Somewhere out to sea a gull screams, and the sound echoes around the cliffs. If Mary is hurt . . . I tilt my head back and pop the pill on my tongue, ignoring the slightly bitter taste as I swallow it.

James takes one as well and we settle back down, lying side by side again with our bodies just touching. Even here in the dark I feel safe with him. I still take a quick look round for the watcher but either he's so well-hidden I can't see him, or he's spying on someone else tonight. Come to think of it I haven't seen him since the swimming-pool.

Would the police arrest him and not tell me?

My eyelids sag again, and I force them open. "The pills aren't working!"

James laughs, "Be patient. I know what'll wake you up. Let's go for a swim."

"You're joking. I'm so tired I'd drown!"

"I'll hold you up, Rubes. Come on!"

I stand up too quickly, feel slightly dizzy, and watch as James undresses down to his pants. He has a muscular body, I remember from the swim at the picnic. The picnic when Linda was alive.

"Your turn!" He starts towards the waves, continuing until he's knee deep, and a couple of yards away.

It's so dark that I can't see anything properly, but I fix my gaze on the vague shape of a figure in the sea, and pull off my work uniform and shoes. I walk slowly down in my bra and knickers, wincing at the odd sharp stone or shell. The heat is heavy tonight, and sweat drips from my forehead.

As I reach the end of the sea wall, James dives into the waves. I stand still, enjoying the cool swish and swirl of the tidal ebb and flow. A small noise makes me turn back to the beach, but I can see nothing in the darkness. For some reason it doesn't matter anymore, and I wade deeper until I'm swimming. The tired feeling is going, and I'm floating along with every sense sharp and alert.

The sea and sky are no longer black, but dark purple, and even red. The cresting waves in the distance are touched with gold, and the beach is far away. I lie back, licking my lips, enjoying the heightened sensations. My fingertips tingle icy cold, and my body's weightless and drifting.

"Ruby?"

"Here. Further along!"

"Do you feel alright?"

"Amazing. You were right. Mary will be okay." I'm so grateful, in a weird rush of golden emotion, that I suddenly decide it would be a good idea to kiss him.

His lips taste of salt and smoke, and he kisses me back. Hard. Our bodies pressed together under the water could be naked, and the waves seem to rush past faster than they should, pushing us closer.

The bright colours of the night merge together, and I wrap my legs around his waist, leaning back from my waist so my short hair floats gently around my face like a weedy halo. There is a reason I should stop, I know vaguely in the back of my mind, but I push everything away except the colours, and the sensations of my body. Everything is better, stronger and sharper than ever before. The sweat is rinsed clean, and our gasps are drowned by the waves.

* * *

"Are you okay, Ruby?"

The first streaks of morning light are visible through the thunder clouds and the heat of the night has turned to the sweat of daytime. The sea is spread before us in a shimmering mass of gold and red. But the colours are quieter, more manageable, and the intensity and connection I had with James is gone.

"Yeah, fine." I force myself to be casual, "Thanks for — you know, keeping me awake."

He leans over, blocking the light, delivering a quick, impersonal kiss to my cheek, "Any time. If you need to stay awake again just call me. I never sleep much."

My body is sore, and my hair is salty and stiff. I rub my forearms without thinking, then notice what I'm doing. "I should go home and get changed."

James helps me up, laughing when I try to shove sandy feet into my shoes. "I'll shower at Black Rock and head down to the office and see what's happening. If I get anything new, I'll ring you at Johnnie's, okay? But try not to worry. The police have Glebe House cordoned off, so nothing can happen there."

My brain is still whirring, but I'm not tired, just disorientated. "We're investigating it at the salon. It's what we decided yesterday. Johnnie started all that, getting everyone to come in and share gossip. One of the clients did say the police might not like it, and we should keep it quiet, though."

"Are you going to?"

I meet those turquoise eyes, slitted against the early sun, and smile thinly. "No chance. Today I'm making it bigger and better, with as many people as I can get until we find Mary and get this bastard."

He grins, and we walk in comfortable silence up as far as Black Rock, before I cross over, almost running up the hill to the salon.

It takes a lot of tea to calm my jittering body, but I wash quickly, pull on a fresh uniform, and use my new keys to open up an hour early. Not that I'm expecting any customers, but I want to be near the phone. Actually I want most of all to take the bus up to Glebe House and check for myself that no victim has been found today. But as James pointed out, the place and the Killing Stone are sealed off by the police.

In the salon window, I carefully pull down one of Johnnie's new advertising boards, and instead stick up the photo of Mary and me. Then I write out a notice:

Can you help? Mary Evans is missing. 23 years old, blonde hair, blue eyes, approx. 5'5". Any information, please call in or telephone Brighton Police Station.

The last is a pacifier to the police. Surely they can't make me take down a notice which includes an appeal to contact them.

I drag out cloths and disinfectant, and clean the salon with vicious energy — mopping the floor, washing the mugs, and sweeping out the whole place. Last of all I get all the paper packaging from the boxes in the back room, and tear it into strips like the pages of a notepad. We only seem to have eight pencils in the whole salon, but I shove them into an empty conditioner bottle and put the whole lot onto the little table in front of the 'waiting chairs.'

Catherine, Eve and Johnnie arrive punctually at half past eight, radiating a kind of ferocious energy, which is just what I need to keep me going. My brain is spinning like a globe and all I can hear is someone chanting her name: *"Mary, Mary, Mary."*

"I'll get the tea done!" I tell them.

Eve follows me down the corridor, picking up a fresh pile of towels, "You've done well this morning, Ruby. I bet you didn't get any sleep either." She eyes me shrewdly, and I nod. "Get an early night tonight whatever happens today."

"We'll find Mary today," I tell her, pouring hot water. I dodge her gaze — I don't want her to tell exactly what I was up to last night — and find myself staring at the concrete floor. She grabs the towels and I hear the tip-tap of her flat shoes on the wooden floorboards of the corridor.

Forgetting the tea, I look at the floor some more. Something's caught my eye. The faded red brick steps down to the old cellar are dirty. Just a bit of sand and grit, but we always keep it spotless.

I kneel down, frowning. The six steps lead down to the boarded-up door. I tread carefully down as far as the barrier, and give it a little shove. Nothing. The boards make a cross and are screwed into position on the actual door. I'm being silly. We had so many people in yesterday. Everyone was grabbing milk stuff, and everyone here would have sand and grit on their shoes at some point. If there was anyone in the cellar they would be yelling blue murder and we'd hear them.

"Mary?" I try calling anyway. No sound. I tell myself I really am losing what little sanity I ever had, finish the tea, and take the tray into the salon.

Mrs Carpenter and her cohorts have arrived, and Johnnie calls a quick meeting. "Ruby, you fill them in on what's happening."

I put my tea tray down and lean against a cherub mirror, brushing my short hair nervously out of one eye. "We haven't had any news, but I spoke to the police yesterday, and they have a new detective on the case. I also spoke to two reporters from the *Herald*, so Mary's story will be front-page news today. The more people who see it the better. With luck, whoever has taken her will either be caught, or get scared and release her." I pause for breath. "Today we need to carry on collecting information, and making sure the search parties cover every single area of Brighton. Does anyone else have any news?"

"Two groups of men went out along the coast as far as Newhaven last night, and this morning my Jon is taking a load from the market in his lorry, so he'll look along the coast road as far as Shoreham," Eve tells us.

Catherine reports that one of her sons was out door-to-door last night. "So everyone in Whitehawk, and further over in White Oak, knows about Mary. They'll get a gang together and search the east side of town after work. Oh, and Tony is over at Cheapside today so he'll cover the roads round here."

"Thank you," I tell them, "I'll get on the phone and ring the local businesses." The door opens and four middle-aged women start shedding cardigans and bags. "Actually, Mrs Carpenter, would you mind doing that while I look after my two clients?

"Of course. We've also spread the word of Mary's disappearance. My sister runs the local WI and she's calling an emergency meeting for this afternoon."

"I'll go down the road to the call box and carry on with the party set. Only another fifty or so to go. I didn't realise I knew so many random people." Johnnie heads for the door, nearly colliding with James and Kenny.

James's hair is still wet and his white shirt is slightly grubby. Kenny's eyes are bloodshot. I flash back to James last night — the colours, the vividness, and his low urgent "I won't let you go to sleep, Ruby, I'll stay with you all night." Well, he kept his promise, didn't he?

"No news from our end, but we brought you the paper," James says, studying the busy salon. "Ruby, you weren't kidding! Oh, and Ted was out last night with a search party, but he's taken another one up to Queen's Square. He said he'd pop in when they're done."

Before he can say anything else, two police cars pull up outside, and I scramble to see if Mary is in one of them. Logically, I know she won't just be delivered back to me like a longed-for parcel, but my heart does a silly flip at the sight of a blonde head, before I sigh with disappointment. Inspector Hammond trails through, minus Detective Inspector Cobbler, but with Eileen as rearguard. Surprisingly, Bill and Ben are with them. The inspector signals to his henchmen. He looks . . . embarrassed, I think. Kenny and James stand frozen on either side of me, like hounds scenting their quarry.

"Jonathon Barton-Gordon, I am arresting you for the murders of Linda Evans, Carla Wilkinson and—"

He doesn't get any further. The crowd in the salon erupts in protest. Many of them press closer to Johnnie, and turn to face the police with their arms crossed.

Chapter Seventeen

Johnnie shakes his head. His face is white and drawn, but his voice is as light as ever.

"Oh dear, Inspector. Have you got yourself into a bit of a pickle? Perhaps you feel the need to prove something to your fellow officers?" He smiles at the mob around him, "Don't worry. I'll be back. Just keep looking for Mary while these idiots are distracted from the real problem in hand."

"Wait! You can't take Johnnie! He isn't the murderer!" I shout.

"With respect, Miss Baker, I suggest you disband your vigilante group and let us do or job." Inspector Hammond's cheeks are flushed red and sweat gathers on his forehead. A muscle is pounding in his throat and the veins in his neck stand out like purple ropes. He seems unwilling to meet my eyes. Even his hands are sweaty — when he puts one on our reception desk to pull out a notebook he leaves a wet print. Why is he so nervous? Is it because of Johnnie or Mary, or is something else going on here?

Mrs Carpenter puts down the telephone, and draws herself up to her full height, hooded eyes flashing. Somehow it doesn't matter that her bosom falls to her waist, or that her hair hangs in grey spikes. She could be ruling the country. She probably should be.

"You ridiculous man. What on earth are you thinking?" Without waiting for an answer she sweeps on, "How did you ever survive the war? Johnnie, my dear, if you leave me the number of your family solicitor, I'll be happy to arrange for him to travel down and join you at the police station."

"Thank you, Mrs Carpenter. You are truly wonderful, but don't worry, Inspector Hammond and I will just have a little chat and sort out our misunderstandings." He looks hard at the bigger man, who flushes again, shifting his feet uncomfortably.

I turn to Eileen, who is silent under her smart hat. "Have you heard something about Mary? You must have something new or you wouldn't come and arrest Johnnie. If you have, you need to tell me!" I shout at him, "Is she *dead*?"

She hesitates long enough for my reporter friends to start scribbling again, but then shakes her head firmly.

"Can we have an official comment, Inspector Hammond? Just so we can let our readers know that you have a good reason to arrest a well-loved local businessman like Johnnie?"

James is good — slick and sharp. He might think Johnnie did it, for all I know, but he can see the mood in the salon is totally against the police.

Eileen breaks her silence and snaps "No comment!" She starts shoving her boss and the other boys in blue out of the door like a farmyard collie herding its charges.

Johnnie's supporters follow them out shouting, all the way to their cars. That group clashes with Ted's search party, which is coming back up the hill. The scuffle quickly turns violent, and I see Ted shouting, and swinging a punch at one of the officers. The crowd in the salon pours out as the police radio crackles.

The roar of motorbikes announces that some Rockers have arrived. When they hear the shouts the police have arrested an innocent man, several tattooed riders wade into the mêlée. Someone throws a bottle over the crowd. It mercifully misses everyone, but lands next to the drain with a crash, splintering glass across the pavement.

"Oh, Kenny, there's Leon! Help him!" Victoria's boyfriend is trying to come in, looking horrified. A couple of rowdy teenagers shove him hard in the race to join the fight. Kenny and I run outside and pick him up, dust him down and bring him in.

"What's going on?" Leon rubs his shoulder. He's hunched in his patched tweed jacket despite the heat of the day. His trousers are covered in dust, and his brown eyes are wide behind his black-rimmed glasses. "Is that a riot? Is that *Johnnie*?" He sounds quite shrill with the shock of it. He rubs a hand across his forehead. "Ruby? I came to see you because I hope I have some information, and we all need to pull together to find Mary. Victoria is devastated so I promised I would help if I could. We really couldn't believe it when Johnnie rang—"

"They've arrested Johnnie, as you can see. The fools." Mrs Acton is sweeping the floor. She glares at Leon, who shrivels under her beady black eyes.

"Quite — err, oh good Kenny and James are here. Now I have discovered something that I hope will be useful—"

More crashes and screams from outside, but in the salon we're all crowded round Leon, even two clients who should be sitting under dryers.

"Ruby, come away from the windows, my dear. I'm worried one of those young idiots will throw another bottle." Leon is still shaking a bit, but he takes his glasses off, wipes them with a very white handkerchief and then pulls a sheaf of papers from his satchel.

"They think Johnnie killed Carla and Linda. They wouldn't say anything else at all," I tell him, and my voice comes out in a squeak of frustration. I cough to clear the tears clogging my throat. "The police never said why they arrested Johnnie but I'm sure they would have told us if Mary was dead. Wouldn't they?"

"Of course," says Kenny. "What's that, Leon?" He eyes the crumpled pieces of paper in Leon's hands.

"I wanted to tell you that I found something. There is a link, a strange one, between the dates that the girls died and the completion of new housing projects. Look!" He spreads the sheets onto the reception desk, and we stare at a map of Brighton and the surrounding area. "As you probably know, I was asked by the police to comment on the possible witchcraft cult that two of the victims seem to have been involved in. The new detective — I can't remember his name — seemed to think there might be a historical significance. There isn't, but I had to oblige."

"Was this after Carla's murder? All the Lady Isabella tales aren't even true. Some posh bloke murdered his wife, in what was probably more of a domestic than anything. Silly girls pretending they can talk to the dead are just stirring up trouble for themselves." Kenny leans against the desk and offers cigarettes around.

Sirens outside indicate that police backup has arrived, but the crowd follows the cars down the hill in a hail of bottles and threats. The roar drowns the other sounds of the street in screams and cat-calls. Revving engines and the blare of hooters add to the mix, as a convoy of motorbikes inches down the hill behind the stragglers. I refuse to think about Johnnie. He's a survivor, and nothing rocks him. Of course he isn't the murderer. I turn my attention back to Leon.

"No — I mean yes, I totally agree with you on the witchcraft front, but look at the completion dates on all these estates. The completion date is when the houses are officially signed off for sale to buyers."

"Bloody hell!" Kenny interrupts as James saunters back in with a black eye. "Every time there's a fight you have to wade right in there. Serves you right, mate!"

"Look at this," I say to James, jabbing my finger at the grubby map. "Leon says that every date on here corresponds with the date a girl was murdered, including Katie last year. Three dates, three deaths. Coincidence?"

James rubs his face. He has a long livid scratch on his arm and his shirt is torn, but his eyes are glowing with excitement. I was right, he's like a hound picking up a scent. "You mean that the murderer has a connection to the building sites?"

"I mean that although it may not be witchcraft, a girl dies every time another few acres of ancient downland is covered in houses. It's like a sacrifice."

We stare at him. "Really?" says Kenny, sounding unimpressed. Leon just shrugs. "It is only a suggestion, and I am aware it is rather an odd connection. However if you consider all the cases, the law doesn't seem to have made any progress into finding the perpetrator, or indeed, the *perpetrators*. The police arrested Carla's dad after her murder because they obviously thought it was some kind of sordid affair gone wrong. Taking inspiration from this other murder last year, I suppose. Now they've taken Johnnie, but we don't know why. Don't get me wrong, I think Johnnie is a great guy, and Vic thinks a lot of him, but there has to be a *reason* for murder."

Leon's soft, slightly accented voice is the kind that makes you stop and listen, and I know he's trying to help, but still . . . "Johnnie is not the murderer." I glare at Leon now. "Even if you have something in these dates, the police have the wrong man. He doesn't care about the houses on the Downs, and certainly wouldn't sacrifice party girls because of it. These girls are part of *us,* they could be any of us. Don't you see?"

"It's okay. Rubes, we'll sort it," James says briskly. "Right, Leon, you need to call in at the police station on your way home and show them what you've found. Do it now and tell them anything else you think is relevant."

"Well, if you think they'll listen to me . . ." He shuffles his papers together, and puts them into his leather satchel before giving us a mock salute, "I'll report back in the morning after Victoria has gone to sleep. She's working so hard at the moment."

The telephone rings again and my heart constricts painfully. Please let it be Mary, and please let her be okay. But it's just another client booking in, and I droop with the usual sag of disappointment. I can't give up, and now Johnnie has been taken from us as well. The police are such idiots. How can they possibly think Johnnie had anything to do with the murders?

I can't give up. "Okay, everyone, if I could just have your attention for a moment—" The salon is filled with chattering women, but as one they stop, and turn to stare at me. "As you are aware the police have arrested Johnnie. I just want to say that we're going to carry on as normal until he is released. We'll carry on with the salon, and with our own investigation into Mary's disappearance and the murders."

They give me a spirited round of applause, and then the noise level gradually returns to normal. Thank God for our extra volunteers. I make them take an hour's lunch break, and serve them tea in the sunshine outside the salon. Eve runs over to Dick's for biscuits, and we continue handing out bits of paper and pencils to everyone who comes through the door.

At four, Ted turns up, looking exhausted but resolute. His little face is still lined with pain, but he is a man on a mission. "Hi, Rubes, I saw Johnnie get carted away. What a load of rubbish. I keep expecting them to pick me up again."

"Why?" I pass him a cigarette and my lighter.

"Oh, Linda, of course — and I didn't tell you before, but I dated Katie a long time ago. It doesn't seem to matter now who knows what. We've searched pretty much the whole town, and knocked on as many doors as we can. The people that live in Green Ridges and the other new estate on the east side were really kind. They've offered to go further, out into the villages, and spread the word. One of them said she knows someone who works in TV so if we could get Mary's picture on the news—"

I grab the ringing phone and indicate that Ted should put his feet up for a minute.

"Hello, Ruby. Leon here. I just wanted to let you know that I stopped in at the police station — with the map, you know?"

"Yes. What did they say?"

He sighs, sounding a bit embarrassed. "Well, they said they appreciated my expert view, but it was unlikely to be connected. I never got further than the desk sergeant, and he clearly thought I was a bit mad. I do have a bit of news about Johnnie, though. He hasn't been charged with anything."

I pick up one of my pencils and chew the end, considering this information. "Well, that's good isn't it? They are idiots. You know, Leon, I think we need to pursue this one. You really could be onto something. I'm going to ask everyone to check on family and friends who work on the building sites. Is that good about Johnnie though? Oh, and is Victoria home yet?"

"Yes, she's having a quick nap then she'll probably call you. If you need us, we're at my place. I have a telephone, so shall I give you the number or do you have it already?"

I take down the number, and thank him.

"Ruby? We will find her," Leon tells me quietly.

I ring off, stare into the slightly dusty ceiling for a moment, and then make another note on my paper. Anticipation fizzes in my stomach. Building sites. If this is something to do with the new developments, as Leon suggests, it might be reasonable to assume that the developers hire passing tradesmen. Therefore, if it was someone working on the sites last year who went away and came back for the extra work this year . . . but the police aren't interested, and they would be the only people with access to Ridgeway's records.

"Any proper news? What did Leon want?" Ted asks from his perch by the window.

I explain the new theory, but he looks unimpressed, stubbing his cigarette out and swinging his legs down from the chair. "I've got use of the van from work, so I might be able to get out to Hove later and have a look around."

"Shall I ring you if we get anything else?"

"Yeah. I've got to go and do some more work now, but I'm staying with my mum. I'll write the address down for you, shall I? And this is the telephone number at work. Oh, and if I *can* borrow the van from work, I'll take another search party from Hove and then along Shoreham Road." He scribbles and then exits with a wave before stomping down the road.

I watch him thoughtfully for a second. He seems genuinely desolate, but what are the chances of being that close to two of the victims? Not that he's hiding the fact . . . I shrug it off and walk over to the basins.

It seems wrong that we are just carrying on as usual, with both Mary and Johnnie missing, but I love the feeling that everyone is rooting for us. As Mrs Acton points out, "There aren't many more places that haven't been searched. I'm sure we'll have her by the morning."

The bedsit seems alien without Mary's chatter, but Mrs Carpenter bought me a basket of chicken and chips with a bottle of coke tucked in the side, and Catherine insisted on walking with me to the door by the alley. Everyone has been so kind. I blink back my tears, put the basket of food carefully on our little table, and avoid looking at the baby crib as I flop onto my bed. The sun has broken through a thin layer of cloud, and lights the room with jewel-like colours. I screw up my tired eyes and concentrate on my stack of notes.

I know the best thing I can do for Mary is get a good night's sleep. The scribbled notes are mostly offers of help, but there are a few things that make me sit up with a jolt: *'Ted Mathews is one to watch. He was walking out with those girls'* and *'Talk to Kerry Anderson in London Road. He works for Ridgeway's and finds all the labourers for the sites. You need to check it out.'*

There is no proper address though, and London Road is at least a couple of miles long. The luscious smell of chips and chicken seduces me into giving up. I eat my supper sitting by the window, watching the sky slowly darkening and the people hurrying past. If I squint I can see that tiny patch of green downland beyond the gaudy new houses. Downstairs in the salon the telephone rings, but I put my head on the pillow and shut my eyes. If I think hard about Mary, maybe I won't lose that thread. She must be alive because I can picture her face perfectly — her long nose, sharp cheekbones, and that droopy mouth that means when she smiles she looks happier than anyone else I know.

* * *

Almost before the sun taps on the window and the sea shimmers into gold, I'm up, washed, and dressed, repeating my routine of yesterday. Today I'm filled with determination. I lock both our doors behind me carefully, before setting the chairs and tables out and opening the salon.

Eve and Catherine arrive as a pair, of course, and bombard me with questions about Johnnie and Mary.

"No news on Mary, and nothing on Johnnie, but that must mean he still hasn't been charged. Is that a good sign?"

"Not necessarily. I'll ring them now, Ruby. They'll take more notice if it's me. No offence," Catherine says, hanging up her coat and stomping over to the reception desk.

I yawn and straighten the chairs. Quickly, I pour shampoo into plastic dishes, and grab the bin of dirty towels to rinse out. I'm just running water in the back room when I hear Kenny's voice in the salon. "I'm coming!" I leave the towels to soak in the sink.

James is with Kenny and I greet him as usual. It's as though the other night never happened. That spark of attraction is still there, but I feel we've had our night on the beach, and anything else would be too much to cope with at the moment. Should I feel ashamed? Or dirty? I do feel a flicker of guilt, maybe, because I'm not a 'nice girl' waiting for marriage and babies. But then I've never been a 'nice girl' and I've always done things my way.

"Rubes, we haven't got anything at the moment, but James has a source at the police station and they're going to release Johnnie later. No charges!"

"Thank God for that!" Eve says.

"Right, see you later. We're going down to Hastings to get a quote off Carla's dad," James tells me, as he and Kenny make a quick exit.

"The only thing you'll get out of him will be 'Bugger off'!" Catherine calls after them, pursing her lips.

"They're only doing their job," I say. "And they have been really helpful about Mary."

"Never trust a reporter, Ruby. They twist everything to suit themselves, and make half the stories up, I reckon."

Several clients push through the door asking after Mary, and I explain today's idea while I'm handing out paper and pencils. "Anything you can think of, or anyone who has changed behaviour and is maybe linked to the new housing developments in Brighton. Especially the Green Ridges one. Just write it down and put in my box as you go out." I point to the empty Estolan box sitting on the reception desk like a little brown pillar box.

The phone rings time and time again, and we are soon buzzing with clients, all of whom are given the same instructions and asked the same questions. "Have you seen Mary? Do you know anyone off the new building sites?"

At about three o'clock, Pearl appears. Her red hair is caught up in a ponytail, and her eyes are shadowed from night shifts.

"Any news? I thought I'd walk down. God, it's hot today. I feel really crummy, and I'm sure it's going to storm." I take her into the back room while we make tea. When we're alone, she lowers her voice, "You're doing good, Ruby. All these old ladies know more than that stupid Inspector Hammond and the whole Brighton force."

"They won't listen to Leon's idea though! It really is the only thing tying them all together — the dates on his map. And yesterday they arrested Johnnie—"

"I know — but, look, Rubes, this can't go any further—"

"What?"

"You remember I mentioned that Johnnie was a poofter."

I study her pale, set face. "Of course I do. I mean it is a bit weird, but I've sort of got used to the idea. Mary was so shocked though. She still can't get past the idea that it's illegal — oh! Do you mean he's been arrested because he's queer? No way!"

"Okay, calm down. Not officially but yes, it does have something to do with him being queer. He generally has a boyfriend down in Brighton and for obvious reasons keeps it very quiet. A couple of months ago he started seeing someone new, but I could tell he was in a bit deep. He told me this bloke was falling for him, and it wasn't an easy relationship."

"Right. What do you mean? The boyfriend is a suspect? Johnnie has been seeing the murderer?" I'm confused. "You think he knows who did it?"

"Nooo . . . Ruby. You can't breathe a word of this because there is a lot at stake. Promise?

I nod, bewildered.

"Johnnie has been seeing Inspector Hammond."

Chapter Eighteen

"Bloody hell, Pearl! Do you think the inspector's wife suspects anything? He said she comes in here to have her hair done."

"I know. Me and Victoria found out. It doesn't matter how, but I needed you to understand why he was arrested. There have been rumours at the police station. I know a couple of people . . . so far it's only whispers at tea-break kind of stuff. But even gossip is dangerous when it involves something like this. Think about it — a senior policeman is going out with another man. If it got out, it would end Hammond's career, his marriage, everything. It would be front-page news and he would never be able to work again. Not only that, but he'd be charged with a criminal offence. You can imagine what they'd do to him in prison!"

She takes a drag of her cigarette. "I suppose, what with the pressure of the murder cases and his private life coming under scrutiny, Hammond cracked, especially with all the interest from other divisions. I guess when he found out that Johnnie has a connection to this case, it was a good way to prove to his colleagues that he had nothing to hide, no bias."

"But Johnnie's been released."

"Hammond's flexed his muscles now. Proved to everyone that he's as normal as they come. Thinking about it, he probably also wanted to be covered if anyone ever linked him to Johnnie again, if Johnnie was down as a suspect in a murder case. That doesn't look good to anyone does it?"

I make the tea, frowning, trying to take this in. *Inspector Hammond?* But it does take care of a loose end. I knew Johnnie wasn't the murderer. Even so, what a risk to take, for both of them. I wonder if they were actually in love? After the initial shock, I even feel a stab of sadness for both of them. Just because you happen to fancy someone of the same sex, it makes you a criminal?

I rub a hand across my tired face, pushing back my hair. So what are we left with? Carla's dad has been cleared as well, and he works in a shop, not a building site anyway.

"Rubes, talk to me. What's going on in your head, sweetheart? Sorry, maybe I shouldn't have told you about Johnnie, but I want you to understand. It's cool. He's one of the good guys, no matter what they throw at him." Pearl pushes back a loose red curl, stubs out her cigarette in a saucer, and takes the tea tray from me, "I'll carry it for you."

"Thanks, I'm glad you did tell me. It explains a lot. Pearl, I must find her. I can't bear to think that she might be . . ." I can't finish, so I swallow hard and make a massive effort to focus.

My cousin looks right at me. Her blue eyes are full of sympathy. I can tell she wants to prepare me for the worst, but she knows better than to try.

I find my voice. "She's alive. I know it," I tell her firmly.

By closing time my box is full and overflowing with scribbled notes. We ran out of paper and Mrs Hayward came back after her cut and dry with a whole load of used envelopes. Her husband runs the post office. I help the others clean up, and then pick up my box and trudge wearily upstairs. Mary has been gone for over two days now, and time is running out.

I put the little pan on our stove and heat a can of tomato soup, grill some toast, and make a mug of tea. Then I change into my pink nightdress, put the food on a tray, and sit cross-legged on Mary's bed to go through the paper mountain. Many of the scribbled notes are just messages of support, the same as yesterday's haul. One makes me laugh out loud: *'Ben Draper done it. He walks round his flat with no clothes on. He is a weirdo and a perv.'*

But in among the mad messages and the sweet ones are a few that make me frown with concentration.

'It's someone we all know, and these crazy people are good at hiding. I know you walk out with Ted Mathews sometimes. He used to work for Ridgeway's last summer. Not pointing a finger, but just saying. Be careful, Ruby.'

Ted again? He seemed truly devastated by Linda's death, but then he never mentioned he worked for Ridgeway's. Yet he was so honest about having dated Katie and Linda. On the other hand, he has use of a van, and that is important. Somehow the murderer transported those girls up to Glebe House because they sure as hell wouldn't have headed up there for a romantic date. Especially Carla. She'd have known all about Katie and Linda. I'm completely confused, my mind is spinning, and the beginnings of a headache are niggling above my eyes.

Leaving the victims for a moment, I run through the rest of our little group. What about Leon? He is a bit odd, but he was the one who pointed out the connection with the building sites. And he's been dating Victoria, so if he was going to kill anyone surely she would be easiest because she knows him.

"*Because she knows him.*" Was it Johnnie, or the police who said that before? All the girls, Mary included, were streetwise party girls. They weren't stupid, or totally naïve. Of course I only know Linda and Mary, but no girl would go off to meet a stranger or someone they didn't trust in the middle of the night, would they?

Which puts Ted firmly back in the frame.

I pick up another note:

'You was asking about witches and that. I don't know about the builders but Carla and some of her friends were into talking to the dead, and they had Tarot cards to predict stuff. It's rubbish of course, but Carla's friend Maddie said she got some information off a bloke she met and she started being a bit queer. Talk to Maddie. She lives up Dyke Hill Road with her dad in Blake Cottages. He runs the farm for the Manson Estate. The police came and talked to her, but her dad hates them and set the dogs on them so she might tell you more.'

Hell! This could be the real deal — a chance to actually get somewhere in my search for Mary. I look at my watch. Half past eight. Plenty of time to get up to Dyke Hill Road if I catch the bus from the seafront. In my mind's eye I'm seeing Linda laughing as Victoria shuffles her Tarot cards, seeing Victoria's pretty, serious face as she explains the Death doesn't mean you're actually going to die. What was it Linda said? No, it wasn't Linda at all, it was one of her brothers. Larry? He came up behind her and made her jump, and said, "Not the bloody cards again, you're as bad as Carla!"

Carla! I yank off my nightie, grab a cotton dress and slip on my flat shoes. I snatch up my purse on the way out. All the time we've been looking in the wrong places, and dismissing this witchcraft thing.

I hesitate at the door to the salon, and then quickly unlock it and go to the phone. I dial the number from memory. "Hello, I need to speak to James. It's Ruby. Is he working tonight?"

"No, sorry, love. Him and Ken have just left. I'd give it an hour and then try Ken's place. You got the number?"

"Yes. Thanks, I will."

I end the call but stand, frowning, cradling the black receiver. The big pink clock on the salon wall shows me I've got ten minutes until the bus goes. Plenty of time, but I need to speak to someone, to let someone know where I'm going. I try another number, and breathe a sigh of relief as Leon answers. "Can I speak to Victoria? Is she there?"

"Of course Ruby. Are you alright?" He sounds as calm as ever, and I imagine him and Victoria drinking a glass of wine as they catch up on the day's events. "Is there any news of Mary?"

Victoria comes on the line and I quickly explain. "I needed to tell one of you what was going on."

I can hear her breathing softly, "Ruby, please be careful. You got all this from one note? How do you know it isn't a set-up?"

Leon says something in the background, and I hear them talking briefly for a moment. "Leon says he'll drive down and run you up to Dyke Hill Road. I'd come too but I've got to be at work by ten. Ruby?"

"Okay. Thanks, that would be great. Tell him I'll be outside the salon."

I put the phone down again, my mind going over and over everything I know, and the whole load of information that I don't. Ted? It just doesn't fit.

I'm heading for the door when the phone rings.

"Hello, Ruby," the watcher says, and this time his voice is softer. Almost caressing. Disturbing. "Have you missed me?"

I let out a long gentle breath, and say nothing.

"I felt that," he tells me. "You need to be careful, Ruby. I like your style but you're going to wind up getting yourself killed if you get too close to this."

"How do you know? Did you kill those girls?" I demand, riled at last.

He laughs, "Do you think I'm a murderer? Takes one to know one. Goodbye, Ruby."

"Wait!" But he's gone and the line clicks into emptiness. I'm left with the familiar churning guilt and frustration. Damn him for being able to play me whenever he likes. And stupid me for getting sucked into his little game. I thought this time I was in charge.

Leon looks slightly harassed when he finally turns up.

"Sorry, I wanted Victoria to have a proper dinner before she went to work, so I thought I'd try a roast chicken." He blushes. "It didn't go very well, I'm not sure I'm cut out to be a cook!"

I laugh, sliding in beside him. "What did Victoria say?"

"She said she'd make some toast on her break." He smiles fondly. "You know, she's going to be one hell of a nurse, the amount of time she spends studying, and all this hard work. I'm very proud of her."

"Me too. Sorry to drag you out, but I think this could be really important. If we go up to Blake Cottages on the Dyke Hill Road, I'm trying to find a girl called Maddie. I'm sure Vic told you the rest."

"I know the cottages, but there are about a half a dozen. Do you have an exact number?"

"No. I was just going to try going door-to-door. If you don't mind staying in the car, I think she might be more willing to talk to me on my own. The note said she lives with her dad, so it might be better if they assume I'm another girlfriend of Carla's."

Leon's glasses flash in the low evening light as he nods. "I agree. You can always call me if you need help."

* * *

The steep Dyke Hill Road winds its way across the Downs, heading north-west. Blake Cottages are just on the outskirts of the town, at the end of a bumpy farm track overlooking green slopes dotted with sheep. I'm a city girl at heart, but the countryside in this area always takes my breath away. I say as much to Leon while he's parking neatly next to a rambling hedge.

"I couldn't agree more. To think of our ancestors making their homes here, herding their animals, burying their dead in those barrows . . . it's something that should be respected and preserved. In fact if you look across the road to that next rise, there is a barrow right on top. It's a perfect place for a picnic. Victoria and I went the other day — so peaceful. We should certainly pay homage to the Ancients!"

I've never heard him speak with such passion before, but it is rather sweet that he is so fiercely protective of the countryside, even if I'm not entirely convinced that there is anything romantic about having a picnic on an ancient burial mound. "How's your book going?"

"Oh, about halfway there. Still stuck in the medieval times at the moment, but I'll get there. Right, I'll wait here and if you need me just shout as loud as you can." He picks up a paper from the back seat, grimaces at the front-page headlines and flicks to the middle.

I stumble over the dusty flint driveway to the first of six terraced cottages. They're all a bit run down and this must be a miserable spot in the winter, but just now the heavy heat of the evening air carries the scent of the pink rambler roses that crawl unchecked across the little flint and brick houses.

I think hard about my best friend, screw up my courage, and bang on the first door. After a good few minutes, just as I'm despairing, a young woman answers. Her brown hair is all scraped into a messy knot, and her face has a pinched, exhausted look. I smell meat cooking and hear a baby's screams. Two toddlers totter into the room behind her, one clutching a wooden train.

"Sorry to bother you. I'm looking for Maddie."

Her sharp black eyes check me over. "You one of Carla's lot?"

"I'm one of her friends, yes."

"Don't get into any of that stuff she was doing, okay? I know Maddie regrets it. She's at number four, and I've just seen her getting the washing in."

One of the toddlers falls over and starts wailing. The woman rolls her eyes and says a curt goodbye before slamming the door.

I'm getting closer to the truth, closer to Mary. I can feel it. Number four has a door of peeling green paint, and so many muddy farm boots piled outside I can hardly get close enough to knock.

A girl of about twenty answers, and I introduce myself again.

"You work at Johnnie's," she says, staring suspiciously at me. Her long brown hair reaches her waist.

"Yes, how did you know?"

"My aunt goes there to have her hair done, and sometimes I pick her up afterwards. Are you really one of Carla's friends?"

She's clearly not a stupid girl, so I go for honesty. "My friend is missing, and I need to find her. Please help me."

"You better come in. Dad's still out with the sheep."

Inside, the cottage is cramped, but clean. The small scrubbed table is laid for two, and the smell of baking bread warms the stone interior, which is surprisingly cool despite the heat outside.

Maddie lights a cigarette. "I only let you in because I know you're not a reporter. What with them and the police, Dad's been going crazy. So do want me to do your cards or the ball? Either would be cool, but we need to get a move on, or Dad'll be back."

I must be looking as stupid as I feel, because she gives a sly smile. "They didn't tell you, did they? I've got the gift. My gran had it too. I can talk to the dead, see things that other people miss, that kind of thing. That's why Carla came, and then she told all her friends."

"You can see . . . things?" I'm determined not to show weakness, because a bit of me is sure she's enjoying seeing me so thrown — enjoying her little moment of power. I play along. "Can you tell me where Mary is by looking at the cards?"

"Maybe. I'll try, but we need to go outside. It's easier on the hill, where the Ancients used to live."

It's so quick and so natural, I almost miss it. *"The Ancients?"*

"You know, people who used to live on the Downs, the ancient tribes. Carla and Katie were a bit obsessed with Lady Isabella at Glebe House, and it's true that is an important site, but Isabella isn't really that important. She was unfortunate, and she did have the gift, but — well, she just married the wrong man, didn't she? She could have taken control at any time with her power. I've spoken to her."

Katie. Obviously. "I see. Maddie, do you know a man called Leon? He's got glasses, tall with brown hair. Or maybe a dark-haired man with a northern accent?"

She frowns and then shakes her head. "No, why?" Then she gives that naughty, knowing smile again. "Although I do know a few men with dark hair."

"Doesn't matter. It was just a thought." Is it really too much of a coincidence that Leon could have used that exact same phrase earlier?

"So did you know Linda, as well? Did — um, did Linda have any gifts?" I scramble frantically for the right thing to say to this self-possessed, self-proclaimed witch. Clearly witches do not have gangs or groups, and I refuse to say 'coven.'

Maddie pulls out a box from under another table. "No, she didn't. Come on. She was just a friend who wanted guidance. They mostly ask for that. 'Who should I see?' 'Does he love me?' Silly. Men are just for procreation, everyone knows that. Linda wanted to know about a man called Ted, I do remember that. I think she was in love with him, but she felt she was too young to settle down."

Right. I follow the witch out through the kitchen door into the sun-drenched garden, past a basket of dry clothes and a mop and bucket. Sanity returns, and the witch turns into a normal, lonely, slightly sad-looking girl.

"We'll sit over there." Maddie walks through a row of beans and pushes through lavender and daises, before settling herself and her box onto a wooden bench, "Wait — no, we need to be closer to *them*. Sit on the grass instead." She takes out a familiar box of shiny cards, and a small glass ball on a wooden stand.

I lower myself cautiously onto the sheep-nibbled green slope. The view is breathtaking. I must be able to see all the way back to Croydon from here! Mary would love it. "Maddie, did you not think it was a bit weird that all the girls who have died, were all interested in . . . um . . . well, they were all friends of yours?"

She glares at me for a second. "The police asked that too. They even wanted to know where I was each time. Dad set the dogs on them in the end. I tried to reach them, the girls, but the channels are blocked. Sometimes it can happen. If you're too close in life, you can't reach them in death."

"Okay. Look, I don't care how you do it, but I need to find Mary. She's having a baby in a few days' time, and she's my best friend." My palms are anchored to the smooth turf, the hard, chalky ground, to reality.

"Sweet," Maddie says. Serene again, she removes the ball from its stand and plays with it. She moves it hypnotically from hand to hand, and the last rays of sun gather and spin in her palm.

"It isn't *sweet.*" I raise my voice, forgetting myself. "You have no idea what we've been through. Our lives have never been *sweet*, but we did what we had to. She's never given up on me, and I won't stop looking until I find her."

Maddie looks pleased at my little outburst, and puts the ball down in the grass. "I knew we had lots in common. Pick a card, Ruby."

I hesitate. She knows a lot more than she's saying, I'm sure of it, so I play along and pick a card. "No way. I had this one at the picnic. How is this going to help me find Mary?"

The girl studies my card, which depicts a bent old man on a mountain top, with a lantern in his hand. "You're very impatient. This is the Hermit card. It shows you are beginning a solitary quest, and need to be alone, isolated even, to complete it. Now pick another and think hard about your friend, her image, her essence and her beliefs . . ."

Her *'essence'?* Sighing, I stretch out my hand and slide another card out of the pack, flicking it over — a figure on a horse, and banner with a rose. Again I hear Linda's laughter, feel the warmth of her leg against mine, her breath on my cheek as we both lean down to look at the card. She was so alive, so real and happy. The scene in my mind's eye shifts and I see Linda tied to the stone, but something is wrong, and this time when I inch closer, her face has become Mary's. My whole body freezes and the green and gold Downs seem to spin slowly around us.

"Let me see," Maddie deftly snatches to card from my fingers. "Oh . . . Death."

Chapter Nineteen

"What's wrong? Death doesn't mean actually dying you know. It means your friend is going to face a transformation, leaving old things behind and taking on a new challenge." Maddie peers at me curiously. "It. Doesn't. Mean. Death. Okay?"

"Linda picked that card at the picnic, the night before she died," I tell her shakily.

"So? Linda was also turning a corner, and embracing her new self. There was this man she'd liked for ages, like I said, but then another one she fancied." Maddie is gathering up the cards now, pausing for a moment to caress the glass ball. "You need to go. My dad will be back soon."

"Maddie, Linda was murdered, just like those other girls, and it just happened to be the day after she picked the card. She went out to meet —"

"Yes, I know, I know, the police told me. She went out to meet a man, or she had lost her necklace or something."

"Don't you care? Three girls have been murdered in the past year and their bodies dumped at the Killing Stone.

There is one very sick man out there who is also probably holding my friend captive, or worse."

Maddie shakes her head. "Nobody has been murdered since Lady Isabella."

"What?"

"Those girls weren't murdered, Ruby. They were sacrificed."

I stare at her, as little chills raise goosebumps on my bare arms, "How do you know?"

She smiles, showing small, even white teeth.

"That's sick. How do you *know*, Maddie?"

"*Maddie*? Where the hell are you?" A voice from the cottage makes her scramble up. The witch becomes a child again. "I've got to go." She grabs her box and runs towards the house. I run after her, trampling plants underfoot.

"Go away! Go round the back gate. It takes you around to number one, and back onto the driveway. Go! I don't know anything else, but I do know that until you open yourself to other possibilities, you won't find what you are seeking."

"My God, Maddie, she's going to have a baby any day now! A child's life is at stake. Not just Mary's, but an unborn baby." I take a risk. "Surely nobody would want to be responsible for harming a baby!"

A flicker behind those hazel eyes says I've got her. "Alright, I will consult the Ancients, and my spirit guides. But I can tell you that all infant life is to be nurtured and a baby boy would never be used in sacrifice."

But a girl would? The sick feeling in my stomach brings bile up to my throat, and I retch. Is this why the murderer is keeping Mary — so he can use her baby as a sacrifice? Sanity and normal, logical thinking have vanished. This can't be happening. Mum creeps back into my head. She always said that, muttered the phrase under her breath, when George started on one of his rants. "*This can't be happening.*" But it could, couldn't it?

Someone bellows again from the cottage and I run across other gardens of flowers and vegetables, jumping a low wall and hurtling around the block of cottages into the driveway. As I pause at the gate, I can hear a ferocious argument from inside number four. Yells and screams pour out and the windows of number one shut with a bang. Finally, as I linger uncertainly by the hedge with the memories of my stepdad raw in my brain, a glass ball comes flying out of Maddie's front door. It shatters against the flint wall into glittering pieces.

I catch the last shout of the man I presume to be her dad. "You are going to get yourself *killed,* Madeleine, playing around with powers you don't understand! I will not let that happen — do you understand?"

The door bangs shut but I can still hear the girl sobbing something that sounds like a curse.

* * *

We're halfway back to the salon, the little Austin Healey scuttling along the road like an over-excited insect, before I can find the words to tell Leon what happened.

"She was really strange. I honestly think she believes she is a witch, but I don't think she had anything much to add after all. We already know that she was friends with all the victims," I tell him. I need to be careful, though. I sift through the conversation in my mind before I speak, choosing the things I want him to know. He sits next to me unperturbed, humming a Beatles hit. "It was weird though. She seemed to think it was all quite amusing, and a bit exciting. I wouldn't say she was upset that anyone had died."

He stops humming. "Really? That's a shame. I know Victoria was really hoping she might give us some clue as to Mary's whereabouts. A witch? Slightly odd in this day and age, but that doesn't mean, as you say, that she has any fresh information." He sighs. "Of course, witches have been in and out of favour over the past few centuries.

They were originally wise women who cured the sick you know. People depended on them."

It's almost dark now, and very soon we're swallowed into the lights of the town and cruising down the hill past Green Ridges. A perfect opening.

"She did say one thing that struck me." I pause and glance at my companion. His expression is as benevolent and relaxed as usual. His glasses are slightly skewed and his hair a bit ruffled. "She was talking about the Downs and mentioned 'the Ancients.' I suppose she meant the historical people who lived there."

He smiles now, turning to me. "And you're worried because I mentioned them on the way up to the cottages. Ruby, I promise you I'm not the murderer, or involved with any silly girls playing witchcraft. And Victoria would kill me if she found out I was!" Leon laughs. "That doesn't make sense, does it? But look, please don't let some crazy teenager worry you. We will find Mary, and to do that we need to eliminate all these red herrings that have the police endlessly chasing the wrong leads. The police are good up to a point, but what you are doing is better. People talk to you, and sooner or later someone will have some information."

I pretend I'm looking out of the window so that he can't see me blushing. "Sorry. I didn't mean it was *you,* I just wanted to know if there was somewhere she could have read about things like that. If so, maybe we can get hold of the book and . . . I don't know. My brain is so tired I don't think it's working anymore."

Leon gives my hand a gentle squeeze. His brown eyes are wide with concern. "Don't give it a thought. I know how worried you are about Mary. Yes, I'm sure I can get hold of a few books that cover the subject in more detail. I believe it was actually Johnnie who first mentioned 'the Ancients' and their presence in this particular area. He is quite knowledgeable about local history — nice chap!"

"Really? I didn't know Johnnie was even interested in history. Oh, but you're right, I am so worried about Mary." *(Johnnie?)* I fumble for a cigarette, covering my frantic thoughts, trying to act naturally. "Maddie said something else that I do agree with though — developers covering the Downs with all these new houses does seem wrong. You were saying yourself earlier about all the history that goes with these hills, but it isn't just that. They're beautiful. When I was talking to Maddie, we were outside and I could see for miles. It was breathtaking." I hold my own breath now, waiting for his answer.

"I couldn't agree more. Such a tragedy that generations that come after us won't be able to see such wonderful sites. But people do need new housing, and it's happening everywhere, not just here — Wales, Manchester, and of course all over the South-east."

Smooth, I think, very smooth and practised, with his soft Welsh accent firmly in place and that pitch-perfect lecturer's voice. Tiredness is kicking in though, and I need sleep to work this out. Can I really go to Inspector Hammond and tell him I suspect an academic is colluding with a slightly crazy teenager to sacrifice local girls. For what purpose? Maddie said she had to consult the Ancients, but perhaps if she has some kind of second sight, then that would be like fortune-telling. Sacrifice suggests cults, and evil. Things like that do not exist.

The car pulls up next to Johnnie's, and I thank Leon and head miserably up to bed. The room is empty and cold without Mary's chatter, and my untouched cold soup has formed a sticky skin across the bowl. I chuck it in the sink, and fling myself onto Mary's bed, hiding my tears in her pillow.

* * *

When I wake, the light is pouring through the windows, hitting my eyes like flame. My watch tells me I've slept until six, and I rub my eyes with both fists, like a child, slowly uncurling from a foetal position. The empty Estolan box is upside down on the floor, and the notes are scattered like snowfall across the wooden floorboards.

I follow my new morning routine of washing and dressing quickly, dragging a comb through my hair and shoving a bit of mascara on to disguise my exhaustion. I hope Mary is comfortable wherever she is. I hope she's not hurt, or hungry, or cold, or having the baby, or . . . or dead.

Downstairs, the salon is warm and smells comfortingly of hairspray, furniture polish and bleach. I sort out a mug of tea, light a cigarette, and start dialling. It's a toss-up who to go for first, but I need some advice. Kenny takes ages to answer and I am about to ring off when he finally offers a sleepy "Hello?"

"Morning, Kenny!"

"Rubes, unless you're actually in my bed I don't want to hear your voice this early in the morning. Or maybe you have news? Is it Mary?"

"No, but I do have news so drag your mind out of the gutter," I tell him firmly.

"Okay, what is it?" Kenny is yawning, apparently still only half awake.

"I went see one of Carla's friends' last night. A girl called Maddie." As quickly as I can, I outline my visit, and then my niggling doubts about Leon. "Do you have anything?"

I can almost hear his brain ticking for a moment. "Not really. They found Derek, Mary's husband, and interviewed him yesterday, but he's up in Liverpool now, working on the docks, so the Liverpool force took care of that. They couldn't find anything to tie him to Mary's disappearance. Apparently he became quite abusive and said he had beaten Mary, and kicked her out because she was having an affair. Do you want me to do some digging on Leon?"

"Why can't the police tell *me* this? How do *you* find out? Okay, I know, your 'source.' But it really annoys me that they don't tell me what's going on." I slump down onto the reception desk chair, twisting the telephone wire in my hand.

"It's because you're not family, I suppose, but you know I'll always let you in on the news. Now what about Leon? Are you telling the police about this sacrifice link? The witch girl up on Dyke Hill Road?"

"Yes. I have to, Ken, because if they get anything that might lead them to Mary it's worth it. Are you putting Mary on the front page again today?"

"No. She's moved down to second page. There was a big car accident on the main road yesterday afternoon, and six people died, including a couple of kids, so they're leading on that."

"Okay. I've got to ring the police before the others come in. Are you coming over here after work for another meeting?"

"Ruby Baker's investigation bureau still alive and kicking? I thought the police told you to shut it down." He sounds amused.

"No chance. Not until we find Mary. See you at half six, unless we get any more information and speak before."

Next, I dial the police station, and for once, get to speak to Inspector Hammond straight away. He's not that impressed.

"We did interview Leon Bellon earlier in the case, and he has alibis for both Linda's and Carla's murders. I agree this sacrifice angle is slightly odd, but I need a bit more before I pull him in for questioning again. He is a historian, after all, and it would be natural for him to have an extensive knowledge of the subject in the course of research and suchlike. The girl you mention . . . mmm, oh yes, Madeleine White. Again she was interviewed—"

"So what *are* you doing to find Mary?" I snap, even though I can see he is being reasonable.

"Everything we can," comes the smooth reply.

I'm tempted to say something about Johnnie, but manage to avoid it. That would just be childish. I put the phone down carefully. My brain is whirring.

* * *

By the time Catherine and Eve come in, I've set up, the salon is ready for customers, and I am in the back room pinning a vast sheet of paper to the wall.

"What are you doing out here? What is *that?*" Eve comes down the corridor.

"This is a map of the murders, and a timeline, and all the suspects, including the ones the police have interviewed. *This* is a list of the people present around the time of each murder — friends, family and so on —and *these* red circles contain people who have a common thread in all the murders." I'm pretty pleased with the way I've converted our back room into a command centre for the investigation bureau.

"This is bloody marvellous, love, and a whole lot more than the police seem to be doing. I hope poor Johnnie makes it in today. Let me see if I know any of the names in the red circles." Catherine leans close to the wall, tracing lines with her finger.

"Isn't he a friend of yours?" She points to Leon's name.

"Yes. I'm not saying any of these people is the murderer, because look — there are ten people in total with red circles. But they do have links, so even if they don't know it, they could have information that leads us to the killer."

Eve joins us, frowning. "Wait, I need to get my glasses! Oh, is that the door?"

We hurry back into the salon as a pale-faced Johnnie strides in.

"You're back!" We fling ourselves at him.

"Did you miss me?" A proper warmth lights up his cat-like eyes, and his cheeks tinge with pink. "Bloody stupid police. I've a good mind to get my lawyer involved after all. Or, on second thoughts, I'll just send Mrs Carpenter after them."

Any awkwardness I may have felt at knowing the real reason for his arrest melts away with the sheer force of his personality. He is Johnnie, and he is back. That is all we need to know.

"Look what Ruby's done!" Eve leads him to the back room, and I follow apprehensively. It is Johnnie's salon, and the investigative bureau was his idea. Nobody speaks while he takes in the huge sheet, which covers most of one wall. Then he shouts, "I bloody love it!" and we all laugh.

His expression changes. "No news on Mary, I assume?"

"No. Today is supposed to be her due date — well, as far as they could tell anyway."

"Damn." Johnnie takes a drag of his cigarette, "But babies aren't often born when they should be, are they? One imagines that very few arrive on the exact date. She could be late, or they might have got the dates wrong."

"Or she could have had it already." I can't see why he's holding her for so long, when he just killed the other girls. My mind flinches from Maddie's ideas on sacrifice. What if she was right? Perhaps this time he wants a baby, and if you kidnap the mother just before the due date . . . "Wait! I need to phone. Oh, how stupid am I?"

I frantically ring the number.

"Sorry, Inspector Hammond isn't available at the moment. Can you call back later?" the desk sergeant tells me.

"It's really important. Isn't there anyone else I can speak to — what about Eileen? WPC Stanton?"

A long sigh floats down the line, followed by the sound of shuffling papers. "I'll see if she is at her desk."

"Thank you." Eve shoves fresh mug of tea under my nose while I wait.

"Miss Baker? Ruby? This is WPC Stanton. We really don't have any news of your friend yet, but please understand we are trying our best to locate—"

"No, wait! Two days ago, Leon dropped in a map of the building sites in the area, and the dates of completion matched the dates the girls were murdered."

"I remember. We did look into it. We questioned the manager of Ridgeway's and several site foremen. As I said, we are trying to solve this case, but it takes time to follow up every lead." She sounds a little impatient.

"Do you still have the map?"

"It'll probably be with the case files. Why?"

I take a deep breath, letting it out slowly as I speak. I need to keep calm and present the facts, even though my heart's pounding so hard I feel sick. "Did it show the *projected* completion dates for all the sites around Brighton, or just the ones that have already been signed off?"

"I really can't remember. Why?" She sounds interested at last and I want to scream with relief.

"Because I think that the murderer took Mary because she is due to give birth, and he wants the baby. That stuff I told Inspector Hammond about earlier, you need to get Leon in because I'm sure he is connected somehow."

"*What* — a *baby?* God, that's . . . okay, Ruby, I'll look into it."

She rings off and I stand with the receiver in one hand, staring at my audience. At least she had dropped the rather too formal 'Miss Baker.'

"You think he's keeping Mary for the next significant date, don't you?" Johnnie asks. He sounds very different from the way he usually does — none of the usual amused drawl.

"Yes, or her baby. Oh, and have you been helping Leon with his book? He said you were really knowledgeable about local history."

"I did give him a bit of background on Glebe House, yes. In fact, I put him in touch with an amateur historian friend, because he was interested in the family who used to own the place. The family even has a distant connection to ours through unfortunate Isabella — some sort of third cousin by marriage. Why do you ask?"

I shake my head, "It's not important now, but did you mention 'the Ancients' to Leon at all?"

"In what context? Ancient peoples? Historical buildings? My parents? Probably but I don't know if I would have used that exact phrase."

"Yes, sort of all those. Oh look, it doesn't matter. God, the police are far too slow. I've got a better idea. Where's the paper?"

I grab the inky sheets, tearing through the headlines until I come to the pages of adverts. A photo of a new house, and lots of copy about how wonderful it is to live in Brighton, near the sea and the Downs. I skim impatiently to the bottom. There it is, in bold, slightly smudged black letters:

Hurry! Downsview is a small deluxe development of just twenty new houses. Add your name to our buyers list and find out if you have secured your dream home on May 24.

Don't delay! Secure your future today!

I dial the number on the advert with shaky fingers. "Hello? I just wondered if you are still releasing the new Downsview homes tomorrow?"

"Yes, we are! You wouldn't believe how many calls we've had, but then it is a beautiful place to live—"

I cut her off, and turn to the others. "Tomorrow. The next development is unveiled tomorrow. We've got twelve hours to find Mary and her baby."

Chapter Twenty

Mrs Carpenter is back in again, so we enlist her services.

"We need everyone out looking for Mary. Tell them that we've found out if she isn't rescued before tomorrow, he'll kill her, *and* the baby."

"Of course. But that's horrific. How do you know?"

"Um . . . just a source. I know it's hard to believe. Tell everyone you can. Oh, wait — Johnnie's back. He's got loads of copies of the photo we've got up in the window. We'll give them out to all our clients, and then we're going door-to-door after we close."

"Here, I'll take some down to Brenda's, and a couple for the ice-cream shop and Dick's." Catherine grabs her coat.

The salon buzzes with activity and chat, and in between shampoos, cuts, and styles, we take it in turns to ring round our friends, updating everyone and telling them how urgent it is.

James says he'll head out along the coast road to check out beach huts, nets sheds, and any other likely places Mary could be kept prisoner.

I'm sure Ted's gang have already searched the coast road, but another look can't hurt. "We need the police to arrest Leon, but they work so slowly. Can you find anything out from your mysterious source? Where's Kenny? Is he not with you at work?"

"No, he's working on something at his flat. I think he might have a lead."

"On our story?"

"You told him to check out Leon, didn't you? Well, he met up with him last night for a coffee. Anyway, Ken asked for this morning off work to follow up on 'something big.' Don't get too excited, he does this on a regular basis, and often it comes to nothing. He's such a hero sometimes! You okay, Rubes? Call me if you need anything."

I agree that I will and as soon as Johnnie is free, I drag him into the back room. "Look, it all keeps coming back to two people. Leon and, oh God, Ted." I tap the red circle with their names in. "They both had the opportunity to get to know the girls we hang out with, and they both have access to vehicles for transporting the bodies."

"They also have an alibi for two of the murders," Johnnie points out drily. "Having been dragged through the wringer myself in that interview room, I wouldn't wish it on anyone who wasn't guilty." He shudders. "I struggle to believe Leon has anything to do with the murders. He's totally obsessed with his damn book, and he's like a walking history lesson. Ted can be a bit moody, but I've never seen him threaten a girl."

I sigh, and fiddle with a loose thread on my pinny. "I really like Ted, but he dated two of the victims, and according to an anonymous note, did some casual work for Ridgeway's last summer. He has also been directing search parties, which means he knows exactly where we are looking. Or where we haven't."

"I don't remember Ted working on any building sites," Johnnie says, lighting another cigarette.

"Hmmm . . . back to Leon. Clearly, he has a thing about the Downs, and talking about 'the Ancients' makes a connection with *her,"* I jab Maddie's name viciously. "That means he might know her, and therefore have a way into another group of girls who would never suspect him until it's too late. Think about it! We've said all along these girls wouldn't go off with someone they didn't know. He isn't lying in wait in the alleys snatching them off the streets. He's probably offering them lifts home, or cheating on Victoria and pretending he's in love with them or something."

Johnnie picks up a pencil and taps his teeth thoughtfully, in a way that reminds me of my cousin. "Any more suspects? If either of Leon or Ted is the murderer, they are pretty damn clever. It makes sense though. If one of them *has* got Mary, and he's hiding her — and bloody well, considering all the search parties that have gone out — we need to follow him, get her out, and then deal with him."

"On our own?"

"If we have to. Ideally the police will pull him in for questioning and keep him for at least twenty-four hours. Even if they don't charge him, he'll be locked up so he can't hurt anyone. And if the date *is* significant, it'll have passed by then. Did you get Leon on the phone just now when you were ringing round?"

"Yes, he was perfectly normal and he said it's Victoria's day off, so they were going out for a picnic and then coming down here to join the search parties."

"Right, that sounds okay. We can talk to him later. What about Ted?"

"His mum doesn't have a phone and there's no answer from his work number."

"Exactly what I was afraid of. Did you say anything when you last saw him that might have spooked him?" Johnnie runs a frustrated hand across his blonde head, making the hair stand up in spikes.

I think about it, remembering Ted updating me on the search, his eyes shadowed and exhausted. "No, I don't think so. He was very organised and told me exactly where he had been—"

"Phone for you, Ruby! It's that reporter boy, Kenny."

"Thanks. Kenny! What are you doing? James said—"

"Ruby, I've got some stuff for you. I took a load of archived papers home to go through, and borrowed some of the nationals from the library."

"And?" I clench my fist around the phone.

"I know you said to have a look at Leon, but nothing popped up so I started messing around with a few more names from our group. I hate to say it, but I found something big on Ted. Of course there are a lot of people with the same name, and trawling through court records and files is not my favourite thing—"

"Get on with it!"

"Sorry. Ted was questioned in connection with the murders of two girls on a building site in Manchester. He was employed as a casual labourer on the site, and it was only reported down here because the father of one of the victims lived in Brighton. I did some digging into the court records around about that time — he would have been seventeen — and he also has a conviction for assault. A street fight. But it looks like you were right about one thing, Rubes, he has an obsession with the building projects."

"Are there any details of the girls who were killed in Manchester?" My heart is thumping and my throat is dry.

"They were found in a shallow grave in the middle of a new housing estate. The estate was built on the remains of a Roman villa, but was thoroughly excavated by archaeological teams before the developers started work . . . blah, blah, some kind of ritual killing was suspected because the bodies were not interfered with and the girls were lying on their backs, blah, blah . . . oh, here it is: 'The two victims were found with their throats cut, and their hands neatly folded on their chests.'"

Bile rises in my throat, and I blink back tears. "*Ted.* I can't believe it. We need to find him."

"I don't like it either, but it adds up. He was with Linda the night she was murdered, and he admitted to dating Katie as well. Do you want me to tell the police?"

"Yes! We need anything that will help get him off the streets until we find Mary." I explain Johnnie's theory, and he agrees.

"I'll ring the police now, and then drag James out. We'll see if we can find out where Ted is now."

"Well, he's not at work, because I just tried there."

"Hell. Speak to you later anyway."

"I know. Be careful," I say, putting the receiver down and dragging my thoughts together. We're getting close — I can feel it. Hold on, Mary.

* * *

I climb onto a chair and clap my hands for silence. The busy salon falls instantly quiet, "All of you know that Mary Evans has been abducted. Through the information you have given us—" I see Johnnie at the back of the room nodding approvingly, "— we are getting closer to finding Mary. But we now know that the man who took her intends to . . . intends to hurt her. We have a deadline and that is midnight tonight. Please, anything more you can do to help, or even just spread the word, would be greatly appreciated — it may save a girl's life."

They burst out clapping as I jump down, and Catherine gives me a hug. There are lots of questions, which I answer carefully. With this new evidence from Kenny, the police will have enough to question Ted, and at the very least look into his supposed alibis again. If he's locked away he can't hurt Mary, and he may even tell the police where she is. But while he's free he could do anything. I wonder again about Leon and Victoria. Maybe

Leon could help find out more about the Manchester murders if they were on a historic site. I also ring Pearl at the hospital, leaving an urgent message for my cousin to call me back on her break.

When Eve returns from a quick lunch, I take some photos of Mary down to O'Hagen's and pick up a hotdog for lunch. I'm not hungry, but I force myself to eat, covering the sausage in thick gooey yellow mustard that burns my throat.

The sun comes out briefly to warm my shoulders and throw prisms of light onto the white wooden panels of the fish and chip shop next door. Over the sea, dark clouds are collecting, and further inland the top of the Downs has vanished behind a stormy heat haze. I lick my fingers, wondering how Kenny got on with the police and how the others are getting on with the search. Part of me wants to be with them, checking every deserted alley, every sheep shack on the Downs.

A fire engine roars past, disturbing the seagulls and sending a rush of dust into my face. I tear the rest of my bun into pieces and chuck it down for the birds before jogging back to work. I jerk to a stop at the turn towards Kenny's bedsit. Flames billow from his building and thick black smoke is spiralling towards the storm clouds overhead. I start running without stopping to think.

"Stop here, please! You can't go down there." A policeman bars my path.

I'm gasping for breath. Sweat pours down my back and under my arms. "You don't understand. My friend lives in that building. Is he okay?"

"The ambulance has taken three of the occupants to hospital. Try not to worry. Hey, aren't you the girl from the hairdresser's?"

"He . . . oh, James!"

James appears from another side street. He shakes as he puts his arms around me. "Oh God, is he in there? He called me half an hour ago to say I should come over, but I got delayed."

"The police say that three men were taken to hospital by ambulance. But they haven't said any names."

A group of bystanders is swelling by the minute, and more police have joined the firemen, who are busy running around with hoses and barriers. Another police car pulls up, and parks diagonally across the road past Kenny's building, blocking the way.

"It's okay. He'll be fine," James says flatly, almost automatically, as he turns from the shouting and the flames. He's back in control, and his hand in mine is steady now, "You go back to the salon so you're next to a phone, and I'll go straight up to the hospital."

"Ring me as soon as you know anything?"

"Of course. *Go!*"

I stagger back to Johnnie's, the flames burning brightly in my head. That fire is no accident. This is my fault, I asked him to investigate. The deadline is creeping closer, and we're a man down.

Chapter Twenty-one

"I need to speak to Inspector Hammond, or WPC Stanton, or . . . um . . . Detective Inspector Cobbler," I say, hedging my bets. I keep one eye on the salon door. The news of the fire has doubled our numbers, so it's standing room only, and every one of the chairs and tables outside is filled. Mrs Carpenter and Mrs Aston are serving tea from a huge urn, and someone else is handing out biscuits. The noise of a hundred different conversations and opinions makes it hard to think, let alone speak on the telephone.

Eventually the desk sergeant comes back on the line, "I'm afraid everyone is out at the moment. Can I get someone to call you back?"

"This is very important. Do you know if Kenny . . ." Hell, I have no idea what Kenny's last name is. "Look, a reporter from the *Herald* has some evidence that a man called Ted," double hell, I'm not even sure what Ted's surname is, "has been involved in two murders in Manchester, and is almost certainly the man responsible for the murders here in Brighton." I sound like a loony, even to myself, and complete the effect by bursting into tears.

"Sorry, I've only just come on shift and there's a skeleton staff manning the station. There's a fire down in Portland Road, and I know the rest of the team are pursuing various leads on the murder case."

"I know! It was Kenny's flat that was on fire. Look, please get someone to call me as soon as possible." The man on the other end slams the phone down, and I take deep breaths, banging a fist against the reception desk.

"Hey, mind the furniture, angel. I take it Inspector Plod strikes again? Or doesn't, to be more exact?" Johnnie puts an arm around my shoulders, and I lean into him with tears of frustration trickling down my face.

"I don't know if Kenny managed to tell the police about this new evidence. Now they're all out and I only spoke to some stupid desk sergeant who has only just come on shift. We're running out of time, and nobody has seen Ted. Victoria and Leon were supposed to come in after their picnic, and Pearl still hasn't rung back!"

"I know. Let's close up early, send all these lovely people out searching and back home, so they can also ring everyone they know. You can go up and get changed into something warm, and man the phone down here. We won't sleep, we'll keep looking, and you can be the command post. How does that sound?"

"It sounds good."

I pick up today's paper from the edge of the desk, studying the headlines. Another piece on Mary. The boys have done well.

KILLING STONE MURDERER KEY SUSPECT IN ABDUCTION CASE

Mary Evans, 23, has been missing for 48 hours, and police say they are increasingly concerned for her welfare. Miss Evans works at popular hairdressing salon Johnnie's on Ship Street, and clients have banded together to help find their favourite stylist.

Links have been made to the three murder cases, and police have sealed off the area around Glebe House as a precaution. All three previous victims were found next to the Killing Stone, but police add they have no reason to assume that any harm has come to Miss Evans.

A close friend, Ruby Baker, says, "All we want is Mary home safely. Her baby is due and we need to look after both of them. I want to ask whoever has taken Mary to consider the implications of harming her or her child. I would like to thank the people of Brighton for helping in the search for my best friend."

If anyone has any information, please call Brighton Police Station.

* * *

Later, as the pink clock on the wall shows half past ten, I'm hunched in a blanket next to the phone, my tired brain whirring. Every so often a call comes through — a search party checking in; the police finally calling back and reassuring me that Kenny did get the message through and they are hunting for Ted; James telling me Kenny is fine, and that he broke an ankle jumping out of the window but is now driving the nurses mad asking for cigarettes; the police again telling me they went to interview Maddie and her father hasn't seen her all day . . .

I make notes on my scraps of paper, frowning at the map I've transferred to one of the walls in the salon. It's pinned up between two golden cherubs, and covered in scrawled writing. Next to it hangs a scale street map of Brighton, which I have divided into squares. When each square has been searched, and the group rings in, I give it a red tick, and they move on to the next one on the grid.

"Ruby!"

I pull my red cardigan tighter around my body, shivering, even though I just heard a rumble of thunder out over the sea. "Hi, Pearl. Oh God, I've been trying to get you all afternoon."

"It's okay, sweetheart, James has updated me, and I've popped down to Kenny's ward. He's doing fine, and driving all the nurses mad. One thing that does worry me is that I haven't heard from Victoria. Johnnie said they never turned up at the salon?"

"No. They were going for a picnic, and then coming to join Ted's search party. Oh!"

"I know. What if they found something? She and Leon would be sitting ducks to a killer. And if it is Ted, he knows all the places we like to go. Anyway, I made a list of places — not party places — but they always went off on long walks across the Downs. Oh God." She pauses and gives a big sniff, clearing her throat. "Shall I read them out and see if anything tallies with your information."

"Yes please." I light another cigarette and turn to the map.

"Right, here goes. Ashford Woods, Glebe House (obviously), a picnic place off Dyke Hill Road next to a burial mound — I remember her saying that one because it struck me as a grim place for a kiss—"

Something clicks in my exhausted fuzzy brain. "Wait, the burial mound is a barrow, isn't it? That's what they call them. Leon mentioned it when he took me up to see Maddie. But there wouldn't be anywhere to hide on top of the Downs."

"Tell the police. They can go straight there and search, just in case. It is just possible Vic and Leon found Mary in a barn or something, and if Ted saw them looking, or was even there himself—"

"Okay, ring me if you think of anything else and—" I don't finish my sentence as a noise behind makes me turn. Then pain explodes at the base of my skull, blocking out the light. I'm vaguely aware of hitting the floor, hard, before I succumb to the blackness.

* * *

I blink hard, but even with my eyes open the room is shadowy, lit by just one bulb. Strange. My head throbs, and when I roll over and stretch my hand out to investigate, my groping fingers meet with hot sticky wetness. My stepdad must have really whacked me this time.

"You can't think that nobody will look in the cellar of the salon."

Mary's voice. It can't be. "But—"

"Oh good, you're back with us. I was afraid I hit you a little too hard, but you really couldn't be allowed to make that next call." Leon beams at me, tapping his knife on one trouser leg. His chocolate-brown eyes are thoughtful. "I would have hated to have lost you. The Ancients were most specific about what needs to happen tonight. They will punish me most severely if I fail."

As if my stepdad wasn't bad enough, I've regained consciousness next to a madman. I stare woozily around the little room, "Where are we?" Is that *Victoria* in the corner? My vision mists again and I shake my head crossly, which makes my brain rattle.

"This is your cellar. Most of the cellars along this road have interconnecting tunnels. I believe originally it was to do with the smuggling trade. And who would have thought that all sorts of things happen at night right under your building?" Leon is smiling again, with that vague expression that is totally at odds with hard eyes. He glances at his watch. "We have to go now."

"The Ancients?" Victoria stares at her boyfriend, with a kind of horrified fascination. "Who are they?" I notice a line of red on her creamy neck, and a dark bruise across her right cheekbone, but she seems to be ignoring the injuries.

I blink slowly around the dark little room, taking in the brick steps, the doorway and hatch, and Mary and Victoria sitting hand-in-hand in a dirty corner. I can't stop myself crying out with relief. Mary's face is filthy, her cheeks striped with tear tracks. But she seems unharmed, and is resting her other hand on her swollen bump. I shut my eyes for a minute. *She's alive, she is alive!*

"I'm so glad you asked." Leon hauls a long length of brown tarp from the other side of the room. "Unfortunately I don't have the time to do them justice now, but the Ancients are an all-seeing, all-knowing force. They existed in this area, and many other sites, long before history even began to be recorded. Now we have come so far from our roots, we think that covering the land of the Ancients in little brick houses is an acceptable practice."

Leon. I was right with my first guess. It seems typical that out of the two red-circled names on my wall of paper, I ultimately picked the wrong one. "Kenny knows it was you," I lie. I'm watching Mary's awkward shifting movements anxiously. She's now sitting with her knees bent under her, cradling her bump, but she looks as though she's biting her lip. "He guessed it was you and this morning he told the police so they're looking for you . . ." My voice trails away. It's worth a shot.

"Really? Last time I spoke to him he seemed at a bit of a loss. Honestly, those two flakes Kenny and James are useless at their job. They are so desperate for a story that they'll believe anything. But I admit Kenny did seem to be on a mission to uncover all sorts of things. Then, when I spoke to him, he seemed convinced that Ted was his man. I may have bumped into Ted and mentioned he was now a prime suspect. Maybe that's why he started the fire at Kenny's house? He was pretty upset that all his friends believed he was a murderer."

"When was this? What are you talking about Leon?" Victoria asks in horror, her face contorted with fear, "Is Kenny okay, Ruby?"

I shoot a glance at Leon, who is still smiling at all three of us. "He's fine. James called from the hospital earlier. Leon, why don't you let Mary and Victoria go? They haven't done anything wrong, and the police will soon find out it wasn't Ted. Listen to the phone ringing in the salon. Johnnie, Pearl, everyone, will be calling me, and when I don't answer the phone they'll come down here to find out why."

"The Ancients sent me down here to complete a task. As I said, if I fail they will punish me." Leon repeats, giving the tarp a little shove with his foot so it sits at the foot of a flight of steps. "There, all ready. We must be quick. You're right, you do have far too many well-meaning friends."

"Where are we going?" Victoria asks sharply, eyeing the tarp.

"Again, another good question." Leon nods approvingly at her. "I knew there were lots of reasons you were my girlfriend, but I just lost sight of one or two of them tonight. Now, *we* aren't going anywhere. Ruby and I are going to pop up to the Witch Stone. Please note its correct name should be used at all times. The papers give themselves far too much credit for invention, and since the actual killing does not take place on the stone itself—"

"We . . ." Words fail me and I struggle into a sitting position. The other two girls are watching me anxiously, and I try to smile reassuringly. "You can't do that—" I'm about to tell him the police will be up there but bite my words off mid-sentence.

"Ruby, I know you may be reluctant to accompany me on your own, so I've brought a little friend." He leans down and peels back the top end of the tarp, "This is Maddie. I think you've already met her, Ruby? I really thought you had guessed the truth when I gave you a lift home, but you didn't, did you? So many silly girls. Anyway, she's coming with us to the Witch Stone."

The cellar is spinning again, and I clench my fingers on the rough brick floor.

A white face with long hair neatly tied behind her, glazed expression and the blood . . . so much blood spattering her body and the tarp. It's Linda all over again, and I hear Mary and Victoria make hushed exclamations of horror. The dead girl is dressed for a night out, with a short green shift dress, pearl earrings, and an armful of beaded bracelets. Her long legs are also bloodstained, but the scratches suggest brambles or wire rather than a knife. The feet are bare, and the painted toenails are dirty.

"She tried to run away, the silly girl." Leon shakes his head. "I always try to kill them quickly so nobody gets hurt. We could learn so much from the sacrifices of the Ancients, you know. I did think she was different, but she simply couldn't accept her destiny in the end. You've nearly ruined everything between you."

"What do you mean nobody gets hurt? She's dead," I point out, frantically trying to marshal my thoughts. My head is still throbbing, and it's so cold down here I'm shivering and my fingers are turning numb.

"I realise that," Leon says coldly, shaking his head at me like a stern lecturer admonishing a stupid student.

"What do you mean? Why did you tell us about the Ridgeway's dates, when it was you all along? Why did you give the map to the police?" I ask him, thinking the longer I can keep him here the more chance someone will come along and find us. The phone in the salon is ringing every few minutes now. It won't be too long. Surely.

Leon shakes his head, and I notice he is taking care to keep his knife in one hand all the time. Are Victoria's injuries a result of an earlier attempt to escape?

"You needed to realise why the girls were sacrificed or there really is no point. It has been very difficult to arrange this last ceremony . . . Mary should have had her baby by now!" He snaps suddenly, turning on her and pointing the weapon at her heart. She cringes away. I struggle up, lurching for the knife, but I'm too weak and Leon brushes me away. As quickly as it started, his anger is over, and he resumes his lecturing tone. It could be a dream, this educated man with a flash of insanity that vanishes into the darkness in seconds.

"As the sun rises on a new day, a special day, the Ancients have asked for three sacrifices to mark the three new housing developments that will be completed today."

"Three?"

"Three. All built on precious historical sites on our beautiful South Downs, but only one here in Brighton. Therefore the Ancients requested one dead, one alive and one newborn. But now it's ruined. Mary hasn't had the baby. *Stupid* girl!"

A wave of sickness leaves me dizzy. Mary sobs quietly into her dirty cardigan sleeve, and Victoria just stares at her boyfriend as if he's turned into some kind of monster.

"Don't worry, it won't hurt a bit. The Ancients knew that when blood was required you just cut quickly straight across the artery." He demonstrates, swinging the knife in a wide arc. We all gasp, shrinking back against the walls.

The dead girl seems to be staring right at me, and she's between us and the cellar steps. In my terror her face becomes Linda's and then my mum's. I blink hard and force myself back to sanity.

As I get slowly to my feet I hear the wail of a police siren, and my heart lifts. But Leon is having none of it. Despite the cool, controlled tones, his breathing is fast and his face glistens with sweat.

"Move it. Pick up Maddie and bring her with us." Keeping the knife near to my chest, he kicks the tarp and the corner rolls neatly over the girl's face.

"What?"

"Either you pick up the tarp, or I just kill you all now. This way, as I said, we leave destiny to the Ancients." Leon nods briskly, as if agreeing with himself, blank eyes resting on my face. "Do it."

The siren gets louder, and I hear cars screech to a stop outside the salon.

Mary moans suddenly, and as I turn to look at her, water trickles down towards her feet. In that split second I'm convinced she's faking it and giving Victoria and me a chance to take down the killer or escape. Then reality asserts itself. You can't fake that. She's actually on the brink of giving birth.

"Her waters have broken," I tell Leon. I can feel my heart racing and fear gripping my body. After everything we've been through to get this far, there is no way one man is going to take it all away from us. "You have to let her go! It's over and the police are here! *Leon!*"

I yell at him, furious and oblivious as the knife swings round and meets my chest. I can hear the sharp sound of fabric tearing and I look down to see I have a gash in my dress from my heart to my waist. That could so easily have been my skin. Blood on my body, blood on my hands.

I glance behind me, and see Victoria crouching next to Mary, instantly smooth and professional, as though she delivers babies every day in a dirty cellar, watched by a murderer and a corpse. "Have you been having pains long?" she asks, glancing at her watch.

Mary nods, relaxing, then screwing up her face as another spasm shakes her body. "It hurts, oh bloody hell it hurts! Let us go, Leon —*please let us go. Help!*"

She moans again. Victoria tears off her cardigan and her white blouse and tells the other girl to breathe slowly and deeply.

Leon rests the knife on the back of my neck. "Pick up the rope on the tarp. Start pulling or you all die right now. Victoria, how long until the baby is born?"

She doesn't even hesitate. "At least three hours, maybe longer. She probably isn't even dilated yet. Look for yourself if you don't believe me!"

Voices are shouting at the front door, and a great crashing indicates they are trying to break the door down. Just a bit longer. Just a bit.

But Leon is frantic. His patronising manner has vanished. It's like being with a trapped fox. "*Faster*, Ruby!"

I do as I'm instructed, feeling the weight of the body, tensing my burning muscles, and hauling with gritted teeth. I take eight long steps up, with the cold blade on my neck, and I hear someone calling my name. James? Johnnie too, by the sound of it. The point of the knife slips a little. There's a sharp sting of pain, followed by a wet feeling across my neck.

Behind me I can hear the girls murmuring to each other. Victoria's saying something about biting down on the sleeve of her blouse. This is not the way we planned the birth of Mary's baby.

"*Move!* Leave the tarp, just move or I will go back and kill them both right now!" Leon slides to knife around to my throat for a second, and as I freeze with fear, he gives a little nod. Then he reverses the blade and before I can duck, cracks it down behind my ear. For the second time, I swim down into the thick blackness.

Chapter Twenty-two

I'm not out for long this time either, but when I struggle back to consciousness, we're in the little white car going at speed up a hill. Houses and a park flash past. The roads are empty and the night is cloudy. Stray drops of rain dance down the windscreen, and the tarmac starts glistening in the yellow beam of the headlights.

We're heading away from the sea, and there is no sign of rescue. I stay slumped in the passenger seat, twisting my wrist to catch a glimpse at my watch. It is already three o'clock. Not long before the sun comes up. Not long before Mary's baby is born. Before she's safe, and Victoria is safe. Whatever happens, Mary is safe. I repeat this like a prayer and then sit up properly, turning to face my enemy.

The car pulls up another hill, turning right towards the road that leads through Green Ridges, and onwards to Glebe House and the Killing Stone. Leon was wrong. The Killing Stone is a better name now that it has been stained with the blood of three girls. But not mine. Not yet. I'm surprised he hasn't anticipated the police presence at Glebe House.

I inch my hand towards the car door handle.

Poor mixed-up Maddie is dead because of what? She didn't go along with his plans?

My breathing quickens and I hook my fingers into the handle and pull. Nothing. I yank the cold metal harder, but the door is locked.

The new houses are dark oblongs on the hill. He's going to drive right into the police and it will soon be over. My heart beats suffocatingly fast as we approach the entrance — and drive right past.

"What are you doing? Where are we going?" I have seriously underestimated this man. This scholarly-looking man who has killed at least six girls, and kidnapped two more. Even now he is humming another Beatles tune as he drives. He wasn't ever going to run into a police cordon. And he's never going to let me live, is he?

I try the car door handle again, and this time he sees and laughs. "If you get out at this speed, Ruby, you're dead anyway. I'd rather have my throat cut, personally." He speaks casually, gently, and if you didn't hear the actual words, you might have thought we were discussing menu options.

"I'd rather not die at all," I retort, feeling the fire return to my belly. I've survived lots of things, and my trump card is that Leon has no idea he is sitting next to a murderer. There is no reason I can't kill him too if I have to. They say it's easier the second time.

Leon laughs, accelerating again, so the trees that line the road become a blur. "You didn't think I was going to risk Glebe House again? I've been up and seen it. Even spoken to Inspector Hammond. All this talk about a killer? It's simply that the Ancients demand obedience, and if they order blood to be shed, then so be it."

I wriggle the door handle again, digging my nails into the metal for more grip, but it stays firmly shut. "Do you speak to the Ancients?"

"Of course! They come to me in dreams. Sometimes they reward me with a good night's sleep, but their punishments — well, you can see their punishments, Ruby." He raises his left arm. The sleeve has pushed up above his elbow, revealing a sickening line of burn marks and scars.

"But you must have done that yourself!" I say in horror before I can stop myself.

He only laughs. "Do you feel sorry for me? Victoria certainly did. Such a shame it didn't work out. Victoria and I are suited in so many ways, but I did have an inkling it wouldn't last quite early on. Do you remember when we had that first picnic by the Witch Stone? She said she would like to live in one of the new houses, or something to that effect. The Ancients told me to kill her instead of Linda, you know, but . . ." He looks less confident for a moment. "I couldn't do it and they were very angry. Do you know something, Ruby?"

Mesmerised by his conversational tone, I shake my head, as we turn along the road that leads across the Downs, past the turning to Dyke Hill Road. I think of number four Blakes Farm Cottages, where Maddie's dad must be waiting for his daughter to return home. I need to get away from this man. The road drops steeply away on our right hand side, becoming chalky cliffs as we climb higher.

Leon continues. "I think, Ruby, that I fell a little bit in love with Victoria."

Even in my cold terror, I'm sure Victoria will be thrilled when I tell her that her nutcase boyfriend did love her really. Then the little trickle of hysterical amusement dries. His warped idea of falling in love probably saved her life. And lost me mine. I won't be telling her anything.

"We're going to the very top now. You will have the honour of being laid to rest on the barrow. We'll be there in a minute. You're lucky that the Ancients have requested fresh blood from a new kill. It's pretty special, and I haven't done it for a while."

I need to do something before I just vomit all over him. The car is bare of weapons, the door handle useless, and clearly nobody coming to save me. Correction, nobody is going to save me but myself. I fling myself past the knife and grip the steering-wheel, swinging it to the right as hard as I can.

The car jolts. Tyres slide on the stones at the edge of the road. The knife burns into my shoulder as a blow hits home, but I hang on, fighting him all the way. He's yelling back at me, but I can't hear what he says. Going at that speed, it isn't long before the car goes straight off the cliff, and after a terrifying moment when it seems to hang in mid-air, crashes downwards in a series of jarring tumbles.

* * *

It's very dark and quiet when the banging and crashing finally stops. The stench of petrol startles me back into alertness, cutting through the fog. I wince as I move my shoulder and lick cut lips. My forehead is sticky with blood. The windscreen is smashed, and the steady trickle of rain pools on the dashboard, dripping onto the seat.

Thunder rumbles again out across the sea, and the thick darkness is blurred by heavy storm clouds on the top of the Downs. Glass crunches as I inch my feet away from the floor, and pain slashes through my shoulder. The whole of the right side of the car is crunched inwards like a tin can, but although the car tilts dangerously into the darkness, I'm still sitting half upright. I blink to my right, watching as trees wave gently in the breeze above and below.

What's below us? I make out the bottom of the cliff through the shadows, many feet down in the scrub. We've come to rest on a kind of plateau, nesting like a huge malfunctioned mechanical bird on a copse of trees. It's hard to fight the darkness that threatens to close down my consciousness. I fix on one thing. Has he been thrown clear of the crash? Is he dead? Please God let him be dead. The driver's seat is empty. I swivel around to see if his body has been thrown clear somewhere.

"Hello, Ruby, I was wondering when you were going to wake up. It's becoming a habit, this nodding off at inappropriate times, isn't it?"

The knife is back at my neck, and I'm back in the nightmare. I put a futile hand up to wipe my face clean of rain and blood.

"That was a silly thing to do. But you can never deny your destiny. The Ancients have decided you will die on the Downs, and you can try to avoid it all you want, but in the end fate will take its course." His eerie calm is somehow more terrifying than his rage. "Look at me."

I turn slowly in my seat to face him. He's crouched outside the remains of my door, balanced on the scrub and rocks. Why isn't he more injured? Or even dead? The clouds flitting across the hot stormy sky mean I only get glimpses of his blood-smeared face, but he seems to be able to move freely, and I suppose if he was thrown clear that would explain why he's in a better state than I am. So no incapacitating injuries for me to take advantage of, whereas I've got a knife wound in my shoulder and another headache. What are the chances? I almost find myself wondering if he does have some kind of diabolical force on his side.

I remember Victoria saying, "Actually it is one thing I don't like about him. He takes too many. Party pills are fine, but he uses them almost every day." Maybe not some kind of divine force, then, but possibly a pharmaceutical one. Great. I wonder what he's taking. The rain starts to fall harder, a steady drumbeat on the car and a soothing river on my cut and battered body. It washes away the last of my dizziness. Time is running out.

"Come on, Ruby. Look, the barrow is just up there. So really if you were going to do something stupid like crash my car, you couldn't have done it in a better place. We'll walk to the top. Move it."

I stare at the winding animal paths up through the undergrowth to the road, and then at the short but steep climb to the top of the Downs on the other side. "I can't walk. I think my ankle is broken."

He tuts, as if I were a reluctant child or mutinous student. "But you must get up there. I think you'll find if it's a choice between dying here or up there, you will able to walk." The knife is at my throat and his eyes are on my face.

I keep myself carefully still and take long deep breaths. I'm not done yet, but if he thinks I am, there might still be a chance. "I'll try."

"Good girl!"

Before I can move to get out, he twists his hand in a grotesque little movement, and I get that sharp, stinging pain again on my neck.

"I said, I'll do it!" I snap, rubbing the cut. It hurts like a bramble scratch, so it must be shallow.

"I'll help you." He leans over suddenly, and picks me out of the car. I scream as my shoulder bashes the door frame. He curses and dumps me on the ground.

"Now walk. Hurry up. It'll be light soon."

He shoves me ahead of him, and keeps the knife pointing into the back of my neck. I stumble and beat the undergrowth away with helpless hands. Once I slip on the wet chalk and nearly fall, but he hauls me up. The stormy heat of the air is smothering, and soon I'm dripping with sweat. My eyes are stinging.

By the time we reach the road, I'm praying for a car, or even the police. Pearl knew about the barrow. By the time the rescuers have finished with Victoria and Mary, they'll realise it was Leon. The road is empty and just a few feet of chalky path lie between me and my destiny. Funny how things turn out.

"Help!" I scream to the rain and the storm clouds, to the distant tumbling sea and the shrouded city on the hill. And then I twist away from the knife and run straight up that stony path to the top of the Downs. Thunder rumbles closer, and suddenly I'm further ahead. I can hear him swearing and slipping. At long last I've got that lucky break. I forget my injured shoulder and my exhaustion, and concentrate on digging into that hill. I'm lighter on my feet than he is and I gain a few more inches when I grab onto a spindly hawthorn bush to haul myself up, and a whole branch breaks off. I twist as I run and fling it backwards, hearing the cursing as it falls back onto Leon. Another couple of seconds saved.

A flash of lightening illuminates the top of the Downs as I finally crest the hill, gasping. I turn my head wildly, looking for somewhere to hide. A mile or so to the west there's a ring of trees, but I would need to run all the way with no cover. Ahead of me I can see the barrow, an unmistakable smooth mound of earth with a dipped top, like a grassy bowl. I head towards the trees, but it's no good. Here on the flat I'm no match for him. Leon finally catches up and grabs me.

Thunder crashes around us as the storm breaks properly. He shouts something as he pulls me towards the barrow. I slip out from his arm and twist away as he plunges the knife at my chest. It's like some nightmare game of chase. But I can only dodge for so long, and this time when he grabs me he tightens his hands around my neck. My already battered body can't fight his iron grip, and I paw frantically at his hands until the red pinpricks appear behind my scrunched eyelids. I can't breathe. He's going to kill me here and now.

But he doesn't. He's dragging me towards the centre of the barrow. I fight every step, making my weight as heavy as I can, hanging onto his arms. In the middle of the grassy dip is a stone. It's not as big as the Killing Stone at Glebe House, but more like those marker stones you see so often on the Downs and on country roadsides, telling you that you have however many miles to Brighton. But it is a stone, and I know why he hasn't killed me yet.

One last desperate struggle. I fling myself at the knife. At the same time I aim my knee upwards with the force of a sledgehammer, right into his testicles. He falters, caught off-balance, before grabbing me with more strength than I thought possible. We fall down together. I'm on top and I can see the weapon. I dive for it again, focusing my whole being on that glittering prize, ignoring Leon's yell of fury, his fist in my face, and the pain that engulfs my entire body in a hot wave.

I feel a squall of rain and see a flash of lightening. Then a huge clap of thunder seems to split the hills apart. In that white light, I seize the knife from the grass, and clench my fist on the handle. I aim wildly at his chest, again and again. Most of my blows miss, but I feel him flinch against me as I strike home.

His own hand closes on my wrist, squeezing, twisting, and my screams echo across the downlands. We roll over and over as the rain beats viciously down. Patches of chalk and flint tear my skin open. The storm is a noisy audience to our tragedy.

I can barely hear the sound of feet, but someone else joins the fight. It's a moment before I realise that he's on my side. I make a grab for the knife but the stranger has taken Leon off me. The man's hair is plastered across his face, and his breathing is as heavy as mine. He hauls Leon away, throwing him down onto the grass not far from the dark shape that must be the milestone.

Leon never moves, but I see his blood staining the ancient turf in the next jagged slash of lightening. Black on black, but his blood is darker. Evil. A sacrifice for the Ancients, or a fitting end for a murderer?

Thunder rumbles overhead. I wait, gasping in lungfuls of the cool air, for the next thread of lightning so I can see my rescuer's face. I've seen it countless times over the last month, but now, looking full on at the dark hair, the deep-set eyes and the sharp face, he's closer than he has ever been. He is younger than I thought. Still in his twenties, maybe. Despite the broad shoulders and height, he moves lightly, even gracefully, like an athlete.

I grab the knife and back away from him. But the watcher never moves.

"Why did you help me?" I gasp out. I'm shaking, as much from the fight as from his presence.

He stays where he is with his brown-and-amber eyes locked on mine. The rain beats down, and I wait for him to speak. To explain. So much emotion passes between us without a word being spoken.

"Who are you?" I think I know of course, but I want him to tell me. Those unusual eyes, the bone structure, and the way he carries himself, can surely mean only one thing.

He takes a step towards me, and I tighten my grip on the knife. He spreads both hands low and wide, approaching me as you would a frightened animal. "I'm not going to hurt you, Ruby."

"Why have you been stalking me then? Stealing my things . . . staring at me . . . I thought you were the murderer!" My words come out jumbled and confused, but I lower the knife uncertainly. "You stole my *knickers* for Christ's sake, you creep!"

He's very close now. But he doesn't touch me.

"George was my dad. He took off when I was a baby, and I don't remember him. But my mam had relatives down South and she kept track of him. Last winter, she was really sick, and before she died, she told me about how he'd run off with another woman — your mam — and she gave me an address in Croydon."

"So? You tracked George down. Hell, when I first saw you properly I even thought you might even be his ghost. You scared the living daylights out of me!"

His northern accent is softer up close, and it's lost that harsh edge of anger. Very carefully, slowly, he stretches out a hand to my bare arm for just a moment. "I am not going to hurt you, and I am nothing like George," he says.

I stay where I am. "Go on. What happened then? You came to find us in Croydon?"

"After she told me, I thought I'd go and see my dad, just to — well, just to meet him. For a couple of days I just followed him around." He gives a wry smile. "I saw the kind of man he was, who he spent time with, but I still wanted something. I don't know what I wanted, really. Some kind of acknowledgement, I suppose."

On the road below us, at the first bend of the hill, flashing police lights and sirens invade our hillside.

"I have to go."

"Why? You might have just saved my life." I squint at him, taking in the sharp angles, the dark eyes that remain fixed on my face.

"Ruby, I saw you kill George. That night I followed him to the King's Head, and I tried speaking to him. He just laughed when I said who I was, and told me to get lost, but he did buy me a drink later, and agreed we could talk on his way home if I didn't bother him in front of his mates."

"You were in the alley."

"Yes. There was a doorway at the far end. When I turned into the alley, you were already attacking George. My dad. I stayed in the doorway and watched."

"You never tried to stop me."

"No. When you ran away, I went to check if he was dead. Another couple of men came down the alley, and saw me bending over his body. That was it. A few days later I was arrested. They kept me in for a few days, but they had nothing on me and they had to let me go. Then I knew I had to find you."

The sirens and lights are closer, but something still niggles me. "Was he dead? When you checked him, I mean?"

Dark eyes meet mine, and one hand comes up to touch my cheek, another feather-light touch that sends shivers around my body. "I'll see you soon, Ruby."

The watcher runs swiftly back across the barrow and disappears down the other side. I realise I still don't know his name. And if I believe him, this is the second time we've committed murder together.

The storm is moving inland now with a crackle of thunder. Overhead the clouds swirl black and thick, but the air is still heavy with summer heat. I lie down on the rain-soaked turf, surprised at the warmth of the earth beneath my body. The downpour beats onto my sore face, as I wait for the police.

Chapter Twenty-three

"Do you think Leon was actually insane or just a drug addict?" I ask suddenly.

We're at the hospital, and Inspector Hammond is sat at my bedside with Eileen. On the other side Pearl is changing the bag on my drip, glaring at them. Matron was pretty good about letting her change wards while I'm in here.

"A bit of both, probably. It seems he was a regular user since his early teens, but we spoke to his mother, and she said he had periods of depression when he was at college. He would go and read in his room for days and keep the door locked." The inspector sighs. "Unfortunately he was also very clever. People like that often are. His research gave him a cause, and he became obsessed. The Ancients you say he talked to would be a classic case of either drug-induced psychosis or part of his personality disorder. As an academic he was free to go where his Ancients told him to. We've already linked him to another murder in Wales, as well as the two girls in Manchester. All connected with new developments on sites that he may have believed had ancient roots," Inspector Hammond said.

"What about Ted? Have you charged him with anything?" I rub my aching head, "Why was he in Manchester?"

"It seems to be pure coincidence that both Ted and Leon were in the area in the same year. We are satisfied that Mr Wallington, Ted, had nothing to do with the murders, but we will be charging him with damage to property."

"The fire at Kenny's flat?"

"Yes. It seems he met Leon by chance, and he told him that you suspected he, Ted, was the murderer, and had told the police. Leon also helpfully mentioned that Kenny was the one who tracked down the evidence, and that he was at home right now. Don't worry, we won't be too hard on the lad. He was obviously terrified, after the last time."

"What I don't understand is why Leon was so helpful when we were trying to find Mary. And he was the one who told us all about the link to the murders and the building sites. He even came down and gave you a map!"

The inspector nods, "He needed to be close to you all, and to find out what was happening. I also believe you mentioned that he said in the cellar that we all needed to understand why the girls were being murdered? That there was no point unless we linked the housing developments with the killings?"

"Oh yes, I suppose . . . I expect he had a blast walking in and out of the police station knowing nobody suspected him."

Eileen snaps her notebook shut, and I ask a final question, "Will I . . . I mean, Leon died while we were fighting so . . ."

The WPC glares at me for a moment, then raps out, "Self-defence, Miss Baker. If you hadn't been able to fight him off you would have been another victim. Of course there will have to be further enquiries, but I think it is safe to say you probably don't have anything to worry about." She pauses, looking hard at me. "With your injuries, it is nothing short of a miracle that you were able to do so."

I squirm in my bed and when they finally leave I fall back against the hard pillow with a sigh of relief. With the police gone and all the difficult questions answered, I can relax my guard, and admit to feeling pretty weak and feeble.

"You ready for visitors?" Pearl demands from behind the curtain. Without waiting for an answer she shoves it open, and Mary creeps in. Her baby's snoozing in her arms.

"Oh she's beautiful!" I clap my hands over my mouth, but it's too late. I'm crying, my best friend is crying, and the baby wakes up. Big bluey violet eyes, tiny rosebud lips, and the palest down of fine hair. She blinks as a tear falls on her pale skin.

"Mary, you're a mum! How did you do that?" I laugh through my own tears.

She grimaces for a moment. "It was awful. Not just the birth, I mean, but being stuck down there. But it was so quick that even when the police came in, just after you and Leon left and they smashed the door open, they said not to move me. Victoria was amazing. She just kept talking all the way through and she knew exactly what to do, and then the ambulance came—"

"Victoria was in earlier. She said it was the best moment of her life, and how proud she was of you. Do you know she seems to have just shrugged off the fact that her boyfriend was a killer, as though it never happened? In fact she seemed more concerned about the fact he killed that cat. Do you remember? On our very first night out."

I sink back and sigh again, my eyes still drinking in the baby. I'm sure Victoria is hurting, but I doubt she'll ever show it. She is one tough nut.

"Crazy Leon. I was such an idiot to let him in, but really he always seemed so *nice*. He said he had found a little highchair for the baby, and would I come out and have a look before he unloaded it from his car. I made him a cup of tea, of course, and had one myself. Victoria said that was when he must have drugged me. The next thing I remember is waking up in the cellar. All the time you were looking I was right next door. I can't believe none of us worked it out!" Mary runs a finger over her baby's cheek.

"Well, we did, didn't we? Just not quickly enough. But his cover as this gentle professor type was perfect. I feel really sorry for Victoria, but you know a strange thing? He said he did actually love her. I suppose that probably saved her from becoming a victim."

"No way! And the watcher? Did you tell the police about him?"

"Shhhhh. No. I'll tell you why later. I feel really bad about Ted."

Mary sighs, "But from what you've told me all the evidence was pointing his way. I'm sure he won't hold a grudge."

"Victoria reckons he just might move on somewhere else, depending on the court case."

The baby starts to grumble and Mary picks her up. "I need to feed her, Rubes. I'm doing it myself, you know," she adds proudly, shifting further up my bed. I make room for her on the pillows, as the baby latches on and begins to suckle.

I feel my mouth stretching into a grin, and a wave of love for both of them nearly has me in tears again. It's okay. Everything is going to be okay.

"What are you going to call her?" I ask suddenly, when the little girl has finished feeding and is dozing in her mother's arms.

"I thought of loads of names, but when I was down in that cellar, it was so dark I kept praying that I would see the sun again, and praying she wouldn't be born yet." Mary's light blue eyes meet mine. "I can understand how people can kill to protect someone, you know. I swore to myself if the baby was born down there I would protect her however I could against Leon."

I nod, and squeeze her hand.

"So anyway, I've decided to call her Summer."

"Perfect," I stroke the soft pale down on the baby's head, and beam at my best friend.

* * *

Two days later we both hobble out of hospital. The sun has returned and the clean, salty air is a welcome change from the antiseptic smell of the ward. Johnnie helps me carefully into the car, and takes Mary's bag for her.

"I can't believe this has all happened. Brighton was lovely and peaceful before you two misfits turned up. Now what do we have? Scandal and murder!" He shakes his head, smiling, and lights a cigarette before settling behind the wheel. "I do hope this hasn't put you off? You are sticking around for the rest of the summer?"

As we pull away into the traffic, I glimpse the sea, lazy blue with the waves dancing in the afternoon light. I see the scattered sand on the beach, the jumbled mass of houses, bars, cafés, shops, and offices that cling dark-shadowed to the long hill, and the people bustling in the heat. I catch the smell of coffee, candyfloss, and hotdogs. Everything that makes up the city by the sea.

Beside me, my best friend grins, and baby Summer snuggles safely between us.

"We'll stick around for a bit."

THE END

Thank you for reading this book. If you enjoyed it please leave feedback on Amazon, and if there is anything we missed or you have a question about then please get in touch. The author and publishing team appreciate your feedback and time reading this book.

Our email is office@joffebooks.com

www.joffebooks.com

MORE RUBY BAKER BOOKS COMING SOON

Printed in Great Britain
by Amazon